Arana's Visitor
Book 1 of the Vadelah Chronicles

ARANA'S VISITOR

Book 1 of the Vadelah Chronicles

Julie Rollins

Essence PUBLISHING

Belleville, Ontario, Canada

Arana's Visitor
Book 1 of the Vadelah Chronicles
Copyright © 2005, Julie Rollins

Library and Archives Canada Cataloguing in Publication

Rollins, Julie, 1961-
    Arana's visitor / Julie Rollins.

(The Vadelah chronicles : bk. 1)
ISBN 1-55306-960-9

    I. Title. II. Series: Rollins, Julie, 1961- . Vadelah chronicles; bk. 1.

PS3618.O549A73 2005   813'.6   C2005-903612-5

Essence Publishing is a Christian Book Publisher dedicated to furthering the work of Christ through the written word. For more information, contact: 20 Hanna Court, Belleville, Ontario, Canada K8P 5J2.
Phone: 1-800-238-6376. Fax: (613) 962-3055.
E-mail: publishing@essencegroup.com
Internet: www.essencegroup.com

Printed in Canada
by

Essence
PUBLISHING

Acknowledgments

I must thank the many people who read my manuscripts and gave words of encouragement...and advice. My volunteer "editors" were exceptionally sharp and helpful.

To those who embraced my stories with such passionate enthusiasm:

The Iflands (Rebecca, Chris, Orion, Adriel, Aidan, Rynnah, Nadia, Rigel, Sumaya, and Charis), the Sabas (Susan, Elise, Elliot, and Erika), the Changs (Naiwei, Benjamin, and Jonathan), the Reasoners (Phil, Jill, and Maranda), the Wiltseys (Tom, Helen, and Hannah), Lisa Marshall, Laurie Sargent, Crystal Linn, Carol Scott, Kathy Roberts, Tom and Patti Lu Deeke, Forrest and Cathy Vail, Tara Banfield, Suzanne Sypert, Amy Ross, Lyra Hall, Stephen Livingston, Christie Powers, and Natalie Bangs.

To Mom and Dad, who raised me in a loving Christian home and never belittled my wild imagination.

To my daughters, Rachel and Rebecca, who love Mommy's stories, and to Ariella, who will soon be old enough to enjoy them as well.

And to my dearest husband, David, who eagerly pursued eye-glazing research, patiently salvaged crashed computer files, and slew the bureaucratic dragons. Ruthlessly honest editor and number one fan, you're the best partner I could ever have. This fragile dream would have died without your help.

To all of you, I say *ramara* for your enthusiasm and help. Take credit for your good work; I'll take credit for anything bad that slipped through.

Finally, I give thanks to You, Father God, for the creative ability You have placed within us all. May the works of my hands bring You glory.

1. The Unexpected Roommate

Darius Blackwell impatiently brushed a hair off the glossy top of his large desk. The reflection of his steel-gray eyes and black hair peered back from the dark polished surface like a ghost.

With a silent sigh, he settled into the cocoon of his over-stuffed leather chair. Little daylight squeezed through the blinds of his spacious dim office. Darius preferred the artificial spotlight that focused on him and his desk. Neatly spaced pictures of missiles, planets, and huge satellite dishes adorned the paneled walls. No chairs stood before Darius' regal desk. The room was not an inviting place. It was arranged to impress, and intimidate, any visitors.

Reaching for the file on his nearly barren desk, Darius opened it and studied its list of strange words. Each had a definition in English. The frigid air pouring from the ceiling vent soothed him as he struggled to pronounce the words.

A knock broke the stillness.

"Come in," he said in an icy voice.

A young man peered in from behind the mahogany door. "Excuse me, sir, but Merloc has a message for you." The man slowly stepped inside.

Darius narrowed his eyes. "Merloc?"

"Yes sir. He says he may need some assistance. An unidentified ship has been sighted near the back side of the moon. One of Merloc's guards is engaged in combat with it, but it's heading this way." The messenger approached the great desk with a reluctant, halting gait.

Setting the file on the desk, Darius backed his chair away and stood. "They found an unidentified ship, and they're shooting at it?" His voice rose in anger. "Did Merloc say why?"

"No sir," the man answered, his face flushed. "But he did say he might need your help if it lands here. He wants you to destroy the ship...and its pilot. Merloc claims it's a hostile alien species."

Darius Blackwell paced the room, fists clenched, as he struggled to control himself. "Merloc's not playing straight. He said his kind was the only other sentient life-form in the galaxy. Now another alien species shows up and he wants me to eliminate it without questions! What is that *melhanor* up to?"

Turning to the blushing young man, Darius asked, "Are you sure you got the translation right?"

"Yes sir. Merloc also warned that if we don't get this ship, it could jeopardize the entire SIRIUS Project."

Darius folded his arms and frowned at his staff worker. "Did he say *how* it would jeopardize the project?"

The worker shifted his weight. "No sir."

"Then you tell our men I want this thing taken alive!" Darius glared at the worker to make his point.

"Do you want me to tell Mer—"

"No!" Darius exploded. "Just *our* men. You tell Merloc we will help—that is all! Do you understand?"

"Yes sir!"

Eyeing his employee, Darius reigned in his temper. "Tell our men to use whatever means necessary to capture this alien. If it lands on Earth, don't eliminate any human witnesses; just take them into custody so we can grill them for information. We can't let this go public, and we certainly don't want the government to realize their little project has been successful. Do you understand?"

"Yes sir!"

"Then go!" Darius thundered.

The young man dashed out of the hostile room.

Darius Blackwell resumed his pacing. The freezing air from the ceiling vent could not cool him down now.

"What are the mel-hanor hiding?" he muttered in an angry voice. "What *are* they hiding?"

David Decker turned on the windshield wipers. What began as a few drops became a hard, spattering rain on the windshield of his old sedan. The rubber blades squeaked and groaned as they smeared grime across the glass.

"I hate it when they do that," he muttered half to himself.

"It's like life. Sometimes things get worse before they get better," replied his middle-aged mother. Nadine Decker's blue eyes still sparkled beneath her dark wavy hair.

Was she referring to his own life's struggles? The vicious taunts and pranks from his high-school peers still cut David deeply. In college, few commented on his skinny body and he'd earned respect for his academic prowess. But this year he was transferring from the community college to a university and he was nervous.

The window cleared and the blades glided quietly over the wet glass.

David glanced into the rearview mirror. His brows brooded over his deep blue eyes, darkened by the storm outside. Although his hair had been recently trimmed, the humid air made his dark curls unruly.

"So, are you and Tyler settled in your new apartment?" Nadine fired off her question without warning.

David moaned. It didn't take her long to hone in on trouble. "No, Tyler decided to save money and commute from home one more semester." *She's going to find out,* he thought.

His mother's eyebrows peaked in the middle of her forehead. "Did you find another roommate?"

David straightened his back. "Yes."

"Who?"

"Todd." *Here it comes.*

"Todd?" Nadine looked sharply at him. "Todd Fox from high school?"

Holding up a hand to fend off a verbal attack, David blurted, "I know, I know. He's not a Christian, and he's a little wild, but he's the best I can do for now. I know what to expect from him; he's not a total stranger. Besides, we talked things over and I laid down the rules. He was quite agreeable. I could have gotten stuck with someone worse." Turning cautiously, he met her with his eyes.

She was smiling. "David, I know you will do the best you can. I've raised you well. Perhaps God has His hand in this. How is Todd?"

No lecture? No disappointed looks? He couldn't believe it. David paused a moment to catch his breath. "He's doing...fine...well, he passed most of his courses last year."

Nadine Decker winced as only a mother can.

"He is doing better than he did in high school," David added. "One of the reasons he wanted to room with me was to stop partying. He figured he could get more done if he left his fraternity. Todd doesn't want to spend the next ten years in school."

Nadine smirked.

With a chuckle, David continued. "He's already saved me money by finding a cheaper apartment. The woman managing the apartment building is one of Todd's relatives. Todd even offered to pay more than half of the rent if I tutor him."

"My, my! He must be serious," Nadine countered in a slight mocking tone. "Did you accept his offer?"

"No," he answered with a straight face.

Nadine stared at him. "No?"

David cracked a faint smile. "I told him I'd tutor him for free if he just behaves." *And he better behave*, he thought.

"Ah, incentive! That was smart and generous. It won't be too much work for you?"

"I think I can handle it."

Nadine beamed. "I've always been proud of your academic abilities, but I'm prouder still of your generosity. You're the best son I've raised."

"I'm the only son you've raised."

She grinned. "Not too bad for a first try, eh?"

"So, when will your car be out of the shop?"

"Tomorrow. Thanks for driving me. I hate missing the women's Bible study." Nadine's eyes gazed down the road. "We had a young woman visit today. She was quite a fireball of questions."

The corner of David's mouth turned up. "Really? What did she ask?"

"Oh, she wanted to know if the Bible had anything to say about life on other planets. She provoked some lively discussions."

"I bet."

Turning, Nadine looked at him. "It is an interesting idea. I have a hard time picturing the rest of the universe *created* without life, yet the thought of intelligent life...how would that relate to us?"

"What did you tell her?"

"The truth. The Bible is silent on the matter, but that doesn't mean it isn't possible."

David nodded. "Well, I'm too busy with life on Earth to worry about life beyond Earth. After I drop you off I've got to go pick up Todd and all his stuff. He's moving in today. Todd doesn't have much. We can probably cram it all into the trunk."

He eased the old sedan off the freeway, wove through the suburbs of Los Arboles, and pulled up to a yellow stucco house.

"Bye, Mom." Leaning over, David kissed her gently on the cheek. "Say hi to Dad for me."

"I will." She opened the door. "Oh, my! It's really coming down. It's so unusual to have rain this time of year."

"Wait." David reached under his seat, pulled out a worn umbrella, and offered it to her. "I've got another one at the apartment."

Nadine sighed and smiled. "Thanks, I'll return it next visit." Taking hold of the handle, she paused. "I love you, Son. You know I'll be praying for you."

"Thanks." He watched his mother until she entered the house and closed the door. For a moment he felt the emptiness in his car, the same lonely feeling he always had whenever they parted.

After listening a little longer to the rain, he drove into the gathering storm. It was getting dark already and soon the sun would set.

A warm, radiant feeling came upon him. His mother's prayers?

David smiled. *Lord, thank You for giving me a mother who prays faithfully. This year I have a feeling I'm going to need all the help I can get.*

The pilot gripped the control yoke with his scaly left hand as his right hand typed on the glowing console, trying to restore the navigational computer. He braced himself as his ship sped erratically through Earth's ionosphere. Glancing at his rear scanner, he observed his attacker.

Broad and flat like a stingray, its black form nearly invisible against the stars, the pursuing craft dogged his every turn. Beams of yellow light burst from its nose, grazing the tail of the pilot's ship.

Inwardly he lamented his predicament. Why hadn't he called for back-up before investigating that suspicious transmission? Now he was cut off from help and growing tired in his constant battle to stay alive. He spun his craft to the right and rolled as another burst of yellow beams streaked by. The computer displayed his every move as his jet-like ship dove and doubled back, ending the brief maneuver with its belly toward Earth.

The black ship followed suit, firing.

His attacker was good, even for a mel-hanor. The ambush from the back side of the moon had taken the pilot by surprise. What was the mel-hanor's little black *crullah* doing here, in the Sanor System? Rolling his craft again, the pilot tried to shake his agile attacker. Another spray of fire grazed the belly of the pilot's ship, but the hull was not damaged. He couldn't fight with his weapons system offline, and his *trelemar* equipment was inoperable.

"Yavana, how can I escape when all my *delah* can do is sub-lightspeed maneuvers?" Looking down at the ominous planet below, he trembled. Even the mel-hanor knew that Trenara was off-limits. Why did his attacker show no fear in following him so low?

Another beam grazed the window and the pilot turned sharply to the left. He felt the g's pulling at his body. "Please, Yavana, I don't want to violate the ancient laws and crash here!"

Sensors showed his silver and white ship descending into the atmosphere. The crullah hesitated and then followed. The delah's pilot leveled out. His attacker would have to kill him before he dared to fly any closer to Trenara!

The delah shuddered and groaned as it took a direct hit. A flashing blue light indicated main propulsion was offline. "Ayeee!" the pilot cried in despair. His ship was going down and there was no way to stop it. At least maneuvering thrusters were online. Lowering the ship's nose, he descended at a dangerously steep angle. He desperately needed to put more distance between himself and the crullah. If he was ever to escape from Trenara, he'd have to get his delah down safely to repair it.

As the air thickened, the cabin shook. The pilot glanced at his rear scanner. Still firing, the crullah glowed red.

The pilot unstrapped his belt and lunged toward the back of the cabin. Unfastening a large storage container, he shoved it into an air lock and jettisoned it. With a graceful leap, the pilot returned to his seat. Zero gravity was easy for him, but he was losing his weightlessness as the increasing air friction decelerated the delah.

Buckling himself in, he checked his scanner. The container drifted off to his left and the crullah veered after it. Internal sensors revealed the relentless rise in cabin temperature. If he didn't get his ship into the correct entry angle soon, it would burn up.

The crullah fired on the storage container, vaporizing it.

The delah's pilot stabilized his ship's attitude. The crullah had taken the bait. Looking down at his instruments, he noted the heat damage spreading over the crullah. "There's no turning back for either of us now."

The dark ship fired, hitting the delah from behind. A loud *whump* resounded from the delah's ceiling as the spine of the craft took the hit. With quick deft movements, the pilot struggled to correct his ship's course. The computer flashed a warning—the deployment motor for the atmospheric wings was damaged.

Turning to his visual scanner, the pilot saw the crullah glow a brilliant white and then explode into a cascade of molten debris. "Well, that's one problem down."

But Trenara loomed relentlessly closer. He was entering the night side of the planet.

The pilot tried to extend the jammed, folded wings with computer commands, but the wings remained frozen. Leaving his seat, he ripped off a floor panel and pulled a lever until it bent. The wings rotated forward partially and jammed again. As he struggled to maintain his footing, the pilot's toenails clattered on the slanting floor. The increasing force of deceleration made it impossible to stand upright. Turning, he stared out the front window at the growing, menacing sphere with its odd sprinkling of lights.

Yavana, it isn't death I fear, it's the terrible unknown I will find on Trenara. As the pilot looked down at the jammed levers, his white face stared back at him from the silvery floor panel. A blue tear fell from his fire-red eye, spattering on the panel. *Arana, I will miss you.*

As he noted the rise in hull temperature, the pilot snapped his jaw. Soon he'd be flying a hunk of molten metal if things didn't change fast! With sudden desperation, he grasped the levers, tugging them with renewed vigor. *Yavana, have mercy. I didn't intend to crash here!* he pleaded silently as he yanked a bar.

The ship bounced and swerved in the thickening air. He could see the top of his delah's nose glowing bright red.

"Yavana!"

David flipped his headlights on high as the old sedan rumbled down the road. The evening light cast the hills in a deep blue and barely lit the scattered clouds crawling across the sky. Like twin swords, the high beams cut into the darkness. The narrow road curved through patches of tall oaks and quivering eucalyptus groves as it wove through the gentle hills.

The countryside always soothed David, but he reminded himself to stay alert for deer.

"I'm having second thoughts about all your rules," Todd Fox said beside him. "You've got more than my old man did. Come on, David, it's 1989, not 1889."

"You agreed to the terms, Todd," David said firmly. "If you're going to stay with me, you're going to learn a little discipline."

"A little discipline," he echoed in a sulky voice. "So, how did the Lady take the news?"

David smiled. "Mom's okay."

"Really?" Todd leaned forward. "I thought she'd have a fit. I mean, well, you know my reputation." He opened a bag of chips and proceeded to munch them.

"She knows all about you." David turned briefly to his friend then looked back at the road. "She's not unreasonable, you know. Not usually."

"Yeah, right," replied Todd without much conviction. He leaned back and munched another chip.

"Are you sure you packed everything?"

"Yes, Mother," Todd answered in a nasal tone.

David laughed. "Well, your step-mother doesn't live too far away. If you forgot anything, we can always go back and pick it up."

"Not tonight."

"Definitely not tonight."

They came to a clearing and the land rose, giving a grand view of the distant hills and sky.

Leaning forward, Todd cried, "What's *that!*"

"Where?" David scanned the road for deer.

"There!" Todd shouted, his finger pressed against the windshield.

David was about to tell Todd to get his finger off the glass when he saw a glowing object near the horizon. "I see it now."

Todd stretched as far forward as his seatbelt would allow. "Is that a shooting star?"

David squinted. "Most meteors would have burned up by now. I'd say it was a satellite, but it's moving way too fast." He pulled off to the side of the road.

They watched in silence as the object grew larger and brighter. A loud *boom* shook the windows. Bracing himself against the dashboard, Todd's eyes went wide. "I felt my brain rattle on that one! It looks like it's headed right for us!"

Before David could answer, the radiant form of a plane streaked by, glowing orange. The wings and tail were unmistakable. It shot off to their left and was lost behind some distant trees.

Todd looked at David. "What was that sound? An explosion?"

David worked to turn the car around, not an easy thing to do on the narrow road. "I think it was a sonic boom."

"Whatta you doin'?" asked Todd in a low voice.

"I'm going to try and find it."

"Why?"

"Because you and I both know that was no meteor."

Todd was silent for a moment. "So, what type of plane do you think it is, or was?"

"I don't know." David sighed. "It sure wasn't a 747."

Todd laughed, but his laughter fell flat. "Do you think it was some hyped-up spy plane, like in James Bond?" His off-key voice launched into the theme song, but stopped abruptly. "Hey, you don't think we could get in trouble for seeing this, do you? If you didn't see anything, I didn't either, okay?"

"I just want to know if there are any survivors." David pressed down on the accelerator until they were clipping along faster than the speed limit. "If someone is hurt, we may be able to help."

"Well, I don't want to get mixed up with the military. If it's one of their top-secret planes, they'll be looking for it. Shoot, they'll probably be crawling all over these hills. I wouldn't be surprised if they're already setting up road blocks."

"You've been watching too many spy movies, Todd. Besides, you don't see any helicopters or police cars, do you?"

Todd looked around. "Well, not yet, but if we do, promise me you'll get the you-know-what out of here."

David smiled at his friend's attempt to temper his language. "I'll promise you this, Todd. If they show up, I'll keep out of their way."

As they drove on in silence, David lowered his eyebrows and frowned. What would they find? Twisted, burned bodies in smoldering wreckage? Pieces of metal scattered over the ground? A finger here, a foot there? David shook his head. *He* had been watching too many movies. Perhaps all he would find would be a crater in the ground. Grizzly images invaded his mind again. *Concentrate on the road, David. Keep your eyes peeled.* He turned up a narrow dirt road.

"Hey, where ya goin'?"

"Judging by the way it went, we need to leave the main road and go this way." David pointed with his finger.

Todd released a puff of air. "I know better than to argue with you on directions. Remember when I got lost on that hike? You tracked me down and brought me back to camp. I was amazed you didn't tell anyone. If it had been me, I'd have blabbed it to the whole camp!"

"You didn't need to be humiliated, Todd," David answered.

The road led toward a farm with an orchard and woods. Scanning to his left and then his right, Todd asked, "How are we going to find it if it crashed in the trees?"

David prayed silently. He felt they had to be close. As they cruised along, they passed a ragged hedge obscuring most of their view.

"Wait. What is that?" David stopped the car at a break in the shrubs.

The land sloped down into a slight dell on the edge of the woods. Resting in the hollow was the plane, glowing faintly.

David whispered. "It looks like a Lear jet—except for that small wing sticking out just below the cockpit." He turned off the car's headlights and the ship's glow became more pronounced.

"Why is it lit up like that?" Todd asked in a hushed voice.

"I don't know. Let's find out."

"Let's not."

"Todd, I've got to make sure the pilot is okay." David took a flashlight out of his glove compartment. "Come on, let's go." Opening his door, he stepped out cautiously. It felt good to stretch his skinny frame after the tense drive.

His reluctant friend joined him and gave a low whistle. "I have a feeling we're going to get in deep on this one," Todd muttered.

Inside the cockpit of his spaceship, the pilot consulted his instruments. In his last desperate push he had succeeded in loosening the wings. He had barely had time to correct his angle and slow his descent, reducing the heat friction that threatened to destroy his ship.

But the moment of relief he felt from landing his craft had vanished now. He was alone, on Trenara.

Snapping his jaw, he read the computer's damage report. The main propulsion unit, trelemar equipment, and navigational guidance could be fixed, but the spine of the delah was severely damaged. Where would he find the materials to repair his ship?

The pilot consulted the sensors' data gathered during the descent. The computer displayed images of landmasses and mineral deposits along with an analysis of the atmosphere. "Whatever else they may say about you, Trenara, you have been blessed with a grand variety of elements. Everything I need is here."

When he narrowed the scan, some took on distinct geometric shapes. Buildings! Inhabitants were nearby. How could he get the materials he needed without running into the natives? It would waste precious time if he had to mine and refine materials. Most of what he needed could be found in these geometric forms, but the inhabitants had obviously made them.

Snapping his jaw once more, he pondered his bleak options. Perhaps he could make contact with a few natives and escape without doing much harm. He unbuckled his belt and walked toward a panel on the rear bulkhead.

Rerouting the power for the main thrusters only took a few minutes. Repairing his trelemar equipment would take longer. There was no sense in fixing it until the spine was repaired. His current priority was to find those repair materials.

The pilot strode up to the ship's portal. "*Toorah barune*," he commanded. The door slid open in response. He stood there, sampling the delicate scents of the night. "*Yavana*," he breathed and stepped onto the soft earth.

The alien gazed up at the starry sky and scattered clouds. So this was Trenara at nightfall. The blue-green band of daylight in the west was nearly gone. Trees rustled softly in the nearby woods. His sonar revealed whatever his adept eyes missed. He strode up to a road and stopped. Strange, wiggly tracks marred the dirt. Bending over, he rubbed the tracks with a scaly finger.

A dog barked nearby.

Straightening, the pilot drew his gray cloak around him. He walked up the road toward a group of farm buildings.

An Irish setter leaped off the porch of a house and bounded through the bushes, barking as it came.

"*Naharam*, naharam!" the pilot cried.

The dog stopped and looked up at him, panting.

"Naharam?" asked the alien in a softer voice. He breathed in the dog's strong scent. Was this one of the natives? He pulled his hand from beneath his cloak and touched the dog's skull with three scaly fingers. Shutting its mouth, the Irish setter cocked its head as the alien uttered dog sounds. The pilot withdrew his hand. "*Dalam*," he muttered in disappointment.

The dog yawned and trotted back to the farm.

Turning, the pilot walked down the road. His sonar detected a large, metallic object, obviously manufactured. It appeared to be some kind of land vehicle.

Two soft fleshy creatures moved near the vehicle. One of the figures held a cylindrical object that stabbed the darkness with a beam of light.

The alien's sensitive ears picked up voices. He approached the two figures and stopped when he was quite close. "Naharam?" he asked.

2. An Alien in the Apartment

"What was that?" Todd asked.

David turned his flashlight in the direction of the sound.

A tall robed figure stood in the light. The gray fabric hung almost to the ground and a large hood hid the face in shadow. "Naharam?" asked the voice again.

"Who is this, some sort of monk?" Todd said with a snort.

Stepping forward, David raised his flashlight.

The stranger flinched, turning his head to avoid the beam. "Naharam?" he repeated louder.

"Is that your name?" Todd asked. "Hey, David, get the light out of his face. You're blinding him."

David lowered the light.

"Naharam?" came the voice, more urgent this time.

"What's he speaking? Arabic?" Stepping forward, Todd tried to peer into the stranger's hood.

"Pull your hood back," David said. He felt strange talking to a faceless robe.

The stranger turned toward him.

"Pull your hood back, like this." David pantomimed his request.

Slowly, the stranger raised his scaly purple hand. Three long fingers and a bird-like thumb grasped the edge of the hood and pulled it back, revealing an avian face. A long pink bill with slits for nostrils graced a white, feathered face set with red eyes.

"What is this?" Todd said with a nervous laugh. "Big Bird? Wait a minute. You don't think that he came from..." He turned slowly and looked at the plane.

It glowed dimly in the starlight.

"Naharam," the tall figure stated. He stretched his right hand toward Todd's head and stepped forward.

Todd jumped back. "No one's gonna suck my brains out!" He turned and ran. David was right behind. They both dove into the bushes.

"*Ahhh!* Let go!" Todd screamed.

David slapped a hand over Todd's mouth. "Shhh! It's me!" He peered through the bushes. "It's still back by the car. It hasn't moved."

"How are we gonna get home without a car?" Todd whined. "Jee–pers, all my stuff is in it."

David eyed his friend, amused Todd had the presence of mind to correct profanity in mid-sentence. "It's not following us. I think we should go back."

"David, we don't know if it's good or bad."

"It hasn't pursued us."

"So? Maybe it just wants to be left alone."

"But it approached us," David countered.

"Yeah, and tried to fry my brains!"

"We don't know that!"

They both stared at the figure standing by their car.

David sighed. "Well, I don't want to walk home. I'm going back." *Lord protect us. Give me wisdom.* He crept toward the car.

"David, I'm the one who's supposed to be crazy and take outrageous risks!" Todd protested, but he joined David and they walked back together.

The stranger's hood was still down and his red eyes watched them.

"Naharam." The alien raised his hand again. This time he approached David.

"No!" David said, surprised by the force behind his voice.

The figure stopped.

"No touch!" David raised his hand in imitation, shook his head, and lowered his hand.

The figure took another step.

"No," David repeated. He pantomimed pushing the alien's hand down.

Lowering his hand, the alien stopped. "No," he replied in a voice identical to David's.

"Sh–oot! It sounded just like you!" Todd stammered.

The alien pulled his hands back and placed them on his chest. "Naharam," he said. Then he extended his arms in a graceful movement toward the men. "Naharam."

Todd scowled. "What does *naharam* mean?"

David shook his head. "Who knows?" The alien appeared to be alone, lost, and unable to communicate its needs. What would happen to it? Pity softened David's cautious heart.

A distant low drumming echoed from the hills.

"Helicopter!" David shouted.

"Chopper!" Todd cried at the same time. "Hey, do you think they're looking for—"

"We can't let them have him," David burst in.

"Why?"

"I can't explain it now. I just know we've got to hide him."

"We?" Todd raised an eyebrow. "You're supposed to be saving me from trouble, not dragging me headlong into it!"

David motioned to the alien. "Come. Into the car. Into the car!"

The alien just stood there, staring at him. A helicopter swung into view, sweeping the nearby hills with a searchlight. David tensed. He had to get the alien out of there. If he was as hefty as Todd then he might be able to manhandle the thing into the car, but he was too small and Todd was scared—like him. *Think, David, think!* he chided himself.

Making eye contact and pointing to the chopper, David cried, "Bad! Hurt! Cause pain!"

Todd got into the act, pointing at the helicopter and acting like it was attacking David.

The feathers rose on the alien's head. He snapped his jaw and pointed toward his ship.

"Delah."

"We gotta hide the plane, er, spaceship," Todd said.

They both raced toward the ship. When they arrived, the alien was still with them. Striding up to the ship, the alien spoke a few words. The ship growled awake. It rose like a harrier jet, followed the robed figure into the forest, and stopped where the foliage of the trees was thick.

The alien gave a command and the ship ascended between the branches of the trees. Clamps extended from its wings and tail, fastening the ship to the trees.

"Hidden from the choppers and hidden from the road," Todd remarked. "The only way you can see it is if you're right under it. Who would think to look for a spaceship here?"

With that done, the trio jogged back to the car. Todd scratched his neck. "Where do we put him? I don't want him in the rear seat where he can suck our brains out behind our backs."

"I agree. Someone needs to sit in back and keep an eye on him."

"Wait a minute, David! There's no way I'm sitting back there with him by myself!"

"Todd, I'm not going to let you drive! If you have a wreck like you did two years ago...."

"I'm not sitting in back with that thing!"

David sighed and held his head. The helicopter droned louder.

"Okay, Todd. We'll all sit in front; is that fair?"

"It's better."

They climbed into the front seat and the alien sat in the middle. David started the car and they were off. No one spoke as they entered the highway. David struggled to convince himself this was all real.

Just before they reached the interstate, he saw flashing lights.

"Uh, oh."

"No," Todd moaned. "And you said I watched too many spy movies. Well, I was right about the road block...and the chopper."

Two cars waited in line ahead of them.

David slowed his sedan. "Quick! Pull the hood over his head and get him to lean on you, like he's asleep."

The first car in line drove off.

Todd raised the alien's hood, then hesitated. His shaking hands tried to pull the alien's head onto his shoulder, but the alien stiffened. "Come on, Big Bird, it's for your own good!" he pleaded. The alien finally yielded.

"If they ask you any questions, he's my brother and he's a monk. Got that?" David glanced at Todd to make sure he understood.

"Yeah, right." Todd added under his breath, "We don't even know if it's a guy or a girl, or if it even *has* a gender!"

The car before them moved on. They were next. David rolled his window down as a highway patrol officer approached him.

The officer held a clipboard. "Good evening, sir."

Trying to appear calm, David replied, "Good evening, Officer."

"We're just checking the area for a plane crash. Did you happen to see anything unusual?"

"No, sir." David's pulse raced.

"Did any of your passengers see anything? Like a flame or an explosion?" He looked at Todd and the shrouded figure in the middle of the seat.

"No," Todd mouthed dryly.

"What about…"

"Shhh," David whispered. "That's Brother Byrd. He's been asleep since we left the house. I don't think he's seen anything."

"Are you sure he slept the whole time? It's not that late…." He leaned closer to the open window.

David winced. "Please, Officer, he was up all night praying, and he spent the entire day working in the fields. Tomorrow morning he has to get up for the five o'clock Mass."

"All right." The officer pulled his head back from the window. He turned to face another car coming down the road. "Move along."

"Brother Byrd?" Todd joked when they were safely on the interstate. "Hey, I didn't know you could lie. Isn't that against your religion?"

"You never read about the Hebrew midwives in Egypt?"

Todd laughed. "Me? You know I've never read the Bible."

"Well, if you did then you would know about the midwives. They lied to save the Israelites' infants from Pharaoh and God rewarded them for it."

"So it's okay to lie…sometimes?"

"If it's to save a life."

"Do you think we saved a life today, David?"

David looked at the large bundle still leaning on Todd's shoulder. "I hope so."

The rest of the drive was uneventful. As they drove down the old streets of Los Arboles, David sighed. "Todd, how do we sneak him into the apartment? We have to get him past Rhoda Stearns."

"Leave that to me," Todd said with an air of confidence. "After all, she is my step-mother's brother-in-law's cousin. We're family!"

They parked, grabbed some of Todd's bags, and sneaked up to the decrepit apartment building.

Peering through the glass door, Todd whispered, "Looks good."

The trio darted through the vacant lobby, rode the ancient elevator up to the sixth floor, and dashed out into the hallway. They almost made it to their room.

"David Decker!" came a shrill female voice.

David froze in his tracks. His forehead tickled as perspiration beaded up on his skin. *No! We were so close!*

A short middle-aged woman bounced up behind them. "Here is the second key I made for you."

He held out his meek hand as she pressed the silver key into his palm.

"Who is this?" She approached the hooded figure.

Todd stepped forward. "My third cousin. His name is John Byrd."

"Nice to meet you, John," Rhoda said briskly. She faced Todd. "Is he staying with you?"

"For a while," Todd offered.

She turned back to the silent figure. "How long?"

"John's not real big on words," Todd jumped in. "As a matter of fact, he's a little strange."

"That's not hard to believe if he's one of your relatives!" she snapped.

David gave Todd a sharp look, but Todd only winked back.

Trying to peer into the long hood, Rhoda said, "Well, John, let me have a look at you."

"You really don't want to—" David began.

"Oh, it's okay, Mrs. Stearns," Todd blurted. "Only don't be frightened. Remember, I did tell you he's a little strange."

David's jaw dropped as Todd yanked back the hood with flare. Fortunately Rhoda had her back turned to David.

"What is this? Some kind of a joke?" Rhoda asked in a sharp voice.

"No, Mrs. Stearns." Todd's face was serious. "John really thinks he's a bird. That's why he always wears this silly suit. The doctor thought bringing him here would help him. We're trying to get John adjusted to the real world."

Narrowing her eyes, Rhoda asked, "He's not dangerous is he?"

"Oh no! He's harmless...just a little confused." Todd placed a hand on the alien's shoulder and smiled.

"A *little* confused? Well, if he's not loud, and he doesn't frighten the neighbors...and you pay your rent on time, I don't care how long he stays with you." Whisking around, Rhoda continued down the hall, muttering, "Poor thing. Todd will ruin him."

David rushed for the door and opened it as Todd hurried their guest in. Once they were inside, David shut the door and wiped his sweaty brow.

"Now, how was that for a story?" Todd spread his arms, waiting for the applause.

"Bravo, Todd." David clapped his hands and tilted back his head. "*Story* is a nice way to describe a lie."

Todd pointed a finger at David. "Hey, I wasn't the first."

"His life wasn't in danger."

"I was more truthful than you! What do you think Rhoda would have done if I told her the whole truth?"

David smirked. "I don't know. It would have been funny to see."

Todd reached for the door handle.

Seizing Todd's hand, David cried, "Wait! I was only kidding!"

Todd laughed. "Relax, will you? I'm just going back to the car to get the rest of my stuff."

"Sorry." David sighed, backed away from the door, and sat in an old folding chair. As soon as the door shut, he remembered he was not alone.

The strange placid figure stood in the middle of the room, staring at him. The alien made the run-down bachelor's pad look rather eccentric.

David massaged his temple with his hand. Where was this thing going to sleep? *Did* it sleep? What would it eat? How long could they hide it? What were they going to do with it? Was it safe?

The room felt too small. Stuffy. Crowded. It was a cage and he was trapped with this creature. What if the alien was a carnivore? What if it thought nothing of killing and eating another sentient being? A whirlwind of fears assailed David. Deep suspicion and dread caused his forehead to sweat again.

Glancing around the room, the alien appeared to feel those same fears. "Yavana," the creature called.

David felt his fears disappear and a warm calm settled on his heart. It was the same experience he had when his mother prayed for him. Stepping toward the serene figure, he looked into the creature's scarlet eyes.

"I'm David." He patted his bony chest with both hands. "Da-vid."

"Da-vid," the alien responded.

"Good! David," he said again, patting his chest.

"Good! David," the alien repeated.

David laughed at the mistake.

Todd burst in with a full laundry basket under one arm, and a large bag in the other.

"Good! David," the alien said, reaching out an arm in the direction of Todd.

"Hey, what have you two been up to?" asked Todd with a serious look on his face.

Smiling, David closed the door. "English as a second language. I got him to repeat a couple words, but he doesn't quite understand them yet."

Todd dumped his burden onto the orange vinyl sofa and sat down.

Looking back at the alien, David touched his own chest. "David," he said. He turned and pointed to his roommate. "Todd," he said.

The alien stretched his hand toward David. "David." He pointed toward the man sprawled on the couch. "Todd."

Todd blinked his hazel eyes. "Go–sh, he sounds just like you."

David clasped his hands together. "Now let's see if we can learn its name." Stepping forward, he pointed to himself. "David." He aimed his finger at his roommate. "Todd." David turned his hand to the alien and waited.

A long purple finger emerged from beneath the gray robe. The alien pointed at David and declared, "David." The finger swung around. "Todd." He pointed to his chest. "Panagyra."

"Pana...what?" asked Todd. He pointed back at the alien.

"Panagyra," the alien repeated.

David scrambled for paper and a pencil. Picking up a new notebook, he opened it. "Panagyra?" he asked looking up at the tall form.

"Panagyra," the alien repeated, patting his rounded chest.

The rest of the evening until midnight was spent teaching their guest the names of the objects in the apartment. David noted that their pupil was an excellent student, and they never had to repeat a word twice. Panagyra grasped its pronunciation perfectly. He never forgot what he learned, although sometimes the interpretation of certain words had to be clarified.

As the night wore on, David's new roommate showed no sign of fatigue.

"I'm starting to worry," Todd whispered, rubbing his eyes. "How do we tell him to go to sleep?"

"Perhaps by example," David suggested.

"We can't just leave him here, awake. What if he gets bored and wanders off or somethin'?"

David yawned. "I'll tell you what. You go to sleep while I stay up with him until six. Then you get to watch him."

"Great," Todd said, catching a yawn too. "It's been a long day." He staggered off to his bedroom. "Take care of yourself." The door shut with a click as Todd locked it.

David spent the rest of the wee hours teaching the alien nouns. Sometimes Panagyra spoke a few words in his alien language, but David was too tired to write them down.

By 5:45 a.m. David was watching the clock and staring at his student in silence. Where did Panagyra come from? Why was the alien here? Was it a *he* or a *she*? The alien seemed content to sit and be stared at for now.

At six David woke Todd.

"Oooh, six already?" Todd moaned as he rubbed his face. Rolling slowly out of bed, he combed his fingers through his tousled blond hair.

"Don't forget we have a guest," David reminded him.

"Ooommph! I was hoping it was just a bad dream." Todd grabbed a set of clothes and staggered into the bathroom.

Lumbering off to his tiny room, David crawled into bed and pulled the sheet over his head.

Todd cried out.

David bolted upright in bed, heart pounding.

"I left all my underwear at home!" Todd wailed.

*   *   *

The late morning sun peeked its way through the blinds, burning through David's eyelids. He moved his head, but the sun kept tracking across his face, pulling him from sleep. A faint mumble filtered through the walls as he rolled onto his other side. David stretched an arm and opened one eye. How late was it?

The clock beside his bed read 11:55 a.m.

Arching his back, he released a deep sigh. He could easily sleep for another hour.

As David pealed back his covers, the aroma of waffles invaded the room. His appetite quickened. Sitting up, David noticed he had slept in his clothes. The events of the previous night assaulted him like a vicious hangover—not that he had ever actually experienced a hangover. Todd on the other hand...what *was* Todd doing?

David got up, opened the door, and wandered into the kitchen.

"Good morning," Todd greeted him in an obnoxious tone. "We can't have you sleeping in all day; you'll miss breakfast. Here, have a waffle fresh from the toaster." He passed David a warm waffle on a plate.

"Where's the thing, er, Pana-gyro?" David asked in a groggy voice, sitting down at the worn card table they used for their meals.

"He, or it, is okay. He's in the living room." Todd set a cube of butter on the table along with some warm syrup. "The guy's staring out the window again like he was when I got up at six. You'd think he'd never seen a sunrise before."

"Maybe he hasn't. At least, not here."

A moment of sober silence enveloped them as David buttered his waffle and covered it in syrup.

Todd sat down with his waffle. "Whatta we gonna do with him?"

"We've got to find out more about him. If we keep teaching him English, eventually he'll be able to tell us more about who he is, where he came from, and what he wants."

"Whoa, David, you're starting to sound like my philosophy teacher. What I want to know is how we're gonna feed him."

"Feed him?"

"Yeah, the dude ate thirteen waffles this morning and he only stopped because I stopped feeding him!"

"You fed him *thirteen waffles*? You're going to poison the poor guy with junk food."

"Hey, it ain't so bad. You're eating one yourself."

David glanced down at his plate. "But I'm not eating thirteen!"

"Anyway," Todd continued, "If he eats like this everyday—shoot, every meal—my budget won't cover this."

"Well, we have a couple of days to figure this out." David rubbed his forehead. "What have you been doing all morning?"

A sly smile crossed Todd's face. "I've been teaching him how to cook."

"Cook?"

"Yeah. First we made an omelet, then pancakes and sausage with a grand finale of frozen waffles. I've never seen anybody eat so much."

"He ate all that?"

"Well, not all of it. I had some pancakes and sausage."

"How much of the pancake mix did he eat?"

"The box."

"And the eggs?"

"Half a dozen, or so."

David stared at the empty box of pancake mix peeking out of the trashcan.

Finishing up the last of his waffle, Todd said, "Now that you're up, I'm gonna go down to the car and see if I can find some clean underwear. Maybe I lost them somewhere in the trunk."

He carried his plate over to the sink. "Oh, and David..."

"Yeah?"

"Don't forget to eat your waffle. It's getting cold."

David looked down at his untouched waffle and proceeded to attack it. After rinsing his breakfast down with a glass of milk he hurried out to the living room.

Panagyra stood before the window, mesmerized. He turned as David approached him.

"Naharam?" Panagyra asked, pointing out the window.

David didn't understand. "Pana-gyro," he began.

"Panagyra," the alien corrected gently.

David nodded. "Panagyra, what is *naharam*?" He sensed the word was important to the alien.

"Panagyra naharam," the alien said, patting his chest. He extended a hand toward David. "David naharam. Todd naharam."

What did they have in common with the alien? David picked up a pillow. "Naharam?"

The alien placed a hand on it. "Naharam, no."

Walking over to the window, David peered down at the crowded street. People? Life? Intelligent life! Panagyra greeted them last night with a question. He wanted to know if Todd and David were intelligent life. Well, that made sense. Panagyra was obviously unfamiliar with human words and customs. Was he here to study life on Earth? Did he have a mission?

Many questions burned inside of David, but the language barrier denied him satisfaction. Absentmindedly, he stripped off his wrinkled shirt and undershirt. Bending down, he pulled a clean set out of a box beside the couch. As he turned back toward the window, he froze.

Panagyra faced him, the gray robe lying at his feet. This was the first time David had seen the alien unclothed. Holding his breath, he walked around Panagyra, amazed.

Although David had wondered what Panagyra's body looked like, he hadn't thought it proper to ask.

Snow-white feathers covered the alien. His purple scaly arms were bare from the elbows to his long fingers. The knees bent backwards, like a bird's, above the scaly legs and toes. Long stiff tail feathers came almost to the ground and David wondered how Panagyra had been able to sit in the car.

But the biggest surprise was the powerful wings that had been hidden by the robe. With the exception of his arms, Panagyra was a perfect scale model of a rock dove—many times larger than life. When the alien stretched his neck, his stature grew to a full seven feet, but when he relaxed his neck, he shrank to about six feet.

By signing with his hands, David coaxed Panagyra to unfold his wings, gasping as they extended across the small room, touching both walls.

Then the alien folded his wings and walked around David, wagging his head in an odd manner. Panagyra stopped in front of David and pointed at his wrinkled pants.

With a sudden burning in his cheeks, David realized the alien was asking him to remove them. "Uh oh, what have I done now?" he muttered. It was one thing to take off a cloak when you're fully clothed with feathers! How could he tell the alien that things were different with people?

Pointing to his pants, David said, "No." Panagyra eyed him. David pointed to his pants again. "Modesty," he said as the fire in his cheeks burned hotter.

"Modesty," Panagyra echoed.

The door opened and Todd burst in with a paper bag. "I was afraid I'd left them at home, but I found them behind the—what the..." Todd dropped his bag and slammed the door behind him. Then he cracked it open, glanced up and down the hall, and shut it again. After locking it securely, he leaned against the worn door and let out a sigh.

"That was close." Todd gathered himself and walked around Panagyra. "Whoa, check out those wings." After he finished his circuit, he rubbed the stubble on his chin and assumed a philosopher's pose. "I say," he droned, "he looks like a giant pigeon!"

David wanted to hit him. "A *pigeon*? That's all you can say? Wait a minute, look at this." David urged Panagyra to spread his wings.

Todd gave a low whistle. "Say, do you think he'd be strong enough to carry one of us? Boy, wouldn't that be a blast! Forget hang gliding. This would be the real thing!"

Panagyra pointed to Todd's chest.

"Hey, David, what does he want?"

David explained the short teaching session he had given Panagyra while Todd had been out.

"He asked you to take off your pants?" Todd bellowed and gave a long sustained laugh.

"Shhh!" David cautioned as his cheeks burned again. "We don't know how thin these walls are."

"You may have a point there," Todd answered, a little more sober. "Still, you, of all people..." He barely suppressed a laugh as he wandered to his room.

David slipped on a clean undershirt. *Lord, don't let Todd do anything stupid. Help us; we don't know what we're doing!*

3. On the Job Training

Darius Blackwell shook his head as he read through the report on his desk. "Idiots!" he fumed.

He looked up at the man standing before him. "You're certain it went down in this area?"

"Yes, sir. It's where we lost radar contact. Our people scoured a ten-mile radius just to be certain."

Standing up, Darius paced on the plush carpet in his office. "No impact craters, no wreckage...it didn't crash. It *landed*. The pilot must have hidden the ship. That means it's alive."

"Do you want Merloc to help search for—"

"No! If he brings a crullah into the area, it will stir up a hornet's nest. There are too many people nearby. The last thing we want are witnesses screaming about UFOs. Even if Merloc could find it, he'd insist we eliminate it."

Darius stopped pacing and turned to the man. "I want all the officers at the road blocks interviewed—again! Run a check on the license plates of every car that went through there. I need some answers and fast! Whatever it is, Merloc is afraid of it and I want to know why. I *will* find out."

"Anything else, sir?"

Darius seated himself and stared off into space. "Perhaps this alien is as ignorant of humans as Merloc was. I bet it's lying low, figuring out its next move. The same language barrier Merloc had to overcome probably faces our little visitor as well."

His gray eyes narrowed into slivers of polished granite. "But what if someone else finds the alien first? That could be a serious problem. If the alien were to befriend some humans...still, how long can something like that be hidden? We'll have to move quickly. Things could turn ugly if civilians become entangled. If only I knew what this alien looked like."

He focused back on the man standing in front of him. "Tell Merloc we killed the alien and destroyed its remains. That will keep him happy."

David wandered into the kitchen for breakfast. It was three days since they'd found Panagyra and they were still hiding him in the apartment.

The great bird stood beside the kitchen counter with Todd, watching.

Todd's strong arms beat some eggs in a chipped bowl. "There's something that really bothers me."

"What's that?" David tensed, wondering if Todd was serious.

The corner of Todd's mouth turned up. "We gotta do something about his name. How about shortening it to Pan?"

"No, Pan sounds too pagan."

"Well, *excuse* me!" Todd mocked.

David rubbed his chin. "How about Gyra?"

"Gyra. I like that." Todd grinned and looked at Panagyra.

With a little effort, they got Panagyra to accept his new name.

David watched as Gyra stretched his wings and paced. "He's getting restless."

"We can only keep him caged for so long." Todd poured the eggs into a hot frying pan.

David stared at the sizzling mass. "But we can't let him out like this."

"No duh! So what do we do? Send him to the zoo? He's as hard to hide as a pink elephant!"

"There's got to be a way." Running his fingers through his curly hair, David prayed. *Lord, if You want us to protect Gyra, You're going to have to help us!*

Todd walked around Gyra. "Maybe we could hang a sign around his neck. 'Alien for rent. Scare unwanted relatives. Entertain your friends. Ten bucks an hour.'" He paused. "Nah, he doesn't look scary enough—unless you're a statue."

David frowned. "*Todd!*"

Todd stopped and folded his arms. "Well, what else can you do with an overgrown pigeon who's sprouted arms? You have any better ideas?"

"Not yet." David circled Gyra. "We need to be able to get him out, but not draw too much attention. You know, your idea of hanging a sign on him might not be so bad."

"Huh?" Picking up a spatula, Todd worked on the eggs.

David grinned. "It just might work. A few alterations and we can transform him into a chicken!"

"A chicken?" Todd flipped the omelette and stared at David.

"Yeah! People wouldn't see an alien; they'd just see some guy dressed up in a chicken outfit."

Snorting, Todd raised an eyebrow. "You mean like those guys in weird outfits who stand on street corners to attract customers?"

"Exactly."

"But who would hire Gyra?"

"My cousin Jeff might go for it."

Todd pressed the spatula onto the frying eggs, making them sizzle louder. "Well, I suppose we could try it. Can't think of anything better. Shoot, who'd really suspect him dressed up like a chicken?"

As David drove his old car down the city streets, Todd leaned back and put a friendly arm around Gyra. The alien looked rather comical in his chicken disguise.

"I gotta give you credit," Todd said, picking at the old vinyl on his door. "It's a great idea. Whether it works or not, it's still a great idea. And you know what I like best? We can take him almost anywhere without hiding him. Boy, won't that be a relief. Fun too!"

David looked at Gyra. "Todd is human. David is human." He gestured to several people outside. "Human." David pointed to his feathered companion. "Gyra is..."

The large bird blinked. "Gyra is phantera."

"Phan-tera," David repeated. He pulled into a park.

As Todd coaxed Gyra out of the car, David stretched and relished the warm sun.

The great bird rubbed his fake chicken comb and adjusted the advertising sign that read, *Eat at Chuckie's Chicken. Home of the famous Golden Bird.* A red apron bulging with candy, plastic toys, and coupons hid the phantera's backward knees.

"Let's go," Todd urged.

A gentle wind sent a few leaves skittering across the gravel path as they walked.

David breathed in the park's pleasant scents. "I can't believe you've never been to Whitefield Park, Todd. Of all the parks in Los Arboles, this one's the best."

Glancing around, Todd said, "I believe you. Most of the parks I've seen are pretty run down."

Swinging his arms, David enjoyed the warm, outdoor air. "Whitefield has always been my favorite. The natural lake, old walnut grove, flower gardens, and lakeside gazebo bring back such memories. There's even a bronze bust of George Whitefield himself."

"Whoever he was," Todd muttered.

David pointed to a path that branched off near the lake. "Up the hill on the right is the best of the gardens. Some benefactor donated a collection of statues, replicas of famous works. Burt the gardener keeps them spotless and guards them like a pit bull. He's got a reputation for being tough on mischievous kids. Even the gangs give him a wide berth."

A young blind woman searched the path with her cane as she strode by.

Todd turned and walked backwards, gawking at the woman. "She's got a lot of guts to come here alone." Whirling back around, he threw his head back and put on a mocking poetic air. "Ah, Whitefield Park—a haven for lovers, bird watchers, wild children, and space aliens."

David chuckled at his friend. "The place is pretty crowded now, but when school starts, it will be almost deserted. When I was little, my family came here for picnics. We'd play ball and fly kites. Dad used to take me out in a rowboat on the lake."

Todd wore a vacant expression.

David cringed. *Great move, David. Just remind Todd about your wonderful happy family—rub his nose in it. How could you forget his biggest heartache? With a father who's as huggable as a cactus, and a mother who bailed out long ago, it's a miracle he has a shred of sanity left. At least his step-mom didn't give up on him.*

They strode into the shadows of the old walnut grove.

"This semester was definitely the toughest schedule juggling I've ever done," Todd complained.

"I know, but the discipline will be good for you." David poked his friend gently in the ribs.

"Discipline. I'm so sick of that word."

David raised a cautioning finger. "It's the only way we can keep an eye on Gyra and be full-time students. I don't relish the idea of taking night classes any more than you do."

"Good-bye social life." Todd kissed his fingers.

Gyra imitated the gesture, causing his two escorts to laugh.

Todd slapped Gyra's back. "Well, at least he cheers me up. It sure is nice to be outside. I was beginning to go crazy in the apartment."

"Todd, you already were crazy."

As they walked toward the lake, a group of youngsters ran to meet them. David tried not to panic as they mobbed Gyra, but the phantera calmly gave out his gifts, as planned.

The children finally raced off to the lake with their candy, toy chickens, and coupons.

David taught Gyra the names of the trees, plants, and animals that lived in the park. When they arrived at the lake, Gyra eyed the ducks that cruised at the water's edge. "*Duca dilu*," he said wistfully.

"Duck," David said pointing to a fat, Pekin drake.

"Duca," Gyra repeated.

"Doo-kah," Todd imitated. "Do you suppose they have ducks where Gyra comes from?"

"Duca naharam?" David asked.

Gyra scratched his neck where the sign rubbed it. "Duca no naharam. Duca *chelra*."

Laughing, the group of children chased each other along the lakeside.

"Hey, Nabil, come here," cried a black kid further down the shoreline. "There's a duck all wrapped in fishing line. Help me catch him."

A little Arab boy ran to the black kid.

David and his friends followed.

A small gathering of children stood on the bank as the little black boy pointed to the Pekin duck sitting offshore.

"The white one, Dewan?" asked the Arab boy.

"Yeah, give me some bread. Maybe we can catch it."

Oblivious to park rules about harassing ducks, the two boys threw bread into the water while the other kids watched.

When the duck wandered within range, Nabil pounced.

The duck released several hardy squawks as its wings splashed water on Nabil and his peers, but the little boy had a good grasp on his quarry and hauled it in.

The children lavished praise on Nabil for his skill as the boy carried the duck a safe distance from the lake. Their squirrel-like chattering died when they saw David and his friends.

"You're not going to turn us in, are you?" Dewan asked with an expression bordering on terror.

"Why should I? You're only trying to help a duck." David chuckled. "Bring her here and let me have a look at her."

The children resumed their jabbering.

Sitting down with the duck on the grass, he fished a pocketknife out of his pocket and proceeded to cut away the line. Fortunately there were no hooks.

"Stupid fishermen," commented a girl. "I wish they weren't allowed to fish in the lake."

"I used to fish here," David said casually, continuing to cut away the line. "The problem isn't the fishing. It's the sloppy people who don't pick up after themselves."

The girl took his gentle reprimand in silence.

"There." Clearing away the last strands of line, David released the duck into a ring of kids.

The children crowded closer to pet the now docile bird.

David balled up the scraps of line and handed it to the girl. "Here, put this in the trashcan by the bench."

"But I didn't make the mess," she protested. "Why should I clean it up?"

"Because if you don't, another duck could get caught in it."

The girl sighed but took the tangled line.

"Gyra," Todd whispered, "Duck naharam?"

Gyra reached down and stroked the duck. His fingers lingered on the duck's head. "No naharam," he said withdrawing his hand. "Duck dalam."

"What'd he say?" Nabil asked.

"Uh, he was saying the duck was...pretty." Todd blushed.

Dewan's black face scowled. "What language was that?"

David looked around at the ethnically mixed group of kids. He had better pick a language they didn't know and fast. Spanish was out, so were Cambodian, Arabic, and Korean.

"Yali Indian." *Forgive me, Lord.*

"Really?" Nabil asked.

Todd glanced over his shoulder. "Uh, David, I think we should leave before—"

"Whatta you punks doing with my duck!" a harsh voice shouted. Old Burt was running up the path, bellowing like an enraged bull.

The children shrieked and scattered into the shrubs.

Picking up the duck, David stood to face Burt.

"If you've hurt my duck I'll make sure they fine you double!"

David whispered to Todd, "Be careful. To Burt, everything in the park is his—*his* statues, *his* flower gardens, and *his* ducks."

Todd trembled and David guessed his friend would rather join the children in the bushes than stay by his side.

Panagyra looked at Todd and David, but was probably too ignorant to be alarmed.

"Just what do ya think you're doing?" Burt demanded. He was the tallest person there, with the exception of Gyra.

"We were helping one of your ducks," David said.

"Oh, really?" the gardener scoffed.

"Yeah, it was caught in some fishing line," Todd added.

"Oh, really?" Burt took a menacing step closer to Todd. "Then where's the fishing line?" he growled.

Todd took a few faltering steps backward.

Burt planted himself before Gyra and glared into his red eyes. "Where did you come from? The circus or the zoo?" The groundskeeper jabbed a gnarled finger at the sign on Gyra's chest. "So, is Chuckie's so cheap that now he's stealing ducks to fry?"

Gyra cocked his head.

"If you want to see the fishing line, you'll find it in the trashcan by the bench." David forced calm into his voice and measured every word.

Burt's hard eyes examined David for a tense moment. "All right," the cantankerous man said. "We'll see if it's there. Come with me and don't even think of running off. If you try, I'll hunt you down and drag you to the station by the ears...for those of you who *have* ears."

Upon reaching the trashcan, Burt pawed at the line sitting on top and frowned.

"Look," David said, opening one of the duck's wings. He showed Burt the cuts and scars from the fishing line.

The groundskeeper's alert eyes met his. "So, you really were helping her, eh?" Todd nodded vigorously. David gave the duck to Burt. The groundskeeper lovingly stroked the duck's feathers and set it down. Wiggling its tail, the fat Pekin waddled into the pond, quacking in a rapid staccato.

"Well, it's nice to see someone doing something good for a change." Burt put out his hand and shook David's with a strong grip. "Good day to you, sir," he grumbled and was gone.

David smiled. Burt never apologized for anything, but David accepted the brief rare expression of goodwill from the man.

"Come on, let's go," Todd urged.

They entered the flower garden and David had to teach Gyra not to touch the statues. He certainly didn't want to get on Burt's bad side. Most of the statues were clothed, but a replica of Michelangelo's "David" stood atop a fountain. Drawn to the nude figure, Gyra circled it, stopped in front, and pointed a finger at it. "No modesty," he declared.

Todd snickered. "You can say that again."

David remembered the time he had taken his shirt off in front of Gyra. "He's saying the statue doesn't have any pants on. He thinks *modesty* means *pants*."

Gyra wandered over to a statue of Venus.

Todd's cheeks glowed pink as his eyes searched the garden. "Gee, David, I hope we don't have to teach him about the birds and the bees," he whispered. "Maybe this isn't such a great place to be right now."

Pointing to Venus, David said, "Female." He aimed his finger at the statue of David. "Male." Gesturing to Todd and himself, he said "Male." Gyra nodded and repeated the exercise.

A young woman strolled down a nearby path. "Female," Todd whispered. Gyra pointed to her. "Female."

"I think that's enough for now." Todd clutched his stomach. "Let's get some lunch."

On the way to the car, Gyra pointed out various people and declared their gender. David marveled at Gyra's accuracy. Different clothes and body weight didn't confuse the alien at all. He identified some people faster than David!

Just before getting into the car, David said, "Todd is male, David is male. Gyra is..."

Gyra glanced at Todd and David. "Gyra is male."

"Do you think he really understands?" Todd whispered.

Rubbing his chin, David said, "Yes, I think he does."

Todd wore a twisted smile. "Well, that's great. I was wondering what you'd have done if you found out Gyra was a *she*."

Stopping at a public library on the way home, David picked up some children's books to expand Gyra's understanding.

Back at the apartment, David poured over the books with Gyra. In no time David covered the alphabet and basic phonics.

"You know at the rate he learns...it's kind of scary," Todd commented.

"Yeah, I know," David returned in a low voice. "I don't have to repeat things. It's like he has perfect memory, but just because he can repeat a word doesn't mean he understands it. I still wish there was a faster way to teach him."

"Here, let me take over for a while." Todd took the book from David and sat beside Gyra. The big phantera crouched bird-style on the ground.

As soon as Todd was settled into teaching, David retreated to his room, sat on his bed, and leaned his slender frame against the cool wall. His gaze fell to the Bible on his nightstand. Picking it up, he caressed the smooth worn leather with his fingers. When was the last time he'd read it? He released a weary sigh. The past week had been incredibly busy. *I'm sorry, Lord.*

Did Gyra's arrival challenge David's beliefs? Before Gyra, David had written off claims of alien contacts and UFOs as pure nonsense. What were the ramifications of alien life-forms, especially intelligent ones?

Doubts crowded in around him. What if Gyra came from a race of beings that were technologically superior and morally barbaric? What kind of a moral code did they have—if any? Would they laugh at Christianity? Did they believe in God? Perhaps they had their own gods. Was Gyra good? Evil? A little of both?

David looked down at his Bible again. Did God give the same guidelines and rules to all sentient life? The cold wall sapped the warmth from his back. What if there *was* no absolute moral code and his beliefs were obsolete, unable to handle change? The stale air in David's room smothered him. He looked up at the cracked yellowed ceiling. His lungs labored under an unseen pressure. Was he a narrow-minded fool? How could he reconcile his faith with the reality of the alien in his apartment? Perhaps all those wacky New Age people were right.

"No!" David spoke with odd difficulty. The pressure increased. His throat felt like a great snake was constricting it.

Sooner or later, people would find out about Gyra. It would be the scandal of the century. The press and conspiracy freaks would have a feeding frenzy. Gyra was a danger to David's faith, to the church, to his family, to all David loved. It would be best if he just secretly surrendered the alien to the authorities.

"It would be wrong to abandon him!" David forced out. He was scared. He was helpless and the situation was hopeless.... Wait a minute. He'd felt this before. These thoughts weren't his own! His throat was so constricted he couldn't speak; he could barely breathe.

But David could still pray. *Jesus, help me!* his mind cried out.

"*Yavana!*" Gyra cried as he burst into David's room. "*Yavana elah David!*"

The malevolent spirit released David immediately. Air rushed back into his lungs.

"Whoa, Gyra, take it easy. David, are you all right?" Todd asked from the doorway.

The phantera raised both his hands and stretched them toward David. "*Ramara sa Yavana. Naphema hamoth David tor mel-aradelah. Dee David sarena.*"

Gyra lowered his arms, placed a gentle hand on David's shoulder, and peered carefully into his eyes.

"What was that all about?" Todd asked with a stunned expression. "The only words I was able to catch were *David* and *Yavana.*"

Rubbing his throat, David gave Gyra's arm a pat. "Let's go out to the kitchen."

Todd microwaved a cup of hot chocolate and offered it to David. "Now, do you want to tell me why you were as pale as a ghost when we came in?"

"I'm not sure you'd understand."

Feigning an arrow wound to the chest, Todd cried, "Oooh! That hurt!"

"All right, only promise not to laugh."

"Cross my heart. Cub scout's honor," Todd replied with the appropriate hand gestures.

David took a cautious sip from his mug and set it down before sharing his experience.

Todd appeared enraptured by David's tale, waiting

until David finished before asking questions—a rare act of discipline for Todd.

"So, this happened to you twice: once right after we brought Gyra home and the other time just now?"

"Yes," David said in a low voice.

Todd wore a serious look. "You think Gyra caused it, like put a hex on you?"

David took another sip of his now lukewarm chocolate. "Yes and no. I experienced something similar a few times *before* Gyra came. Each happened just before or after a major turning point in my life. Christians call it 'being attacked.'"

Todd leaned forward. "What did you do to get rid of it?"

"Since my throat was being choked, I prayed to Jesus in my mind and it left."

"Whoa, this is too weird." Todd shook his head. "How does Gyra fit in?"

"At first I thought he might be the cause of it, but I don't think so now. Gyra looked distressed too. I think someone is trying to keep us from learning about Gyra. They're trying to plant fear in our hearts."

Todd raised an eyebrow. "Someone or something?"

David was embarrassed to use the word *demon* in front of Todd, yet that was exactly what he thought it was. "There's a lot more going on than we know, Todd. A whole lot more."

4. A Close Call

Glancing at his watch, David rose from the couch. "Time to go. I don't want to be late for my first class, even if I hate going to school at night. Make sure Gyra stays out of trouble."

Todd put an arm around Gyra. "Don't worry, we'll be fine."

"With you? I worry!" David grabbed his backpack.

"Thanks for the encouragement!" Todd yelled as David headed out.

David shut the door, paused, and hurried down the hallway. *Lord, look after them. I can't be in two places at once.*

Todd waited until he was certain David had left the building. "Come on, Gyra, let's go cruisin'." He didn't have a car, so his idea of *cruisin'* meant a ride on the bus.

Once Gyra was dressed in his chicken outfit, they hopped on the local transit, drawing more than a few stares. Getting off at Main Street, Todd and Gyra strolled down the sidewalk.

The streetlights cast a sickly orange aura around them. Todd pointed out the window items on display.

A woman walked by with a bulging belly. "See that?" Todd whispered after the woman passed by. "She's pregnant. She's gonna have a baby."

"Pregnant," Gyra repeated.

Walking along the storefronts, Todd spied a hooker standing on a corner. "The place has sure gone down hill the last few years."

Gyra cocked his head. "Where is the hill?"

"It's just a saying, an expression, a...never mind. It means the place ain't as nice as it used to be."

Todd moved on. "Look." He pointed to an elderly man using a cane. "That man is an old man. I am a young man."

"How can you tell?" Gyra asked, wagging his head in an odd manner.

"Easy: the gray hair, his stooped walk, but especially the wrinkles on his face. Old people have wrinkled skin."

They paused before a smoke-filled bar. "Leroy's

Lounge" proclaimed the rusty sign. Heading for the open door, Gyra asked, "What is in here?"

"Wait a minute!" Todd grabbed him by the apron. "You can't go in there unless you're twenty-one."

"Twenty-one what?"

"Twenty-one years."

"How long is a year?"

"Three hundred and sixty-five days. A day is twenty-four hours and an hour is sixty minutes." Todd didn't have a watch on so he was at a loss as to how to proceed.

Gyra nodded. "Then I am seventy-three years and forty-three days old."

"How did you figure your age out so fast?"

"Easy. I fixed it and added. Do you not know how?"

"Yes, but not that fast." He put an arm around Gyra. "Come on."

As they entered the dim room a low voice assaulted them. "Wait a minute, birdie. You don't show a face and an ID, you better not come in here."

"It's okay, Uncle Frank," Todd called.

"Todd? Todd Fox?" The bartender swore. "I haven't seen you since last year. Where've ya been?"

"Keep'n my nose clean." Todd sat down on a barstool.

Frank stuck his thumb toward Gyra. "Who's your buddy here?"

"Gyra. He comes from another country, so I thought I'd show him around the place."

Frank frowned. "Is he a minor?"

"No, but, hey, we're only gonna order soft drinks, so don't worry."

Still frowning, Frank asked, "What'll you have?"

Todd glanced at Gyra. "How about two root beers?"

"Two root beers coming up."

Leaning closer to the phantera, Todd spoke in a low tone. "This is a bar. People come in here to order drinks, meet people, and have fun."

The Gyra looked around. "Drinks like root beer?"

Todd winced. "No, drinks like real beer, wine, scotch, whiskey...drinks that have alcohol in them. It makes people feel good, forget their problems. Sometimes they get a little drunk, like that table over in the corner."

Gyra followed Todd's gaze. Two women and two men laughed uncontrollably. One of the girls fell to the floor still giggling.

"Is she sick?" Gyra asked.

"No, just drunk."

"Why?"

"Huh?" The question caught Todd off guard.

"Why would she want to get drunk? It makes her act sick."

Todd's lips tightened into a sad smile.

The phantera's keen red eyes examined another table. "Why does the female over there have water on her face?"

Turning, Todd saw a young woman staring into her drink, tears rolling down her face. "She is very sad." He stared at the sticky counter. How could he explain the facts of life to Gyra?

"Water comes out of your eyes when you are sad?"

"Yeah, it's called crying." Todd took the two root beers, but he didn't feel very thirsty.

"Phantera do something like that when they are sad too. Why is she sad?"

"I don't know." Todd took a sip of root beer anyway. Setting down his mug, he paid Frank. When he turned back to Gyra, Todd found himself staring into empty space. "Gyra?"

The big bird had wandered off to one of the tables.

Sipping his drink, Todd watched. Let Gyra explore a little. He'd bail the alien out if he got in over his head.

The phantera towered over the seated crying girl.

"Hello, I am Gyra. Todd says you are very sad."

She glanced up at him and turned away, blushing.

"Why are you so sad you crying water on your face?"

Staring into her drink, the girl winced. "Where do I begin? My boyfriend beats me. If I leave him, he'll kill me. If I date anyone else, he'll kill them."

Gyra eyed the bruises on the woman's arms and face. "Your boy does not sound like a friend."

She dried one eye with a cocktail napkin and gave a weak smile. "No, I guess he's not. All the same, I'm afraid to leave him."

"I could help you leave your boy." Gyra put a hand on her shoulder.

Todd realized Gyra was mimicking the way *he'd* tried to reassure the phantera.

"How old are you?" the girl asked.

"I am seventy-three years and forty-three days old," Gyra answered.

She smirked. "Are you an engineer?"

"What is an engineer?"

Her smirk turned into a frown. "Where're you from?"

"Arana."

"Where's that?"

Gyra fingered his bill. "Far from here."

"Must be. Listen, pal, if you want to live to be seventy-four, you'd better leave me while you can. Just forget about me. Besides, you're too old."

Gyra cocked his head. "What is *too old*?"

A tall man dressed in black leather strode into the bar. "Take your creepy claws off my girl, Big Bird."

Todd leaped off his stool. Now was the time to intervene.

Gyra apparently did not realize that the brooding man was the abusive boyfriend. Turning to Todd, Gyra pointed at the towering enormous beer-belly before him, and declared, "Pregnant."

"No, no, Gyra, that's not pregnant, that's fat." The words were out of his mouth before he could call them back.

The big man swung around and glared at Todd. "Who you calling fat, runt?"

"Please," Todd said, "I was only trying to help my friend. He's a foreigner and can barely speak English."

"I don't care what planet he's from—"

"Arana," Gyra said.

"Shut up!" the biker shouted.

Gyra looked up at the ceiling. "I see no door. What is there to *shut up*?"

"He doesn't understand, Ed," the girl pleaded in a ragged voice. "Please, just leave him alone. He didn't do nothin'."

"He's still got his paw on you." Ed took a step closer.

"Is this your boy who is not a friend?" Gyra asked.

The girl nodded slightly and hung her head.

"We're in trouble," Todd whispered.

The bar went silent except for the tapping of Ed's steel-toed boots. He was almost as tall as Gyra. Squinting as he faced the phantera, Ed asked, "You lookin' for a fight, you big chicken?"

"Oh God!" Todd breathed in terror. It was the closest he had come to praying in a long time.

Gyra blinked. "What is a *fight*?"

Ed's expression went blank. He broke into a hoarse laugh and spit tobacco juice onto the floor.

Cocking his head, Gyra asked, "What is that smell from your mouth? It is new to me."

"No!" Todd muttered, covering his forehead with his hand.

Ed stopped laughing. "I'll show you what *fight* means." His bloodshot eyes narrowed maliciously. "Move away, woman." Reaching down, Ed grabbed the girl by the arm and yanked her aside.

"Oww!" she cried through clenched teeth.

"Frank!" Todd whispered to the bartender. "Why don't you do something?"

"And have Ed's gang trash my place? No way!"

A righteous anger welled up in Todd, but he didn't know what to do.

The feathers rose on Gyra's head as he faced Ed. "I will not let you beat her."

Face flushed, Ed wrinkled his nose like a mad dog. His thick fingers dug further into the girl's arm. "Just try and stop me!"

Quicker then Todd would have expected, Ed's right fist shot for the girl's face.

"No!" she screamed.

Ed's hand hung frozen a mere inch from the girl's face with Gyra's claws firmly wrapped around it. The biker's face paled a little, but he recovered and yanked his hand back. Releasing the girl, he spat on the floor. His right hand flew forward again, then veered away as his left fist went straight for Gyra's belly.

Once more Gyra neatly grabbed Ed's fist, but this time when the biker tried to pull back, Gyra didn't let go.

Cursing, Ed swung his right foot for the alien's knees, but Gyra grabbed the biker's boot with his clawed foot.

Todd hoped the tables blocked most people's view of Gyra from the knees down.

Spitting and screaming, Ed squirmed, but he couldn't break loose. He swung at Gyra with his free hand, but Gyra caught it too. With only one leg to balance on, Ed struggled in vain to break the alien's grip. "I'm gonna snuff you!"

"What is *snuff*?" Gyra asked.

"Shut up!" Ed screamed.

"You still have not told me what that means," Gyra replied in a calm voice.

"Aarrgghh!" Spitting tobacco juice at Gyra's vest, Ed

kicked at the phantera with his free leg, but found himself flung to the dirty floor.

Todd breathed when he realized Gyra had dodged the booted foot.

The biker rolled to his feet and stood up. Snatching an empty beer mug, Ed hurled it at Gyra. The phantera caught it and set it down gently on a table.

Ed grabbed a chair and heaved it, but the alien caught it too, and put it down. The biker stood panting for a moment, brown juice running from his mouth. Slowly, he reached behind and under his jacket. Out came a large knife. A grin spread across his unshaven face.

The people behind Gyra moved away, but the phantera never turned.

With a wild look in his eye, Ed said, "Time to carve up a chicken dinner." He approached Gyra holding the knife in front of him.

"Look out, Gyra!" Todd yelled. "He's gonna throw it!"

"*Yavana hamoth!*" Gyra cried.

In an instant, the biker hurled his lethal missile with deadly accuracy. Too hemmed in by the tables to dodge the knife, the phantera snatched up a wooden peanut bowl. The tense moment of silence was broken by the *thunk* of steel into wood.

"So *that* is what *snuff* means," Gyra said in a low voice. He pulled the large blade from the bowl.

The yellow-toothed grin on Ed's face drooped into a frown as he panted heavily. With a yell, he charged the phantera, but stopped when Gyra held up the silvery blade to examine it. Beads of sweat ran down Ed's face and his skin lost its reddish color.

Gyra looked at the biker, looked at the knife, and turned to Todd. "What should I do?"

"Get rid of the knife," Todd said in a shaky voice.

"Should I put it where he cannot reach it?"

"Sure! Fine! Just do it quick!" Todd just wanted to take Gyra and run.

"Okay." Gyra flung the knife at one of the hefty wooden beams spanning the ceiling. The blade sank two inches into the wood.

Pausing just long enough to see his knife was gone, Ed launched himself at Gyra with hands outstretched to throttle the great bird.

Grabbing both arms, Gyra promptly threw the biker back onto the ground. He rolled Ed onto his beer belly and pounced on him—like an eagle on a rabbit. Seizing Ed's flailing legs with one hand, and the thick hairy arms with his other, Gyra's long fingers secured the limbs like living shackles.

Todd crept over to the pay phone, punched in 911, and sneaked back, leaving the receiver off the hook. Now what could he do?

Screaming like a burned cat, Ed issued an unabated stream of profanity until a beer bottle crashed down on his head.

Gyra looked up.

Ed's girlfriend said, "Thanks, I owe you one." She tossed the broken bottleneck onto the floor, went back to her table, and sat down.

Todd rushed over to Gyra. "You were incredible." He stared down at the still body. "Is he dead?"

"I do not know what *dead* means."

"Has he...stopped completely?" Todd kicked away some of the larger pieces of glass.

"His insides still move."

"Fine." Todd glanced around.

The other bar patrons appeared to be getting over their shock and murmured quietly.

The wail of a distant police siren grew louder.

"Let's get out of here," Todd said in a hushed voice.

No one stopped them as they fled out the door. They were only a couple of shops away when the police car pulled up to the bar.

Officer Graham stepped into the dim bar with his partner. "I got a weird call," he announced. "What's up?"

A hush descended upon the place and numerous patrons slipped out the door.

"Over here," a lone girl responded. She pointed to the unconscious biker on the floor. "My name's Irene. He started it. Tried to take me away by force, so I cracked his head with a beer bottle. It was self-defense."

"Steve, call for a paramedic," Officer Graham told his partner. Turning back to the girl, his practiced eyes noticed the bruises on her arms and face.

Setting his jaw, Officer Graham looked around the nearly empty room. "Anyone else see this?" The remaining people turned away or stared into their drinks.

"I did," said the bartender. "She's telling the truth."

"Do you want to press charges?" the officer asked the girl.

For a moment, Irene stared in silence at the inert form at her feet. "Yes," she said quietly.

Officer Graham watched, amazed as Irene uncurled from her cowering position. She looked at him, face growing firm with resolve. "I'll tell you about all the beatings and threats. And if you wanna make a bigger bust, just search his place on Eleventh Street."

She rubbed a bruise on her wrist. "His bike is hot too. You'll find it parked illegally on the sidewalk just outside."

Officer Graham allowed a slight smile to break through his professional demeanor. "You're one brave lady."

Irene looked away. "No, not really."

Down the block, Todd led Gyra onto the bus heading home. As soon as he found a seat, Todd took a deep breath and let out a moan.

Gyra remained standing.

"Finally we're safe," Todd said.

Eyeing him, the phantera said, "I do not understand. We were not safe before we left the bar?"

"Yes and no." Todd glanced around to see if anyone else was listening. "The way you handled that guy was great, but the police were coming and I didn't want them asking us a bunch of questions."

"Did police make sound that scared you?"

Todd smiled. His friend's perception amused him at times. "The police ride in a car that makes the sound you heard. It wasn't the sound that scared me, it was what the sound meant. I was afraid of the police."

"Are police bad?"

Todd noticed an elderly woman peering over her newspaper. "No, Gyra, they are not bad—not usually. As a matter of fact, I called them while you two were fight—er...figuring things out. I just was trying to save you a lot of unnecessary hassle."

"Hassle is bad?"

Todd laughed. "Yes, hassle is *very* bad. Hassle is having to fill out endless forms, standing in long lines, and dealing with bureaucrats...." Todd babbled on with his definition of "hassle," not caring if he left Gyra in the dust on the road to understanding. He just wanted to keep his friend from raising any more suspicions.

As they got off the bus, Todd finally ceased. He was exhausted to the bone.

"That man said many new words when he fight me," Gyra said. "What do they mean?"

Todd stopped walking. "Gyra, those words should never be used."

Cocking his head, the phantera assumed his typical "I do not understand" pose.

Okay, try it again. Todd sighed. "The words that man spoke were bad words. He spoke those words because he was a bad man. Bad people say words like that." Todd winced. He knew he was being simplistic. Wasn't foul language a vice he indulged in from time to time? What would Gyra think if he heard Todd cuss later? Even David let a bad word fly on rare occasions.

He continued walking in silence until they reached the apartment building. In the elevator, Todd thought he would collapse from fatigue. Finally the door opened and he plodded down the hall. Almost home. They were out of the woods now.

Once inside the apartment, Todd promptly locked the door and crashed onto the old couch.

David wandered in from the kitchen. "Short class tonight. Just a brief orientation and then we left to pick up our books."

He walked up to Todd and towered over him. "Are you all right? You look like death warmed over. What happened?"

"Man try to snuff Gyra," the phantera commented.

Todd moaned and pulled a pillow over his face.

5. A Major Breakthrough

"You took Gyra to a *what?*" David was stunned. He felt betrayed.

Todd held up his hands. "We were just strolling by the bar and he asked to see it."

Cringing, David rubbed the curls sticking to his forehead. "Great, just great. And I suppose you ordered him a round while you were there?"

"No, David, I didn't! All we had was root beer, honest! I haven't had a drink all summer."

David folded his arms, reining in his anger. Perhaps it wasn't as bad as it sounded. "All right. Tell me what happened—*everything.*"

Todd gave an account of their adventure, sprinkled with many apologies. "I thought for sure we were going to lose him," Todd added when he finished.

David sighed. Todd's remorse was deeper than any tongue-lashing could produce. There was no sense in laboring over his friend's poor judgment. "I don't know whether to praise you or scold you for calling the police. Who knows what they would have done with Gyra. Still, the Todd I knew a few years ago would have run off and climbed into the nearest hole."

Todd's eyes watered as he wiped his nose on his sleeve.

David put an arm around his friend, remembering the last time Todd had cried in front of him. Todd still hurt from his father's second divorce and was full of bitterness toward his father. He rarely cried, but whenever things got rough, he came to David.

Sighing deeply, David closed his eyes. Was he really the only guy Todd could trust, the only one his friend could open up to? *God, may I never violate that trust!*

"Todd sad," Gyra declared. "Todd have water on his face. Tears."

The two guys laughed and the mood was gone.

"Oh, that reminds me—" David dashed off to the kitchen and brought back a pile of books. "I checked these out from the library after I went to the bookstore." He rummaged through the small stack. "Ah! Here's a book on grammar, one on basic math, advanced math, simple science, and after that, chemistry and biology."

Todd fingered through a book. "Boy, you sure went hog-wild, didn't you? Wait a minute. You forgot my favorite subject."

"Which is?"

"History!" Todd stuck his tongue out in distaste.

David chuckled. "Actually, I did think about it, but I didn't want him to find out from a book. I figured it might soften the blow if I told him myself."

"Hey, we're not that bad!" Todd protested.

Counting on his fingers, David said, "Nazi Germany, the Inquisition, slavery, human sacrifices, the gladiators, communism, genocide..."

"Okay, okay!" Todd held up his hands in surrender. "I get your drift."

"We'll start him off with grammar first." David handed Gyra the book.

The phantera opened it. He turned the pages slowly at first, then faster.

David looked on, amused. "My counselor says you should always take your English classes first. Then you'll do better in your other classes."

"So, that's my problem," Todd said with a smirk. "No wonder my reports never got A's."

"No, Todd, that's not why. It's because you didn't start your reports until 11:00 the night before they were due." David wore a firm smile. "But not this year."

"Yes, Mother."

"That was a good book," Gyra said. "It will help me speak more clearly."

David and Todd looked at each other.

"You finished that whole book?" Todd asked.

Scratching the white feathers on his neck, Gyra said, "Yes, but it will take a few minutes for me to understand all the details. Why do you look surprised?"

David answered. "We've never seen anyone read that fast before."

"Whoa," Todd spoke in a hushed voice. "This dude's gonna pass us up real fast."

"I think you're right, Todd." David rubbed his chin.

"The only thing slowing him down is us."

Gyra cocked his head. "I do not understand. My fast learning scares you?"

"A little," David said slowly. "Humans tend to be wary of someone who is stronger or smarter than they are. They're afraid of being hurt."

Fingering the tip of his pink bill, Gyra said, "I see. I will not try to hurt or control you. I want very much for you to...I do not have the words for it. I need more words."

David held up a finger. "Wait a minute." He ran back into his bedroom, snatched up his dictionary, and returned.

"Are you sure you want to do this?" Todd asked. "He'll end up with a bigger vocabulary than we have."

"It will help him to communicate," David said to reassure his skeptical friend. He gave the large book to Gyra. "This book doesn't have all the words we speak, but it has most of them."

Cradling the dictionary, Gyra looked up at the ceiling and said, "Harana nal ramara sa Yavana."

He turned to David. "Thank you. This means a lot to me." His purple scaly fingers paged through the book.

Todd and David exchanged glances once more.

"Let's have some ice cream," Todd suggested. "All this studying makes me hungry."

David followed him into the kitchen where Todd pulled out the Rocky Road and Chocolate Mint. They were on their second bowls when Gyra burst into the kitchen, dictionary in hand.

"I have so many questions," the phantera jabbered. "But I have to tell you something first. My name is in here."

"What?" Todd leaped up.

"Let me see," David asked as he took the book. He searched the g section.

Gyra stopped him. "No, not there." Turning to the p's, Gyra pointed to a word. "Here!"

"Panegyric," David said.

Todd laughed. "Close, but it ends with a *c* sound."

"It is a form of my name," Gyra insisted.

David lowered his eyebrows. "How do you know?"

"Because of its meaning."

Shaking his blond head, Todd said, "I don't understand."

"Panegyric, second meaning: 'elaborate praise or laudation.'" The phantera looked expectantly at the two puzzled faces before him. "My name means *high praise*."

"We can see that," Todd said, pointing to the page.

"No, you do not understand." Gyra lowered his head until it was on the same level as David's. "My name means *high praise* in Ramatera."

Todd blinked. "What's *Rama-tera*?"

"It is the common language of the naharam, the language of the flexible tongues."

"Great," Todd said in a flat voice. "Go back and read some more."

Gyra took his book and returned to the living room.

Todd gave David a skeptical look. "Why do you suppose he's so excited about a coincidence in words? I mean even some of our *human* languages share the same words."

David rubbed his chin. "I don't know. Many of our languages are interrelated so you'd expect to find similarities. Perhaps it makes him feel better to see something familiar, something that reminds him of home. Maybe it makes our world seem a little less alien to him."

Todd sighed and dished up a third helping of ice cream. "Yeah, I guess if I was marooned on some strange planet, I'd grab on to anything that seemed familiar too."

Glancing at his watch, David announced, "Lights out at eleven. I want to make sure you have plenty of sleep for your first class tomorrow."

"Aye, aye, sir," Todd responded with a salute.

"I plan on making this a habit. You can study while you watch Gyra. Besides," David grinned mischievously, "soon he'll be able to tutor you."

Todd chuckled. "Well, it's about time he started to pay me back for all the things I've taught him." He slowly stirred his ice cream. "David, how smart do you think Gyra is? I mean, how far can he go with all the things he's learning? Do you think he's smarter than Einstein?"

David rubbed his left temple. "I don't know. Actually, I was wondering what he thinks about humans. You've got to admit we're kind of crazy no matter how you look at us."

Todd shrugged his shoulders. "I don't know. Maybe his planet's got problems too."

David flinched. "Exactly!" Springing up, he carried his bowl to the sink and began to wash the dishes.

Todd cocked his head, the way Gyra did when he was confused, and resumed eating his melting ice cream.

With suds on his hands, David worked the sponge over his bowl. There was no reason to trouble Todd more. Thinking of the possibilities of a highly intelligent depraved species made him shudder. Some thoughts were best left unspoken. Over the next two hours, he chatted with Todd about trivial matters.

Later, the phantera crept back into the kitchen.

"You have words for terrible things." Gyra's speech was slow, cautious. "Do humans engage in all these things: abortion, adultery, bigamy, genocide, homosexuality, incest, infidelity, murder, rape, slavery, torture?"

Turning to David, Todd grimaced. "So much for history."

David looked up at the phantera. "Yes, it is true. Some humans are incredibly evil, but most people don't do those things."

"Are you an evil race?" Gyra asked.

"We are a fallen race. Sometimes we want to do good, but we don't."

"Ain't that the truth," Todd breathed.

"I did not find words for some of the things I wish to talk about. Therefore I will use a few Ramatera words and explain them. *Naharam* is our word for all sentient beings. Those naharam who embrace evil are called *mel*. They do the horrific things I found listed in your dictionary. They do them without shame."

"Some of our people may do those things without shame, but most people would feel guilty," David offered.

"Then not all of you are mel-human. If you had been mel, I could not have expected help."

Sitting down at the table once more, David said, "Now that you can communicate better, can you tell us why you're here?"

"I come from a planet called Arana. I never intended to land on Earth. I was scanning an asteroid belt in the Hollun System when I picked up a distant transmission. Someone was talking about the next visit to Earth.

"Since all planetary governments forbid visits to Earth, I decided to investigate. So, I set a course for the back side of your moon. Coming out of *trelemar*, I was ambushed by a ship we call a *crullah*. It is used by some of the mel species. Its pilot was a *mel-hanor*.

"The crullah fired, disabling my weapons. Since I had no way to defend myself, I fled. My trelemar and navigational equipment were also damaged, so I had to fly by sight and sensors while the crullah followed relentlessly.

"I came toward Earth hoping the mel would drop his pursuit. Until now, all have honored the law against visiting Earth, naharam and mel-naharam alike, but this mel showed no fear. He pursued me into your ionosphere, down to the mesosphere. Hitting my craft again, he knocked out my main propulsion system. I jettisoned a cargo container as a decoy. He did not have time to scan it, and guessed I was in it. Turning, he attacked the pod instead of my ship. Then the crullah burned up."

Todd's hazel eyes went wide. "It burned up?"

"His ship could not take high temperatures as well as mine. My ship is called a *delah*. It is made for interplanetary travel and defense.

"After the crullah burned up, I was able to unfold my delah's wings manually. My ship had been heavily damaged and I was barely able to land."

"So, what do you plan to do now?" David asked.

"I need to learn more about your metals and gather some to repair my ship. Then I must leave Earth as soon as possible. I do not know what harm has already been done, but I do not wish to add to it."

Todd gave David a puzzled look.

David held up a hand to stifle Todd's questions. "I will give you some more books to read tonight," David told Gyra. "We will discuss them in the morning."

He went to the living room, brought back the rest of the library books, and set them on the table.

Turning to his roommate, David said, "Todd, it's time we went to bed."

Next morning, Todd rushed off to school while David took his turn "walking the phantera." Although David enjoyed morning strolls, the cool air reeked of industrial stench as he escorted Gyra down the city streets.

"Todd told me that humans go to bars to order drinks, meet people, and have fun," Gyra stated. "But when I looked around, I saw unhappy people sitting by themselves, while others were inebriated. Those who were drunk were laughing at the time, but they would suffer a hangover the next day."

"True," David commented with a wry smile.

With an inquisitive tilt to his head, Gyra asked, "Had they never been to a bar before?"

"They'd probably spent a great deal of time in bars. Why do you ask?"

Gyra wagged his head. "Very strange. They go to bars to drink alcohol, which makes them sick the next day. The people they meet are often troubled themselves and are not good mentors. They go there to have a good time, but get hurt—Ed tried to beat a girl and kill me. I do not understand why people continue to use a bar if it does not fulfill their expectations."

"Todd neglected to tell you that some people get drunk to forget their problems," David said.

"No. He told me. But they will remember when they are sober again," Gyra countered. "Then they will have to face their problems with a hangover. This human custom makes no sense!"

Chuckling, David said, "You aren't the only one to think they're worthless. Not everyone goes to bars. Did the books I gave you last night help?"

"Yes. The metals I need for my ship are aluminum, titanium, chromium, and tin."

"Hmm, most of those should be easy enough." David rubbed his chin. "The only thing I don't know about is the titanium. I know it's used in some drill bits, but that would be an expensive way to buy it. How much metal are you going to need?"

"Two pounds, five pounds, one pound, and a half pound."

"Hold on, Gyra! I need to know how much for each metal."

"But I just told you." The phantera blinked his scarlet eyes. "I gave you the weight in the same order as the metals. Did you forget so soon?"

"Yes! Human memory doesn't work the same as yours." David blew out his breath. His friend was a walking computer!

Scratching at the sign's strap around his neck, Gyra said, "I'm sorry. I did not know. The books helped me a lot, but I still have enormous gaps in knowledge regarding human physiology and customs. It is not my intent to offend."

"I know." David put a hand on the phantera's shoulder. "By the way, out here you should be careful what you say."

Gyra stopped. "Why?"

"Because you never know who might be listening. It could be a mel-human."

The phantera swung his head back and forth. He went rigid. "There are two people around the corner to the left and three people coming up behind. How can you tell if they are mel?"

"You can't."

"*What?*" Gyra cried as the feathers rose straight up on his head. "You mean you live with mel-humans all around you, not knowing who they are?"

Laughing softly, David resumed walking. What kind of planet was Gyra from? "Sometimes you can guess pretty accurately, but most of the time you don't really know. On the streets, you can pass right by a murderer and never know it."

Gradually Gyra's feathers smoothed out. He followed, silent for a while. "I thought your mel-humans would all be in the same location; places that have 'gone down hill,' like the region where the bar was. I had no idea mels were everywhere. Are you afraid?"

"Sometimes, but most of the time I don't think about it."

Gyra scratched his feathers again. "How difficult it must be to live here."

Two women came around the left corner. Remembering Gyra's warning, David stopped. After the women passed, he whispered, "How did you know there were two people coming?"

"I heard them," Gyra whispered back.

"You *heard* them?"

"Yes. You have a word for it: sonar. I bounced sound waves off that shop window to hear around the corner."

Stunned, David asked, "What else can you do?"

"What do you mean?"

"What else can you do that we can't?"

Gyra's nails clattered softly as he moved down the sidewalk. "Since I don't know everything you can and cannot do, I am unable to answer your question completely. However, I can deduce a few things from common observation.

"I can rotate my head three hundred and fifty degrees, I can fly, I can hear far above and below your range of hearing, at close range I can scan a person's insides with ultrasound, I can see in darkness one hundred times darker than you and I appear to have superior olfactory senses. Do you smell the dog that was here half an hour ago?"

"No." David staggered and placed his hand against a tree. What kind of a being was this phantera? At least Gyra didn't appear to be hostile. "It's a good thing we didn't know all these things about you earlier."

Gyra cocked his feathered head. "Why?"

"Because we would have been terrified!"

"Why would these things terrify you?"

David took a deep breath. "When we first saw you, we didn't know if you were a mel-phantera."

Gyra eyed him. "You do not look well. Your heart is beating fast—now it is beating even faster. Are you still afraid?"

Struggling to slow his breathing, David faced the phantera. "Yes," he confessed. "I'm still a little scared."

"You do not trust me, and yet you are trying to help me." Gyra cocked his head again. Was that a sad look in his eyes?

David swallowed. "We trust you some, but deep trust takes time. Come on, we should head back."

As they turned around, Gyra scanned the area. "Time is something we may not have. How are you protecting me from the mel-humans?"

"Well, we added this vest, fake comb, and wattle to

make you look like a chicken."

Gyra fingered his pink bill. "But chickens are not known for their fierceness, unless they are fighting cocks. They are commonly viewed as cowards. I do not understand."

David's desire to protect Gyra began to replace his fear of the alien.

"Everyone knows you're not a real chicken."

"They do? Then why do I wear these things?"

"Because you're advertising for a store that sells chicken dinners. People think you're a human in a chicken suit. If they knew you're an alien, many would be terrified."

"They are afraid of aliens?"

"Not everyone. Some people worship them, thinking they bring enlightenment."

"No naharam should be worshipped," Gyra stated. "What would the mel-humans do if they found me?"

David crammed his hands in his pockets. "It would depend on the type of mel-human. Some would see you as dangerous and try to kill you, the New Agers would set you up as a god, the skeptics would say you're a fake and ignore you, and still others would want to study you so they could make a name for themselves. The government would whisk you away into seclusion, worried you might pose a threat. They'd try to learn all about your technology and abilities."

Gyra trembled. "So many different mel-humans on the same planet. Earth is indeed a place of firsts."

6. Crisis at the Clinic

A few days later, David and Gyra strolled the city sidewalks once more. This time they took a street David hadn't walked in years.

A few crows cawed in the branches of a huge dead oak.

"Todd and I figure we'll go shopping for your metal on Friday," David told Gyra. "It's the soonest we can fit you in. Our schedules are pretty tight and I don't want to give Todd any excuses for cutting class."

The phantera turned to him. "I am grateful for your help."

Half a block down the street, a car pulled to the side of the road. A young woman stepped out of the car, slammed the door, and watched as it sped away. She stood rigid, hunched over. Her shoulders trembled.

"She is pregnant," Gyra commented. "And crying. Do you know why she is crying?"

The woman turned and faced a faded pale building. "Westside Women's Center" proclaimed a blue and white sign above the entrance. On the wall, a red and white sign hung: "No Trespassing. Violators will be prosecuted to the fullest extent of the law." A well-built security guard stood near the glass doors, arms folded, while a closed-circuit TV camera stared down from the roof.

David's stomach felt sick. "It looks like she's going to an abortion clinic." *God, why did I come down this street?*

"She is going to kill her baby?" The feathers went erect on Gyra's head, and he snapped his jaw. "Why? How could she?"

"A lot of people don't know what really goes on in an abortion," David said. "The schools and the media never give a blow-by-blow description of what happens. A lot of people never see it from the baby's point of view. They believe the unborn child is just a blob of cells, even though the baby has a beating heart and brain waves by the time a women has an abortion."

"But why would she want to kill her own child?" Gyra asked.

David grimaced. "She doesn't want to be pregnant and have a baby." Sighing, he ran his fingers through his hair.

"Some women see a baby as an impossible burden, an obstacle to their education or work. They may feel they can't afford to raise a child and they have no choice. Others are pressured by their husbands, parents, or boyfriends to have an abortion." David released a frustrated sigh. "The worst excuse I've heard was that it was for 'the baby's best interest.' Adoption is far more merciful! Abortion is a hideous, painful way to die."

Gyra pointed toward the woman. "She does not appear to have made up her mind."

The woman started for the stairs.

Gyra darted down the sidewalk. "I must stop her!"

"Gyra! Wait!" David dashed after him.

"No time to wait!" the phantera called back.

Trying to catch up with his friend, David yelled, "You'll get in trouble! It's against the law!"

The girl turned around and saw Gyra. "What are you doing?"

Gyra grabbed her hand.

"Hey, buddy! You're on private property!" yelled the guard.

The woman screamed at the giant bird. "Let go of me!"

"I won't hurt you!" Gyra pleaded. "I have to show you!"

The guard pulled out a radio, contacting the police. "I have an anti-abortion nut assaulting a client—hurry!"

The phantera slipped one hand on the woman's head and the other on her belly.

Her distressed face went blank.

"Gyra, what are you doing?" David cried.

"My God," she breathed. "What was I going to do?"

The guard trotted down the stairs. "Ma'am, are you all right? Sir, you are under arrest for assault." He seized one of Gyra's arms and slapped a handcuff on it.

David cringed. *Lord, no! Please!*

The woman whirled around to face the guard. "They lied to me! The whole damned clinic lied to me!"

The guard stepped back. "Whoa, ma'am, don't you worry. You'll be safe. The police are on the way and your identity will be protected. We'll make this jerk pay!" He yanked Gyra's other hand into the handcuff.

The big bird did not resist, but tilted his head as he looked down at the metal cuffs.

"They told me it was nothing, that it wasn't a baby, but it is! Let him go! He didn't hurt me!"

The guard drew himself up. "Wait a minute, ma'am, I saw him assault you. If you don't press charges, we will, for trespassing and disrupting our business. Now come along, you have an appointment." He took the girl's arm in one hand, held Gyra with the other, and pulled them both toward the clinic door.

"If I don't go in there you'll charge him with disrupting business?" the woman said, her face flushed. "You son of a—" With that, she gave the guard a left hook, catching him completely by surprise.

The large man lost his footing and fell back onto the steps.

David saw his chance. "Come on!" he yelled and yanked at Gyra. They both raced down the street.

"Wait for me!" screamed the girl.

Looking back, David saw the woman right behind him and the guard still struggling to rise. Joined by the girl, Gyra and David turned a corner and covered another block before coming out on a main street.

"Are the police bad now?" asked Gyra.

"Yes," David answered between pants. "Right now the police are definitely bad."

"Then I suggest we stop running."

"Why?"

"Because a police car is approaching from around the corner."

David stopped and the girl almost ran into him. With only seconds to act, he dashed into a dark open doorway, pulling Gyra behind him.

David looked around and smirked. He had stumbled into a bar. Well, Todd *would* have the last laugh.

Gyra hid behind David and the woman. "Here it comes," he whispered. A police car sped by without its siren.

"Hey, you guys gonna order something?" asked the bartender.

"No, we were just looking for a bathroom," answered the woman. "But I think I've changed my mind."

"Let's go," David whispered.

Sticking his head out the door, Gyra did a sweep. "It is safe."

"Let's cut over to Jackson Park," David suggested. "It's overgrown with shrubs and weeds."

Crossing the street, they entered the park. The man-made lake had been drained long ago and they walked on its sandy bottom. David scanned the area. "This is the perfect place to hide. The park's size will make it formidable to search."

Plunging deep into the thick bushes, they sat down to wait.

"Now I can talk," the girl said. She turned to Gyra. "I want to know how you let me see my baby."

David shivered. What was she talking about?

The phantera eyed the young woman. "I don't know if we can trust her. She might be mel."

"Hey, I've been accused of a lot of things, but never of being male! You especially ought to know that." She rubbed her belly.

David almost laughed. "Not *male*. He said *mel*. It means *bad* in his language."

Her face bore a determined look. "I still want to know how he let me see my baby, and how he knew that police car was coming before we even saw it."

Coughing nervously, David said, "My friend has some special gifts."

"I'll say." The girl turned back to Gyra. "Can you let me see my baby again?"

"My hands are bound," Gyra answered, showing her the handcuffs.

Her brown eyes softened. "Oh my gosh, I'm so sorry! If it hadn't been for me, you wouldn't be in this mess."

"If we had not met, your baby would be dead."

David cradled his head. Gyra sure could be blunt. Attempting to change the subject, he said, "I'm David."

"Debbie," the girl replied with a tight smile as she shook his hand.

Placing his hand on the phantera's shoulder, David said, "This is my friend Gyra."

Gyra stretched out both hands and took Debbie's.

"This is the first time I ever shook hands with someone in handcuffs." Debbie promptly hung her head and her long dark hair closed over her face like a curtain.

Longing to help the girl, David scooted closer.

"Debbie, I don't want to pry, but if you need anything— prenatal care, a place to stay, counseling, baby stuff—I'd like to help."

Debbie's head remained bowed, shoulders trembling.

David rested a hand on one shoulder and Gyra put both of his hands on the other.

"My boyfriend told me to get an abortion or move out," she said between sobs.

David fished a tissue out of his pocket and handed it to her. He hoped it was a clean one.

Taking it, Debbie crumpled it in her hand. "He expects me to call him when I'm finished. I have no place to go and I haven't found a job. Even my parents don't want me. What am I gonna do?" She blew into the tissue without even looking at it.

David rubbed her shoulder. "I'll help you find a place to stay. For tonight you can stay with me."

Debbie looked up at David, eyes narrowing like a cornered bobcat's.

He recoiled. "Don't worry, I won't make any moves on you."

"David is not a womanizer," Gyra offered. "He told me he is a virgin."

"Gyra!" David felt his cheeks burning.

The phantera cocked his head. "What is wrong?"

"That's not something people talk about."

"Why? Are you ashamed?"

"No, it's just that people don't go around talking about their sex lives."

"Some people do," Debbie said with a soft laugh.

David sighed. "I know, but I'm trying to teach him the proper way for people to act."

She frowned. "You say that like he's not human."

"What do you think he is? Some alien from another planet?" David blurted the truth, hoping she would dismiss it as ridiculous.

But Debbie just stared at him with those wary eyes. "A few weeks ago I would have thought the idea was crazy, but I've been hearing too many weird things the last week." Her eyes held him.

"Things?" David's throat tightened. "What things?"

"Mysterious objects tracked across the sky a few miles from here, a sonic boom when no military jet was around, and high-up people frantically searching for a downed 'plane' but keeping its identity hush-hush."

David's stomach turned to stone. He wanted to turn away from that piercing gaze, but was afraid. "How do you know this?"

Releasing him finally, she looked down as her long hair formed a curtain again. "My boyfriend, Wayne, works at the air force base on the edge of town. He was a nervous wreck last week. I asked him why and he told me all this. Said he couldn't share any more."

"Are you going to tell him about us?" David asked in a tight voice.

"And let him gloat to his friends about finding you? No way! Wayne tried to make me kill my baby so he wouldn't have to pay child support. I'm not going to give that jerk anything to crow about." Her hand went to her belly again. "I just wish my baby had a better father."

"Well, I think he's going to have a good mom."

"Me? I don't know anything about children. My family was a mess." She blew into the tissue again. "I think this Kleenex is finished."

David took back the soiled tissue. "Well, you can talk to my mom. She's a fountain of wisdom when it comes to kids. I'm sure she'd love to help."

Debbie smiled. Her eyes were still red-rimmed, but the tension had left her stocky body. Turning to Gyra, she said, "Thank you for showing me my baby. You kept me from making the worst decision of my life." She reached out and placed her hand on the alien's shoulder. "Your secret is safe with me. If I can ever repay you, I will."

The phantera nodded.

"Hey, Gyra, can you see if there are any police cars out there?" David whispered.

The phantera raised his head just clear of the bushes. "Two are cruising the street and one is parked near the clinic. There's a strange van parked in front of the clinic. It has a pole extending vertically from its roof with a big dish on top."

"Great," David breathed in disgust.

Debbie's brown eyes widened. "Is it the military?"

David shook his head. "Worse. It's the news! Our faces will be plastered all around town by nightfall."

Shaking her head, Debbie asked, "How can that be? They didn't get there until after we left."

"Then I suppose you didn't see the surveillance camera mounted on the roof?" David blew out his breath. *God, spare us. What will my parents think?*

Debbie's face paled. "I've got to get to a phone—fast!" She stood up.

"Wait!" David hissed. "The police are out there looking for you. Why do you need a phone?"

"I have to get a hold of Wayne. If I can reach him in time, I might be able to keep him from talking."

"Where is he now?" asked David. "Think!"

"He'd be at work on the base."

"Would he have access to a TV or radio?"

"Not the regular type. Hey!" She brightened. "He won't have a chance to find out until he gets home."

Sighing with relief, David said, "Great, we still have some time. When does he usually get home?"

"He's been working late the last few weeks, coming home about eight."

"Good." David clasped his hands. "We can wait until dark, then sneak back to the apartment. You can call your boyfriend from there. He should still be at work. What are you going to tell him?"

Debbie's face hardened into a fierce expression. "I'm gonna tell Wayne if he doesn't keep quiet, I'll tell the press he was pressuring me to have an abortion—and I'll make him pay child support."

Rubbing his chin, David asked, "Do you think it will work?"

"Sure will! It'd embarrass him to no end if his friends heard about it. Several of them are already on his case for how he treats me. His job would become a living hell."

David looked up at the sky. "It's going to be a long time until dark."

"Well, does anyone have a good story?" Debbie eyed David and Gyra. "It would make the time pass easier."

Chuckling, David said, "Gyra here has one that will definitely keep you occupied."

David was relieved when the sun finally set. "Now we can leave."

"I have been thinking," Gyra said.

"What?"

"You waited until it was dark because then it would be harder for the police to see us, right?"

"Right, especially you." David rubbed his curls. "You stick out like a sore thumb."

"I do not understand."

Waving him off, David said, "It's slang, meaning something that is hard to hide."

"That is what I have been thinking." Gyra looked at the silvery cuffs on his hands. "It would be easier if you two went by yourselves."

"And what would you do? We can't leave you here," David protested.

"I could meet you at the apartment."

Scratching his shoulder where a shrub pricked him, David asked, "And how would you get to the apartment alone?"

"I would fly."

David's mouth fell open. "Fly? Of course! You do have wings, don't you?"

"If you wish, I could carry you one at a time."

"No!" Debbie said in an urgent voice. "I have a...fear of heights."

Gyra cocked his head.

"I'll have to stay with Debbie," David answered. "She doesn't know where we live. Do you think you can find your way back to the apartment by yourself?"

The phantera nodded. "Of course. Why do you ask?"

"I'm just afraid you might forget."

"Phantera do not forget. That is not one of our weaknesses."

"Right," David answered, chagrined. Mulling over the idea, he tried to anticipate any problems.

"Gyra, I like your idea, but it wouldn't be good if people saw you land near the apartment. Once you were on the ground you'd still have to take the elevator. Why don't you land on the roof? No one would expect you to come down the stairs."

"What if the police are already at the apartment?" asked Debbie.

David fingered his chin. "Hmm. We don't know how much they know. It's better to be safe than sorry. Gyra, you land on the roof. Todd or I will come and get you if it's safe. If we don't, or if someone else is already up there, fly back here and we'll meet you as soon as we can. If none of us can make it," David grimaced, "we'll send someone to find you. They'll say *naharam* as a sign, okay?"

Gyra nodded and spread his enormous wings. "I will wait for you. Yavana guide you!"

Leaping into the air with his powerful legs, the phantera completed his first downstroke from a height of ten feet.

"Wow," David whispered, watching the strong wings. They beat faster than he would have expected for their enormous size.

"I almost wish he had taken me with him," Debbie said.

"Me too. Let's go."

Arriving at the apartment building, David peered into the lobby. Nothing unusual. They took the elevator up to their floor and stepped out.

"So far so good," David muttered.

Scanning the hall, Debbie muttered, "Doesn't look like a bad place."

He opened the door.

"David! Where have you been?" Todd cried from inside.

David raised his hands to calm his roommate. "Shhh! Is it safe?"

"Better than being out on the streets. I heard some wacko pro-lifer in a bird suit attacked a woman and guard at an abortion clinic. At first it had me worried, but then I remembered Gyra was with you, and I knew you wouldn't have let anything like that happen to...where's Gyra?"

Motioning for Debbie to follow him in, David shut the door.

"Who's the girl?" Todd asked as if Debbie were an irrelevant intrusion.

"This is Debbie. Debbie, my roommate Todd," David said as the two shook hands. "She's the girl who was at the clinic."

Todd's eyes froze on her. "Oh sh–oot!" He spun on David. "Gyra?"

"He's okay. He should be waiting on the roof."

Wagging his blond head, Todd muttered, "I never thought he'd hurt someone."

Debbie put a hand on her abdomen. "He didn't. He just touched me and showed me my baby somehow. It was so weird, yet...wonderful. I could see my baby's form in 3-D. And then I *felt* him. I can't really explain it, but I felt his mind, and he felt mine. He was so curious. And then he sensed my fear. My fear became his fear. Then all went blank and I saw the guard coming to arrest Gyra. My moment of joy turned into horror when I realized what I was about to do."

Todd scowled. "And then Gyra attacked the guard?"

"No way!" Debbie flashed Todd her fierce brown eyes. "He didn't hurt anyone. *I* slugged the guard. The jerk tried to drag me into the clinic. I snapped when he referred to killing my baby as a business. He acted like my appointment gave them a legal claim on my son!"

"Well, this isn't the first time the press has messed things up," David commented.

Todd grimaced. "That's a nice way of putting it."

The phone rang and everyone froze. "Was I mentioned anywhere in the report?" David asked.

Staring at the phone like it was a venomous snake, Todd replied, "They said there was another man, but the camera didn't get a good picture of his face."

"So, they don't know who I am?"

"I don't think so."

The phone rang again. "Are you going to answer that?" Todd asked.

"Maybe you should."

Todd picked up the phone. "Hello? ...Oh." He smiled. "Hi, Jeff, what's up? ...David? Sure." He held out the phone. "It's your cousin."

David's hands were sweating as he took the phone. "Hello?"

"David! It's Jeff. What's going on? The police told me someone in a chicken outfit advertising my place beat up a woman and a clinic guard. I've got a bunch of angry feminists picketing my place. What happened?"

Rubbing the damp curls on his forehead, David pondered how much to share. *Lord, show me what to do.*

"Jeff, where are you?"

"At work. I've got to keep an eye on those feminists."

"Jeff, listen carefully. Gyra and I were at the clinic this morning, but Gyra didn't hurt anyone. He just talked a woman out of an abortion. The problem was he walked onto the clinic property to do it. The guard flipped out and tried to drag the girl into the clinic. She punched him and then we all ran. I'm really sorry you got involved like this, Jeff...Jeff?"

From the other end of the line came the last sound David expected to hear. Starting as a wheeze, it grew in volume until he realized it was a laugh—a laugh so strong it had taken Jeff's breath away.

"Jeff? Jeff, are you okay?" Howling laughter forced David to pull away from the receiver.

Finally controlling himself, Jeff said, "Had you worried, didn't I? Today's been an interesting day. I knew those press people were up to no good when they refused to show the whole film on TV. They gave some lame excuse about protecting the woman's right to privacy. Those creeps didn't want anyone to know what really happened. Listen, next time you see Gyra, tell him I'm proud of him."

David straightened. "You are?"

"Sure. It takes a lot of guts to do what he did. I only wish more people were willing to stand up for what's right."

A thought crossed David's mind. "You said the police came and talked to you?"

"They did more than that! When I told them Gyra wasn't here, they took me down to the station for some friendly questioning. Someone from the clinic arrived with the video from a surveillance camera, so the police asked if I could identify Gyra from the film. I said I'd try. I told the police someone else might have rented a bird suit, copied the vest and committed the 'crime.' When they asked if I had any suspects, I said I have a lot of competitors who'd love to see me get this kind of publicity. That's true too. Some of the local joints are owned by the mob. So, they set up the video and ran a short clip. I saw you in the background."

"You could tell it was me?"

"Only because I recognized your jacket. Anyway, they wouldn't show Gyra attacking the guard on the film. I smelled something fishy. After raising a big stink, saying I couldn't identify my employee unless I saw the whole scene, they played it. Then I nailed them."

David blinked. "You nailed them?"

"Yeah, I pointed out that the guard was dragging the girl by the arm—like you said. You should have seen the look on the detective's face! He was stunned. I told him I didn't think my employee assaulted anyone, but if that girl turns up, the clinic could have a major lawsuit on their hands. Then I said, 'If the clinic wants to press charges, then they better be ready for the whole truth because I'll countersue to clear the name of my business. Just tell them to contact my attorney.' I don't think you need to worry about Gyra now. Our 'friendly neighborhood abortion clinic' is backpedaling fast for the moment. Now that they've made their noise, I think they'll just lay low."

"Thanks, Jeff, I really owe you one."

"Think nothing of it," Jeff said. "One of the feminists insisted I show my remorse by giving a donation to their cause. These people are shameless! If the feminists boycott me, so be it. I'm going to give a donation to the local maternity home. So, don't worry. I can hold things down here. Just take care of your friend."

"Thanks again," David added before hanging up. He pulled his shirtsleeve across his forehead. "I'm starving. Let's get something to eat."

"What about Gyra?" Todd asked.

"Oh yeah. Go up on the roof and get him."

7. An Unexpected Conversion

Savoring his slice of pepperoni pizza, David recounted the day to his friends.

"I thought of you when we hid in that bar, Todd," David confessed.

Feigning astonishment, Todd cried, "You took Gyra to

a *what*? What were you thinking?" He chuckled. "You, David Decker, of all people!"

"It was not as bad as the last time," Gyra added.

"I should hope not!" Todd helped himself to another piece of pizza.

Debbie smirked. "How many is that now?"

Gazing up at the ceiling, Todd counted on his fingers. "Five, but who's counting?"

"Seven. I am," Gyra answered.

David and Debbie laughed as Todd's face went blank. "Well, that's what you get when you have an alien in the house," Todd retorted. "Hey, David, when you didn't show up, I figured you might've gotten stuck somewhere with Gyra. Seeing your backpack was still here, and knowing you'd be bummed if you missed your first session of Art History, I took it upon myself to intervene. I went down to school, sat in on your class, picked up your course outline, and bought your textbook."

"Todd, I'm amazed!" David exclaimed. "Thanks, I owe you one."

Looking over at Debbie, Todd wiggled his eyebrows. "Someone's got to look out for you, David."

Debbie merely yawned. "Well, I'm stuffed. Thanks for dinner. Where do I sleep?"

Todd's eyes bulged opened. "*What?*"

David took a deep breath. *Here we go.* "You can sleep in my room—"

"*What?* Wait a minute!" Todd protested.

"And I will sleep on the couch," David finished.

Standing up, Debbie wiped her mouth on a paper napkin and said, "I better phone my boyfriend now—or rather my *ex*-boyfriend. I should have ditched him a long time ago."

"Phone's by the sofa in the living room," David said. Debbie walked out.

"What about your rule: no girls?" Todd hissed.

Grimacing, David faced his friend. "I know, but she has no place to go. Her boyfriend told her to get an abortion or get out, and her family doesn't want her. I promised I'd find her a place to stay. It's too late to do anything tonight, but don't worry. Tomorrow I'll take her over to Mom's and she'll help Debbie. If Mom can't, she'll know someone who can."

Todd watched him out of the corner of his eye. "So, she'll only stay tonight? On the couch?"

"No, I'm sleeping on the couch. She'll take my bed."

Todd waved his hand. "Yeah, right, that's what I meant."

Debbie stomped back into the room. "That dirty little creep!"

Frowning, David asked, "What happened?"

"Before I even had a chance to talk, Wayne gave me this line about how we should 'cool our relationship' and that I should move out so he can have time to think! But when I told him I didn't get the abortion, he got real quiet! I explained what happened at the clinic, except for the part that would give Gyra away. I told Wayne if he so much as lets out a peep, I'll tell his friends and co-workers what a cruel manipulating coward he is: using a girl and kicking her out on the street because he got her pregnant! Then he got scared and even asked me to come back, but I told him I didn't want anything to do with a man who would murder his own son—unless, of course, he wanted to pay child support. Anyway, you don't need to worry about him for a while. I've got him right where I want him." The fierce triumphant fire in her eyes faded. "He would have kicked me out even if I'd had the abortion."

"The jerk," Todd muttered forcefully.

"He wanted me to kill my baby and then dump me out like trash!" Debbie cried, her body convulsing with each sob.

Bowing his head in prayer, David put his hand on her shaking shoulders.

"I hate him, I hate him!" After weeping for a good ten minutes, her raspy voice lamented, "I feel like I'm never going to stop crying!"

Reaching out, Gyra placed one hand on her head, the other on her belly. Debbie stopped sobbing. Her eyes opened, staring as if they beheld some wonder before her. Tears continued to flow from her eyes, but a gentle smile of joy lit her face.

After a moment, Gyra withdrew his fingers. Debbie seized a purple hand and gazed up into Gyra's eyes. "Thank you," she said in a soft voice. Standing up, she slipped off to Todd's room.

Todd began to follow with a worried look on his face, but David seized his roommate's shoulder.

"It's okay," David whispered. "She doesn't know which room is mine. If you want, you can take my bed tonight."

Todd wagged his head. "Nah, I'll sleep on the couch."

"You sure?"

"Yeah, I'm tough. Besides, I take naps on it all the time. I'm used to it." Todd walked out to the living room. "Nighty night!" he crooned.

David threw out the empty pizza boxes and turned to Gyra. "How did you get the handcuffs off? I forgot all about them until you touched Debbie."

"I had plenty of time to get back," Gyra answered.

"But how did you get them off?"

"I found a way."

"Gyra, you're holding out on me. What happened?"

Staring at David, Gyra said, "This is not something we phantera share freely. It is one of the reasons we are hunted by the mel-naharam."

David folded his arms, waiting for an answer.

Gyra snapped his jaw nervously. "While flying back, I saw a large building under construction. A few men welding metal beams took a break and left their equipment out. I landed quietly and used a blow torch to cut the handcuffs off."

Holding up a hand, David interrupted. "Wait a minute, you may have been able to cut through the links, but the metal cuffs would still be on your hands. Even if you could keep the flame off your skin while cutting the cuffs, the heat would have traveled through the metal and burned your wrists."

Gyra bowed his head. After a moment of silence, he walked over to the gas stove and turned the flame on high. "Please, tell no one what you see unless it is absolutely necessary."

David's stomach tightened. "What are you doing?"

Gyra placed his hand in the fire. The flames licked around his large purple fingers, but the phantera never flinched or cried out. The scaly skin didn't even blister. After several minutes, the phantera withdrew his hand. "Touch it."

David obeyed. A little soot rubbed off the cool skin, but the purple hands were undamaged.

"How much heat can you take?" David whispered.

Gyra held up a finger and winked. "That is classified information. I showed you this secret because I trust you."

David blushed, deeply honored. What could he do in return? Then he knew. "Gyra, I have one more book for you. It may take you a while to read—well, maybe not! Anyway, I want to know what you think of it."

They crept out to the living room where Todd lay sprawled on the couch, eyes closed.

David slipped into his room, picked up his Bible, and returned. Giving his beloved book to Gyra, he said, "Here, I hope you enjoy it."

"Thank you, David." The phantera opened it. "You always bring such interesting books."

David smiled. "Goodnight, Gyra."

"Goodnight, David," the phantera answered. "Goodnight, Todd."

"Goodnight, Gyra," Todd replied.

The next morning, David woke with a start. He had slept well enough, but a sense of urgency stirred him. Rolling out of bed, he headed for the door in his pajamas. What was he doing? There was a woman in the apartment! *Way to go, David. Just waltz out there in your jammies. Wouldn't that impress her!* Throwing on some clothes, David combed his hair before peering out the door.

Todd lay asleep on the couch, Debbie's room was still silent, and Gyra sat staring out the window, his long tail fanned out behind him.

Tiptoeing over to the phantera, David whispered, "Gyra?"

"Yes, David?" Gyra did not move. Though the phantera faced the window, his eyes didn't appear to be focused on anything.

David bent over. "Gyra, what are you doing?"

"I am making connections."

"What do you mean?" David noticed Gyra was cradling the Bible with one hand while the other held a crumpled paper towel.

"The book you gave me has so many messages, hidden and obvious," Gyra said in a low voice. "The more I review it, the more connections I see. But there are parts I do not understand."

David nodded. "People have spent their entire lives studying the Bible."

"A phantera could spend an entire lifetime studying it too. Do you believe what is in this book?"

David saw Todd roll over. "Come back to my room. I don't want to wake Todd...yet."

Once they were in his room, David shut the door.

"So, do you believe this book? Are you a member of the Way? A Christian?" Gyra pressed.

A chill ran down David's spine. Was the phantera testing him? He didn't know what the alien's response would be, and he couldn't read Gyra's face. The big bird suddenly seemed very menacing to him—that seven-foot frame, those red eyes, the long beak with a subtle hook on the end....

David felt an invisible veil torn from his mind. An intense battle raged in his little room. *I will not be swayed by the hosts of hell. Come what may, I will tell the truth.* Looking Gyra straight in the face, David declared, "I am a Christian; I believe that the Bible is true."

Was that a wind that passed by, or did he just imagine it? His mind felt clearer, his spirit emboldened.

"The demons are gone. They failed in their mission," Gyra said, eyes bright. "They were trying to keep you from confessing your faith in Christ. Do you know why?"

"No."

"Because we are brothers in Christ!" Gyra pounced on David, embracing him. "I would greet you with a holy kiss, but my anatomy doesn't allow it."

David gasped in shock. "You mean you're a Christian? How did this happen?"

"I read your most wonderful book!" Gyra held out the Bible. "The wisdom and truth in here are of God. I did not think your people understood Him so well. In the dictionary, I found names for many gods. I didn't know if your people were polytheists or monotheists who worshipped a false god. But now I see there are some who know the true God, and you are a minority. You are scattered among the ignorant, like wheat among weeds."

Pointing to the Bible, David asked, "How do you know this is the truth?" This time David was the skeptic who needed to be persuaded. He wanted to know *why* Gyra believed.

Gyra placed a hand on the book. "It lines up with the history I learned from my people, it addresses the necessities of life, it is harmonious with the ancient phantera prophecies and even fulfills some of them. Everything is connected as a unit from the beginning to the end. This book contains words of power that open the eyes of my soul."

David grinned. May it never be said that Gyra had made his decision on a whim. But he was not finished testing the alien. "Why do you think Jesus died for phanteras?"

"Phantera is like your word *deer*. We do not change it to show plurality."

"Sorry," David said.

"No offense taken. To answer your question, Jesus became a naharam, correct?"

David nodded. A human was a naharam.

"Then He died for all naharam," Gyra reasoned.

Rubbing his chin, David frowned. "I don't understand your logic."

"Are you of Jewish descent?"

"No."

Gyra held up a finger. "And yet His death still applies to you."

"But He was human." David raised his finger. He loved clean fair debates.

Gyra wagged his purple finger. "But He was a naharam too!"

"He was a living being and angels are living beings, yet He didn't die for the fallen angels." David wagged his finger back.

"Ah!" Gyra cried in a triumphant voice. "You are good, but you argue on the wrong side this time. Angels, *aradelah*, are on a different level than naharam. The demons saw the face of God and still rebelled against Him. But humans did not know all the ramifications of their sin and were partly ignorant of God. They weren't beyond saving. Jesus became a naharam, not an aradelah. And, as a naharam, I lay claim to His death, burial, and resurrection. He is *Vashua*, the Mystery, the Provision, the Restorer."

David was stunned. "You have a name for Him?"

"Yes, but not much more. We have waited a long time to learn the meaning of His name." Gyra held up the leather-bound book. "Here is the end of our waiting."

"Wow," David whispered. "Gyra, do you know what Jesus' name is in Hebrew?"

"No, I have not learned Hebrew yet."

"It's *Yeshua* and it means *God saves*."

Blinking his red eyes, the phantera said, "I think I know why our languages share some words. During the time of the Tower of Babel, God confused your languages. It seems that fragments of the original language were scattered throughout your various tongues. I have reason to believe that your original language may have been Ramatera—the language of the flexible tongues. We even share similarities in a few letters of our written languages."

David scowled. "But we use Latin letters—definitely not the oldest characters of human writing. Even the Greek and Phoenician alphabets are older than Latin."

"Perhaps some of your written characters and languages are still influenced by Ramatera." Gyra rubbed the tip of his bill. "It is a mystery."

They both fell silent for a while.

"Remember when we first met?" Gyra asked.

David smirked. "How could I forget?"

"You humans seem to find ways to forget a lot of things! Remember when I asked if you were a naharam?" David nodded. The phantera looked down at the Bible. "I raised my hand to touch your head, but you ran away."

"You terrified us." David chuckled. "We ran and hid in the bushes. As I recall, you tried to touch us again."

"Yes, I did. I wanted to do *rhutaram* on you. It is the

way phantera normally learn languages. We can assimilate an entire language in an instant."

"Sounds painful," David joked.

"No, it is painless for both the phantera and the host."

David braced himself. This could be scary. "Is it like mind reading?"

"No, I would not pick up your thoughts. That is a different technique called *falarn*. In falarn, I would only share your current thoughts."

David's spine tingled at this revelation. "Gyra, why didn't you try to do your rhutaram later, when you started to talk?"

Scratching his head bird-style, the phantera said, "It was obvious you did not trust me."

"You could have tried while we were asleep," David quipped with a wry smile.

"No, that would not be right. It would have violated what little trust there was. Rhutaram and falarn must never be forced on someone unless it is extremely urgent. It would abuse the gift God gave us."

"Did you use falarn on Debbie?"

Gyra nodded gravely. "It was a matter of life and death for her child. She expressed a desire for it the second time."

"Do you access all of a person's thoughts, going into their past?"

Gyra snapped his bill. "We are strictly forbidden to press into past memories, but if someone wants to share a memory, they can bring it up and we will see it."

David eyed Gyra thoughtfully. "Do you still want to do rhutaram?"

"Yes."

"Why?"

Looking out David's sunlit window, Gyra said, "Because there are still words I do not understand—your slang for instance—and some words have multiple meanings. Many times I do not know which meaning is being used in a situation. Also, your non-verbal communications are often a mystery to me. Rhutaram will fill in some of those gaps. If you do not wish to do it, I will understand."

"Gyra, you know more words than I do, but if this will help you, then go ahead."

Gently, the phantera placed his scaly hand on David's head. David felt as though a feather brushed the top of his brain.

The phantera withdrew his hand. "Thank you. I know it was hard for you to do this."

David blinked. "That's all?" He couldn't believe it; the procedure was so fast and simple.

Picking up the paper towel Gyra had dropped on the ground, David noticed it was stained with blue, purple, and yellow blotches. "What is this?"

Gyra looked at the towel. "I was crying."

With a frown, David asked, "Why?"

"Didn't you cry when you first heard that Jesus died?"

David grew misty eyed. "Not the first time, but I did later when I was old enough to understand."

Taking the crumpled towel, the phantera unfolded it and placed a curved fingernail on the blue stain. "Here is where He was betrayed." Gyra fingered the large purple stain. "And here is where He died." The phantera hung his head in silence.

David pointed to a bright yellow spot. "What about this?"

Gyra eyed the stain and tapped it with a long finger. "Here is where He rose from the dead!" The phantera jumped up and danced about with his hands up in the air. "He rose from the dead! He rose from the dead! Hallelujah!"

Laughing, David joined in. Gyra leapt so high, David was worried the phantera would hit the ceiling.

David was panting when they finally stopped. Glancing at the rumpled paper towel, he said, "So, your tears change color depending on what you're crying about?"

"Blue is sad, purple is very sad, and yellow is very happy."

"Are these all the colors you can cry?"

With a snap of his jaw, Gyra said, "No, there is one more: red."

"What does it mean?"

The phantera shuddered. "Red means the depths of pain, sorrow, and agony. Jesus sweat blood. It is similar with us when we are in great distress. It means our *crealin* organ has ruptured. We usually die from it."

Staring down at the towel, David remarked, "Well, I'm sure glad I don't see any red here."

"No red," Gyra said, rubbing the purple spot.

Todd knocked on the door and poked his head in. "What's going on? I thought I heard a wild rumpus or something."

Patting the smooth feathers on the phantera's back, David said, "Well, Brother, let's go eat breakfast."

8. A Forced Vacation

While Todd rummaged through the cabinets for cereal, David went to the refrigerator and got the milk. Gyra was setting the bowls on the table when Debbie poked her head into the kitchen.

"Good morning!" she said.

Todd let out a yell and then checked himself. "Sorry, I forgot we had a woman in the house."

David frowned. "You didn't remember? It's why you slept on the couch."

Rubbing his tousled hair, Todd said, "I used to fall asleep on the couch at home all the time. It wasn't such a big thing."

"You need to find yourself a wife," Debbie said in a dry voice.

Todd blushed, but quickly recovered. "I don't need one as bad as David does. Anyway, he's the one who's been having all the luck with women lately." Glancing at David and Debbie, Todd whistled "Here Comes the Bride."

"Todd Fox!" David shook his finger at his friend in mock anger.

The three sat at the table while Gyra stood.

"Four places?" Todd looked up at the phantera. "Are you eating with us?"

"Gyra eats once every two to three days," David explained to Debbie. "He only has one meal, but he eats enough to bust a cow!"

"You're just jealous because I don't have to eat three times a day," Gyra bantered.

"Gyra, you used a contraction!" Todd nearly shouted. "You used two of them."

"And I'm surprised you even noticed, Todd!" David stared at his roommate with equal amazement.

Setting down his spoon, Todd jabbered, "Listen to the way he talks. He has more feeling and his words flow so much better. He sounds...natural. Say something, Gyra."

"Something," the phantera repeated.

Todd groaned. "No, no, no!"

"It was a joke, Todd." Gyra winked.

Todd's face went blank. Then he laughed.

David explained rhutaram and how Gyra had used it that morning. He thought it best to mention Gyra's "conversion" later.

After they finished breakfast—Gyra was last—they started clearing the table.

The phone rang. David ran to the living room to answer it. "Hello?"

"Is David Decker there?"

"Speaking."

"David, this is Maria. I work for your cousin Jeff; he asked me to call you. Listen carefully because I don't have much time. Some scary men are questioning Jeff right now about Gyra. They're not from the local police. We think they're from the federal government. They forced Jeff to give up his records on Gyra and it looks like they're headed for your apartment next. Jeff says you should take a quick vacation—now! Don't wait to pack, just leave! I have to go before they look for me."

Click. She hung up before David could ask a single question. Every muscle in his body was rigid with dread.

"Who was it?" Todd asked, coming in from the kitchen.

Gyra poked his head through the door. "It's time to go."

Coming alive, David slammed down the receiver. "We've got to leave! They're coming for Gyra!"

"Who?" Debbie asked.

"The government! Todd, grab one set of clothes and your jacket—that's all. We don't have time for anything else. Debbie—"

"All I've got is myself," she finished for him.

"Gyra," David shouted. "Get that cloak you wore the night we met—and your chicken disguise."

Diving into his room, David snatched up a change of clothes and a jacket. He hesitated a moment before grabbing his pocketknife and sunglasses. As he burst into the living room, he barked, "Let's go, we haven't much time!"

The four stole out of the apartment building as quickly as they could without looking suspicious. David prayed they wouldn't meet Rhoda on the way out. He figured the drive from Jeff's restaurant was five minutes at the most. Jeff would stall them as long as he could, but for all David knew they could have been on their way when Maria called.

They made it to the car safely and saw no one unusual. Gyra wore the hood up on his cloak. "Can I sit in back this time? It will make me less conspicuous."

David nodded. "You can have the whole back seat. The rest of us will sit up front."

Sitting on the left side, Gyra let his tail cover the seat on his right. He hunkered down, making himself appear smaller. David drove onto the street.

"Now where do we go?" Debbie asked.

Donning his sunglasses, David said, "To my parents' house. I don't want anything to happen to you and I promised to find you a place to stay."

"I'm really sorry I got you into this mess." Debbie lowered her face.

Gyra reached out and touched her shoulder. "Don't worry. God has His hand in this."

Todd glanced at David.

David kept his eyes moving from his passengers to the rearview mirror to the traffic around him. "If we're being followed, I'll know real soon."

After they arrived at the Decker's home, David handed Todd the keys. "Stay in the car with Gyra. If you see anything unusual, get out of here." He nodded to Debbie, who got out and followed him to the house.

Fidgeting, David knocked on the front door.

"I want to give you something," Debbie whispered. She thrust a wad of papers into his hand. "It might come in handy."

David stared down at the wad. It was money. He flipped through it. "Debbie, I can't take this! This is four hundred dollars! What were you doing walking around with four hundred dollars in cash?"

"It was the last thing my boyfriend gave me. I don't want it."

With a jolt, David understood. This was the money Wayne had given her for the abortion! The clinic didn't accept checks or credit cards; they wanted untraceable cash. Stuffing the wad into his wallet, David promised, "We'll use it wisely."

Debbie hid behind her long hair, shifting her weight.

The door opened.

"David, I thought you'd be in school. Who's this?" Nadine asked.

"Mom, I don't have time to explain everything. We have an emergency." David stepped inside, pulling Debbie after him. He hastily explained what had happened at the clinic without mentioning that Gyra was a space alien.

With a serious look on her face, Nadine said, "David, I never taught you to hide from the law. Why are you teaching Gyra to run from his problems? He needs to face them head on."

"Normally I'd agree with you, Mom, but I'm going to have to ask you to trust me on this."

"David Decker, I am your mother. Keeping such a serious secret from me is wrong." She let a dreadful silence permeate the air before continuing. "You know I trust you, but I would turn the question around and ask do *you* trust *me?*"

Another tense silence filled the space between them. David saw the trap, but couldn't avoid it. "Yes, I trust you." He bowed his head. *Here it comes.*

"If you trust me then tell me what is really going on. Besides, I can help you better if I'm not left in the dark."

David sighed. He didn't have much time. "Debbie, go get Gyra—fast!"

Debbie's sturdy legs flew out the door.

"I didn't want to tell you because I was afraid you'd think I'm going crazy." David took a deep breath. "Gyra is an alien."

"An illegal alien?" Nadine's brown eyebrows went up. "What country?"

How tempting it would have been to lie, but David quickly committed himself. "No, Mom, he's an alien from outer space. He came from a planet called Arana." It was do or die now.

Nadine's surprised look turned to a scowl. "Is this all just a prank?"

Gyra came in the door. "Mrs. Decker, I've heard so much about you from David. He really is a good friend and he talks of you often."

Leaning toward her son, Nadine whispered, "Flattery will get you nowhere!" She held out her hand to Gyra. "Nice to meet you. I think what you did for Debbie was a wonderful thing. It's too bad others don't appreciate it."

David felt a renewed sense of urgency; time was slipping away. "Gyra, we have to convince my mom you're a space alien and we've got to do it fast!"

Turning to David's mother, Gyra asked, "Mrs. Decker, if I did things that no human could, would that convince you?"

Nadine crossed her arms. "It might."

"Then I will give you a short demonstration."

Removing his robe, Gyra showed off his backward-bending knees. He turned his head around like an owl and flexed his six limbs simultaneously. Spreading his wings, he leaped and stirred the air with his great wingstrokes, hovering a few feet off the ground.

The wind sent paper and magazines flying off the coffee table. Gyra dropped back to the ground.

"He flew from Jackson Park to my apartment. I saw him," David added.

Nadine's stoic face revealed nothing. "Impressive work, but not good enough to convince me you're an alien."

"Gyra can read your thoughts," David offered.

Scolding David with her blue eyes, she said, "He could

use some occult method to do that. You know better than to fall for that."

"How can we convince you?" Gyra asked.

"Wait just a moment." Nadine went into the kitchen and returned with a sharp knife.

"What's she doing?" Debbie whispered.

Wagging his head, David muttered, "I don't know."

Nadine fingered the knife's edge. "Do you bleed?"

Gyra nodded. "Yes."

She took hold of one of his long fingers. "If I give you a slight cut, will it endanger you?"

"No, but it will hurt." He tilted his head then straightened it. "You are a wise woman. You may cut me."

Nadine drew the knife across the underside of Gyra's finger. The blade slid deeper and the phantera blinked.

Nadine stopped. A blue-purple liquid ran from the cut, dripping onto her palm.

Cradling the bleeding hand, she whispered, "So, it's true. David, get me a paper towel."

David snatched one from the kitchen and returned.

"What do you know about him, Son?" she asked, blotting the finger.

"He's intelligent, moral...and he became a Christian last night."

Nadine shot him a startled look. "He what?"

"Look, Mom, I don't have time to tell you the whole story now. The government is after him and we've got to go!"

With a countenance as hard as granite, Nadine declared, "I won't abandon a brother to them for experiments!" An amused smile crept onto her face. "I have an idea that may buy you more time."

"Please, make it fast!" pleaded David. "Once they search the apartment, they'll come here."

"Take your Aunt Alice's car. She's touring China for a month and left it with us. Alice said we could use it. The police won't be looking for her Chevy Blazer."

As Todd and Gyra hurried into Alice's car, Nadine gave David a bag full of food and a couple of blankets. Debbie watched in silence.

"Don't tell me where you are going," Nadine said. "If you need to contact me, call your old friend Steve in Colorado. We'll use him for messages. I'll tell him a little about what's going on. Can I drive your car while you're gone?"

"Sure," David answered, slipping behind the wheel of the blue Blazer. He passed his car keys to his mom.

Nadine placed Alice's keys in David's palm and squeezed his hand. "I will pray for God to protect you, and give you wisdom."

Returning the squeeze, David replied, "I love you. Make sure you use a different pay phone each time you call Steve."

He started the engine and drove the Blazer out of the garage.

Debbie waved as the blue Chevy drove away.

Nadine sighed. "I feel like going for a drive."

"A drive?" Debbie asked in surprise.

"David did say I could use his car while he went on vacation—and he never did tell us where he went." Nadine winked. "There's no need to wait around for someone to find us. Why make it easy on them? If they want to question us, they'll have to catch us first!"

Debbie smiled. "Let's go!" She was beginning to really like this lady.

Ten miles later, David finished telling Todd what had happened in the house.

"It was so weird to see her with that knife in her hand. I really didn't think she'd cut him," David concluded.

Scratching behind his ear, Todd said, "I still don't see why that convinced her. I would have believed when I saw him fly."

"She is a wise woman," Gyra replied.

Todd glanced back at him. "Why do you say that?"

"She looked where most people would not normally have searched for proof. Mrs. Decker sought out my weakness, not my strength."

"Gyra's right," David said. "If someone made a fancy robot, or an elaborate costume to dupe people, they might focus on wowing them with superhuman powers, but who would think to make it bleed?"

"Sometimes you learn more about someone from their weaknesses than from their strengths," Gyra commented.

Todd peered into the bag for something to eat. "So, what's this about Gyra becoming a Christian?"

David couldn't resist smiling.

Thirty miles later, Todd leaned against the window, hand propping up his head as his forehead glistened with sweat. "I don't know David, this is all too weird. How do you know he didn't do it just to be polite?"

"I may not wish to offend," Gyra broke in, "but I will not deceive you to spare your feelings. Why is this so hard for you to believe? Aren't you a Christian too?"

David tried to rescue his friend. "No, Gyra, he's not."

Cocking his head, the phantera eyed Todd. "Why?"

David was about to reply when he stopped. No, this was Todd's job. He would have to answer for himself.

"Why aren't you a Christian, Todd?" the phantera repeated.

Todd blew out his breath loudly. "I respect David, and his mom, but I just don't think it's for me."

"Why?"

Throwing his hands up in the air, Todd replied, "Because I just can't see myself going to church and being a goody two-shoes. I don't want to give up having fun, I want to enjoy life."

"I have never been to a church," Gyra said in a subdued voice. "I thought you liked to do good things. I don't know what fun things you would have to give up. Do you really think that David, Mrs. Decker, and I don't enjoy life?"

David smirked. Gyra could boldly tread where no Christian had gone before.

Todd fingered a smudge on the window. "Sure, they enjoy life. It's just that I choose to enjoy it differently."

"How?" Gyra prodded.

"Like...like...I used to drink a lot of beer with my fraternity buddies."

"Getting drunk, falling down, and throwing up is enjoying life?"

David tried so hard to stifle a laugh that tears came to his eyes.

"I didn't get that drunk...too often," Todd stated.

Gyra pressed on. "I thought people got drunk to forget their pain. That's what you and David told me."

"Well, yeah..."

"But it sounds more like you were *running* from life than enjoying it. How can you really enjoy something when you're inebriated?"

Todd stared at his hands in silence.

The phantera continued. "I'd think you would want to be sober to enjoy every nuance life has to offer. Christianity is about a relationship with God, a relationship we were created to enjoy. Do you enjoy your times with David?"

"Yeah, usually." Todd turned his head toward the distant pale foothills. "He's the best friend I ever had."

A somber silence enveloped the three. Shaking his blond head, Todd said, "Gyra, I can't explain it. I'm just not ready now. Maybe sometime later, but not now."

David released a silent sigh. His prayers would not be answered today.

As they drove through a rural area, David spied a salvage yard sign and pulled off the road.

"Whatta you doing?" Todd asked.

David pulled a piece of paper from his pocket and glanced at the list. "Going shopping."

Thirty minutes and twenty pounds later, David crammed a box of metal scraps into the back of the Chevy Blazer. "I decided to err on the heavy side," he explained wiping his brow. "I didn't trust the guy's scales."

"Shoot! Did you get everything?" Todd asked, hopping out of the car and examining a piece of aluminum tubing.

"Everything except the titanium. I didn't expect to find that at a junkyard. Gyra will have to separate the chromium from the stainless steel and the tin from the solder."

They jumped back into the car and were off again.

"Well, David, I just have one question now." Todd fingered the molded plastic around the window.

Eyeing his friend, David asked, "What's that?"

"Where are we going?"

David smiled. "I thought you'd never ask."

9. Chaos at the Convention

"Mr. Blackwell, we have a lead."

Darius took the report from the man standing before his desk. Opening the folder, he searched through it. "Give me a summary."

"This David Decker is a friend of Gyra's. We ran a check on his car's license plate. He was there at the road block."

Allowing himself the mere hint of a smile, Darius said, "At last, a real break."

"We checked his apartment and his parents' house, but no one was home. We've alerted all the local authorities to seize David Decker's car and detain any occupants for questioning. He can't get far. Our team is investigating Decker's background, and they're looking into his room-mate's as well."

"Notify me immediately when you've seized them." Darius peered up at his assistant. "You may go now."

The man left.

Leaning back in his chair, Darius turned a page on the report. "We shall have to talk, Mr. Decker. I don't know how you've hidden an alien for so long—especially one that looks like a giant bird. I'm sure you'll have a fascinating tale. I can't wait to meet you."

"I thought we'd drive to Cabrillo Bay," David announced.

Todd pulled an apple out of the food bag. "Why there?"

"It's a nice quiet place and reasonably far away. There's a cheap motel near the beach. The town is pretty small. Its only attraction is Marine World Park, but I don't think it'd be wise to go there."

Todd bit into his apple, mumbling with a full mouth, "Unless we dressed Gyra up...as a seagull or something."

"Don't even think of it!"

Gyra stared out the window from beneath his hood. *Yavana, is this why I crashed here? To discover Your great revelation in David's Bible and take it back to my people? But how can I be the one to bring it? Perhaps I am just a link in the process.* He leaned forward. "David, could you buy me a blank book?"

Turning his head slightly, David asked, "Why?"

"I'd like to make a Ramatera New Testament. Since I don't sleep at night, it will give me something useful to do."

David's dark curls wiggled in the wind from the open

window. "Sure. We'll pull over at the next stationary store and buy what you need."

Sighing in relief, David shut the door to their motel room and locked it. They'd arrived at Cabrillo Bay under the cover of night. Since it was the off-season, David paid only half the normal price.

Gyra stood beside the table and began to write in his book.

"Don't you need to see my Bible?" David asked.

"No," the phantera answered. "My photographic memory can call up a flawless image of every page."

Todd wandered over to watch. "Check it out! What *is* this?"

"Ramatera," Gyra answered without breaking his pace.

Scowling, Todd leaned over and asked, "Is it some sort of picture writing, like hieroglyphics?"

David looked at Todd in surprise. He hadn't expected such a sophisticated question from his friend.

"No," Gyra replied. "Each symbol represents a specific sound, like the letters you use in English. The characters by themselves do have a separate meaning, but we don't normally use them that way. What you see are words spelled out phonetically."

Todd wore a crooked smile. "Wow, what would my English teacher say about this?" He held out his palm to David. "I forgot my money, but if you give me your wallet I'll get dinner."

David was tired from driving, so against his better judgment, he tossed his wallet to Todd. Grinning, Todd squeezed the wallet and left. David watched Gyra for a while in amazement before crashing on a bed to rest.

An hour later, Todd returned with take-out Chinese food and a large plastic bag. He tossed the billfold back to David.

Sitting up on his bed, David asked, "What's in the bag?"

Todd gave him a crafty look out of the corner of his eye. "I am about to turn our friend into a master of disguise." He pulled out a plastic duckbill. "Here is Gyra the Delinquent Duck." Todd twitched his eyebrows before reaching into the bag once more. "And here's Gyra the Secret Seagull." He displayed another bill. "Gyra the Illegal Eagle."

David fingered the plastic beaks. "Where did you get this stuff?"

"There's a little costume shop in town called Props R Us or something like that. They have lots of great gag gifts. I could have gotten more, but I thought this was enough for starters."

Todd dumped the bag upside down over the bed and more objects fell out. "I also bought these to help in a pinch. Here's a can of gray spray paint for hair. It washes off with water. I got a can of black too."

Holding up three elastic strips, David asked, "What's this for?"

"To hold the fake noses in place. I didn't know how big his head was, so I figured we'd attach it ourselves. I also got some orange latex and glue to make his feet webbed."

Gyra set down his pen and eyed the stretchy material.

"Todd, that was very...creative of you," David said.

"Thanks, but I couldn't have done it without Debbie."

"Debbie?" David looked up at his roommate.

"You know, the money."

"*How much?*"

Todd's hazel eyes winced. "You really don't want to know."

David reached for his wallet. Sighing, he brought his hand back empty. "You're right, I probably don't want to know, not tonight anyway. Let's eat and go to bed. I'm exhausted."

"Me too." Todd opened up the dinner packages. "So what's our plan?"

"We'll hang out here for a few days and go back to Gyra's ship after things cool down. Oh, and we still have to find some titanium."

Looking around the room, Todd wrinkled his nose. "We're not staying in here the whole time, are we?"

"Of course we are—until you figure out how to make Gyra invisible." David sniffed the delicious aroma of food. "I'm starved. What did you get?"

"Mongolian beef, diced chicken and almonds, and a side of rice. Aaaagh!" Todd cried. "They didn't give me any plastic forks, just chopsticks! I hate chopsticks! I don't know how to use them."

David bolted upright in bed. Todd groaned and covered his face with a pillow. An alarm blared just outside the window as shouting echoed from down the hall.

"What does that noise mean?" Gyra asked, his pen hovering over a page in his book.

Leaping out of bed, David unlocked the door and peered out.

A gang of teenage boys laughed at a red-faced kid.

"I don't believe you set it off!" crowed a boy.

"You're the one who dared me! You didn't think I'd do it, did you!" the red-faced kid retorted.

With a moan, David shut the door.

Todd rubbed his eyes. "What's up?"

"We are. A kid set off the fire alarm—on a dare."

Todd grimaced. "Uh oh. We better hustle Gyra out to the car. When the fire engines come, they'll be checking all the rooms. We went through this at the fraternity all the time."

Gyra clutched his book and shrouded himself in his cloak as David grabbed their few belongings. They slipped out into the hall.

The sun hovered over the dusky hills when they crept into the car.

"Now what?" Todd asked.

Sirens wailing, two fire engines and a paramedic vehicle roared into the parking lot.

David ran his hand through his curls. "I don't want to walk back to our room in broad daylight. Gyra looks too weird, even when he's covered with a cloak. Let's go for a drive."

David and Todd sat in front while Gyra rode behind. The Blazer's rear windows were tinted, making it difficult for anyone to see their strange, hooded passenger.

"Hey, check it out!" Todd pointed to a gathering of people near a large tent. "What is it? A circus or something?"

"There's a sign." David slowed down. "It says 'UFO Convention.'"

With a wicked gleam in his eye, Todd asked, "Want to have some fun?"

"No, Todd. We don't want to attract attention."

"Just think what would happen if a *real* alien showed up," Todd chuckled.

"It would be funny," David admitted.

"Sh–oot! Look at the outfits those people are wearing!" Todd crammed his finger against the glass. "Some of them are dressed as aliens."

David turned off the road and into the parking lot.

"Whatta you doing?" Todd asked.

"I'm dying to stretch my legs and I bet Gyra is too. This is one of the few places where Gyra can almost be himself."

Grinning, Todd smoothed his unkempt hair with a hand. "Well, that's a change of heart! David, sometimes you surprise me."

David parked the Blazer. "Let's go," Todd said, leaping out of the car.

More hesitant, Gyra set down his book, peered out the door, and swept his head back and forth. "I see two police cars," he whispered.

"It's okay, Gyra," David reassured. "They always have a few around during big events like these."

"They're not looking for us?"

"No, not in particular," Todd said in a low voice. "Just don't do anything to draw attention to yourself. They'll think you're in a costume like the rest of those people."

Gyra crept out of the car and joined them.

Entering the tent, David saw it was filled with people. Booths sold everything from New Age crystals to models of flying saucers. One booth peddled books on UFOs and psychic phenomena; another sold videos on the Bermuda triangle; beyond them, another advertised a support group for people who had encountered aliens.

"What a joke," Todd whispered as they passed the support group booth. He pointed to a popcorn vender. "Now there's *my* kind of stuff."

David exchanged glances with Todd. Gyra was not with them. Spinning around, David spied the phantera talking to a woman at the support group booth.

"You have seen an alien?" asked Gyra, cocking his head.

"Yes," the woman answered with a salesman-like smile.

"What species?"

"They called themselves the arilena," she answered politely. "They had white skin and large black eyes."

Gyra shook his head. "I am not familiar with the arilena."

"Here's what they look like." The woman proudly displayed a drawing of a slender humanoid figure.

Fingering his bill, Gyra asked. "What did they say?"

"They told me not to be afraid—they want to help us. Soon, they will reveal themselves to the world to bring peace on Earth."

David felt a riling in his spirit.

Watching the woman with his red eyes, Gyra asked, "Did they mention anything about the ban on visiting this planet?"

"No." The woman's eyebrows lowered.

Turning to a series of astronomy charts, Gyra asked, "Where did they say they were from?"

"The third star in the tale of Scorpio." She pointed to a white dot on the chart.

Gyra blinked. "We call that star Talup. It has no planets. The nearest inhabited planet is Balada, home of the friganar. They hate space travel and don't look like your drawing at all."

All traces of the lady's smile vanished.

"Are you certain this is where they came from?" Gyra gazed at her.

"Yes." She narrowed her gray eyes. "I gave this information under hypnosis. I know it's accurate."

Gyra looked at David. Cheeks glowing red, the woman said, "You don't believe me, do you. I thought at first you were one of us."

"Come on, Gyra, let's go." Todd tugged on the phantera's cloak. They moved down the aisle.

The phantera turned to David. "She was wrong, but she didn't want to know she was wrong. Why?"

David shrugged his shoulders. "Some people only believe what they want to believe."

Posters and drawings of aliens, mostly humanoid, met them at almost every booth. "It appears humans are trying to make aliens in their own image," Gyra commented. "The vast majority of drawings and statues look like altered humans. I see no bird aliens, although there are some reptilian and insect ones."

They passed a booth selling occult objects. "That stuff gives me the creeps," Todd whispered.

"Oh wow!" exclaimed a girl seated in a booth selling New Age books. "That's the best costume I've seen yet. It looks so real!"

Gyra strode over to the red-haired girl.

"Boy, you look so convincing," she continued. "I wish you were real."

"Why?"

"Why?" The girl giggled. "Because then I could say I've met a real alien."

Gyra eyed her. "So you *haven't* met an alien?"

The girl sighed. "No. So many people have, but not me."

Cocking his head, Gyra said, "I don't understand why you're so eager to meet one."

"Because everyone I know talks about how wonderful they are. Just a few had bad experiences. The aliens are going to save our planet from disease and pollution."

The phantera watched her in silence for a moment. "What would you do if you met an alien?"

The girl's eyes lit up under her red wavy hair. "What would I do? I'd do whatever it asked, I'd tell the world whatever it wanted me to say, I'd..."

"Worship it?"

"Of course!" the girl exclaimed clasping her hands together.

"No alien should be worshipped," he said in a low voice.

The girl froze and her smile drooped. "Why do you say that?" Her green eyes narrowed into a cautious expression. "Have you met one?"

Gyra turned to David.

"Go ahead," David whispered. "You can probably get away with saying anything here."

Looking back at the girl, Gyra said, "Yes, I have met many aliens."

"I knew it!" the girl said in a hushed voice. "What was the most exciting alien you ever met?"

The phantera motioned for her to lean closer. "Humans," he whispered.

The girl's face went blank; then her eyes grew very large. "Oooh. You're saying you are an...one of them." Leaning back, she frowned. "How do I know you're not just saying that to make me feel good?"

"Would you like to share my thoughts? It's called falarn."

"Kinda like a Vulcan mind meld?"

"Sort of." Gyra cocked his head and looked at David.

"Sure," the girl scooted closer. "I'll try anything once."

Todd looked ready to protest, but David held up his hand to silence him. Spreading out his fingers, Gyra laid his hand on the girl's head.

Yavana, guide me, Gyra prayed before he began.

"Will this hurt?" the girl asked as she gazed up into his eyes.

No, he answered from within her mind.

"Wow!" she breathed.

What is your name? Gyra asked.

Can't you read my mind?

I only know what you are thinking now.

My name is Sharon.

Well, Sharon, since you want to know so much about aliens, let me share some of my memories with you. As I remember them, you will see them, like watching a movie.

Todd glanced around as the phantera and Sharon remained locked in falarn. "Her eyes are closed. What do you think he's doing?"

"Your guess is as good as mine," David replied. How long was Gyra going to stand there?

No one else asked the two still figures what they were doing, but three people smiled and nodded their heads as they strolled by.

After a few minutes, Gyra took his hand off the girl's head.

"Wow, what a trip!" Sharon whispered. She looked up at Todd and David. "You're still here? I'd have thought you would've left hours ago!"

Scowling, Todd sputtered, "Hours ago? You couldn't have been doing your thing for more than five minutes."

"Really?" The girl blinked her long eyelashes. "Wow, I thought I was gone for hours. I saw so many things." She gazed at the phantera, smiling. "Thanks for showing me all that, Panagyra. I may be human, but I won't forget this. Ever!"

"What's going on, Sharon?" called a firm voice from down the aisle. A middle-aged woman strode up in a long flowing dress. "I sensed a disturbance in the vibrations around here." Clutching at one of the many crystals adorning her neck, the woman declared, "Your aura has changed!"

Todd's face wore a puzzled expression as he glanced at David. David sensed a writhing even stronger than before. His spirit pushed back on some unseen force.

Staring at the stocky woman, Gyra whispered, "David, she has demons all around her!" Rose glared at Gyra in silence as the wrinkles hardened about her eyes.

"Rose, meet Panagyra," Sharon said with enthusiasm. "He not only reads thoughts, he can share his too."

"Is that so?" Rose raised her nose and narrowed her dark eyes. "Then let him read this!"

Sharon appeared oblivious to Rose's hostility. "No, no, no, Rose, he has to touch your head."

"Very well." Rose stepped forward. "Are you willing to try it on me, or do you fear Rose the Prophetess?"

"I do not fear you or your host," Gyra answered.

"Then read my mind!" As she moved closer, David was almost smothered by her heavy perfume.

Stretching out his hand, Gyra placed it on the wild brown hair covering Rose's head. Her eyes became slits and Gyra gave a startled blink. Then the phantera closed his eyes as the woman opened hers wide.

Springing back as if she'd been shocked, Rose stared at him with a pale face, panting. Gradually, she steadied herself and found her voice. "You lie!" she hissed. "The Masters are good, not demons! You're a fake, an unbeliever who has come to mock us!" Rose's face hardened into an expression of rage. Her hand trembled as she drew herself up to her full height.

"Brothers and Sisters, those of you who look forward to the New Age, to world peace, to true inner enlightenment, I am Rose Celeste, the Prophetess!" she declared loudly.

People milling around nearby stopped and turned their heads. Rose's mouth turned upward into an unpleasant smile. "Yes, I am Rose Celeste, *the* Rose Celeste, the same who appeared on the New Day America show, the same who foretold of Senator Cadwin's demise, and the same who predicted the terrible earthquake in Chile."

More people moved closer to listen, some nodding their heads.

"I must now warn you of yet another danger." Rose's hideous smile broadened. "An enemy has come to mock us, to disrupt our peaceful cause. Will you let him succeed?"

"No!" a few voices called back. The crowd began to grow.

Rose aimed a finger at Gyra. "Behold the monster! A wolf dressed in...dove's clothing! He came to spy, to mock, and to deceive those who are vulnerable."

Sharon sprang to her feet, shouting, "No, Rose! He knows what he's saying. Just give him more time to explain—"

"Never!" the medium snapped. "He calls the Masters *demons*, and the wisdom of the ancients *lies*! He's a right-wing fundamentalist, come to proselytize us. His self-righteous judgmental beliefs enrage me!"

"I thought we tolerated all beliefs," Sharon protested, growing red.

"All beliefs but *his*. We do not tolerate those who have no tolerance for others."

Sharon shook her head. "You're wrong, Rose."

"Who are you to judge me?" Rose spat. Turning to those people around her, she announced, "I am deeply offended by this bigot's costume. See how he mocks our belief in aliens and world peace? He sneaked in wearing the skin of a dove so he could spew out hatred! Am I the only person outraged?"

"I think we should be leaving," Todd whispered.

"I think you're right," David replied, yanking on Gyra. They tried to back away.

"He's an alien!" Sharon yelled, but she was drowned out by Rose's overwhelming voice.

"Who else is outraged?" Rose challenged. A few raised their voices.

Rose's voice became a shrill cry. "Will you just sit around while our rights are being trampled? We have a right to be here!"

"Stop him!" called the woman from the support group. "He humiliated me, treated me like I was a lunatic." She burst into tears.

"See how he preys on our most vulnerable?" Rose cried.

"The mean-spirited jerk," a man seethed.

With Gyra between them, David and Todd moved quickly away. Eyes flashing, Rose barked out, "Action, people! We must take action! This impostor and his friends must not prevail!" She seemed to feast on the rising anger of the crowd.

David ducked as someone hurled a banana. A glass bottle shattered on the floor beside Todd. Some black-clothed teenagers with pierced body parts jeered at them.

A man in a tie-dyed shirt stepped between David and some of the aggressors, pleading, "Wait, let's not resort to violence!"

"Hey, hey! Ho, ho! Fundamentalists got to go!" a thin man chanted from a booth. Others picked up the chant as David and his friends beat a retreat to the far exit.

A woman leaned out of a booth selling music CDs and screamed, "Racist, sexist, anti-gay! Born-again bigots go away!"

"Give me justice!" wailed the woman from the support group.

"Don't let them get away! Fight for your rights!" Rose crowed above the chanting, jeering crowd. "They have created a disturbance. We must press charges. We must hand them over to the police!"

A young man snatched up several soda cans and flung them at Gyra, over the loud protests of the vender. They all missed the phantera and one demolished a stack of books arranged in a neat pyramid.

"Come on, this is no way to act!" shouted a woman struggling to protect her hanging crystals. Several venders cowered behind their tables.

Hurling his final soda, the young man snarled, "Stop the enemies of world peace!" before the vendor pinned him to the ground.

The spinning can came straight for David's head, but Gyra paused, grabbed the can in midair, and tossed it aside.

The more rabid members of the mob rushed after them. David spied a few policemen behind the crowd.

"Gyra," David yelled. "Meet us at the car. *Get out of here!*"

Spreading his wings, Gyra ran ahead. Somehow, Sharon had already reached the exit when Gyra dashed past her. Sharon's mouth opened as her gaze rose higher and higher, a look of delight on her face. Then she quickly averted her eyes, like a child worried about giving away a friend's hiding place.

Todd grabbed David's arm and yanked him to the side. "Not that way," Todd said, keeping David from leaving the tent. "Quick, double back down the side."

"Why?"

"As soon as they don't find Gyra they'll turn on us,"

Todd whispered loudly. "If we follow them out, we'll be prime targets. Doubling back will give us the time we need."

David nodded. He'd have to give Todd credit for this one. Fortunately, the booths were empty as everyone watched the mob at the exit.

"Where is he?" a man called. "He disappeared!" A tumult arose.

"Get his friends!" Rose shrieked. "They're accomplices!"

Roaring vile slogans, the mob searched for the objects of their wrath. They rushed with renewed vengeance when they spied David and Todd. But Todd had led David almost to the entrance.

A great *snap*, like the breaking of a mighty tree, cut through the tumult. It was followed by an ominous creaking from the tent supports. The mob stopped and stared upward. David and Todd paused just outside the tent to watch.

"Look!" A man pointed to a shadow darting on top of the tent. "What's that? Someone's on the roof!" A mighty *crack* tore through the air as the support pole shuddered.

"It's falling!" a woman screamed.

Sure enough, the great pole fell like a mighty pine. No one was in the area where it smashed several booths into the pavement.

The crowd churned, a sea of confused voices. People dashed for the exits, but most were trapped inside. Venders cried out and tried to protect their booths. One man remained rooted to his spot, looking upward, mouth agape.

A great rush of wind blasted out the openings. The huge canvas covering fell fast enough to gently blanket most of the people in the convention.

The few who made it outside were too busy helping the cursing, screaming masses trapped underneath to notice Todd and David's escape.

Reaching the car, David found Gyra hiding behind it.

"Wait, please wait!" Sharon ran up, panting. "Take me

with you!"

"No way," Todd breathed.

"They'll blame me too!" Her whole body shook as she fingered her red, disheveled hair.

David knew she was right. "Okay, hop in!"

As they drove off, a police car started up its engine, pursuing them with lights and sirens.

David floored the pedal. He couldn't let them read his license plates. Fortunately, Alice's Blazer had good pick-up and it roared onto the road. Turning onto the highway, he raced toward town. Maybe he could lose the police in traffic before they were identified.

"I saw you fly, Panagyra," Sharon said.

Todd looked back. "Is that how you got away? You did a great number on the tent too."

"I had to stop them without hurting anyone," Gyra answered. "It was the only option besides surrendering myself."

"Don't even think about that," David said as he skidded around a corner.

Gripping his door, Todd cried, "Easy David! We may have seatbelts on, but we're still getting thrown around. If you crash the car it'll be a long walk home."

"David, I've made an observation," Gyra spoke in a calm voice.

"Not now, Gyra!" David wove around a van.

"It may help our situation."

"Okay, shoot." David's hands perspired madly and he was afraid he'd lose his grip on the wheel.

"I've noticed that cars use glass for their windshields. Do the police use glass too?"

"Yes!" David shot back impatiently.

"If you let me stick my head out the window, I can shatter his windshield with a sonic blast."

"Go for it!"

Todd and Gyra exchanged places—not an easy thing to do in a car chase—so Gyra could use the passenger side window. The wind ruffled the phantera's feathers as he poked his head out and wagged it back and forth.

"It has a protective coating on it," shouted Gyra.

"Great," Todd lamented. "We're through."

"I can't break it open, but I do believe I can disable it effectively." Tracking the car with his head, the phantera inflated his chest and released a loud tone.

David glanced in his rearview mirror.

The entire windshield of the police car cracked into thousands of tiny pieces. The glass remained in place, but was impossible to see through. Their pursuer skidded to a halt.

"Well done, Gyra!" David cried. Todd whooped and Sharon cheered.

Slowing down, David entered a busy street. "Just in time. Thank you, Lord."

Sharon sighed. "I'm sorry for what happened."

"Hey, it's not your fault," Todd said. He moved up and changed seats with Gyra again.

"But I feel so bad," Sharon said in a low voice. "You know, I used to believe all that stuff Rose said about fundamentalist Christians. She called them 'mean-spirited hypocrites,' but she was always taunting me, saying I didn't try hard enough to be a successful channeler. All my friends are gonna hate me now, but you know what? I don't care. I just don't care anymore."

"Doesn't sound like they're very forgiving," David commented.

"Them? Forgiving? Ha!" Sharon found David's eyes in the rearview mirror and laughed. "They're always trying to prove they're more spiritual than the next person." She brushed some of the hair out of her eyes. "When that big ol' tent went down, I felt like my whole life went *whoosh* with it. Funny thing, I don't have any remorse. You'd think I would feel *some* remorse, especially after spending so much time and money on all those seminars."

"What *do* you feel?" David turned onto a side street.

"I feel like...I've been released, like something reached down and plucked me out of there." She turned and smiled at Gyra.

"Naharam are not to be worshipped," Gyra reminded her.

"I know, neither are the spirits," she answered. "I remember what you showed me. Tell me more about Yavana, especially Vashua. You said He visited here once."

"You have a name for Him in your language. Haven't you heard of Jesus?"

"They say he was one of the masters, a great prophet," she answered in a subdued voice.

"*One* of the masters?" Gyra wagged his head. "He is *the* Master, God in the flesh, fully human and fully divine. He came from heaven. *He* is worthy of worship."

Sharon was silent for a time. "Some Christians say channeling, fortune telling, spells, and crystals are wrong. What do you say?"

"Yavana says they are wrong."

She cringed. "Why?"

"Because they keep you from coming to Him. Channeling invites the mel-aradelah, the demons, to control you. With fortune telling, you try to see the future without trusting Yavana to show you what you need for each moment. The mel-aradelah only see part of the future and will lie to control you. Those who cast spells seek to control their world. They are trying to be little gods and don't trust Yavana to take care of them.

"Crystals are not bad in themselves, after all, Yavana made them! But when people use them for spiritual healing, they are using them like little gods. They do not go to Yavana for their healing."

David glanced in the mirror. Tears rolled down Sharon's

cheeks, blurring her makeup. "I thought all this time I *was* seeking God, that I *was* doing good, but He hated all of it!"

"No, Sharon," Gyra reassured in a gentle voice. "The way you sought Him was wrong, but your desire to know Him was not. He's forgiving and compassionate. Vashua came when naharam were lost and rebelling, not when we were good. It is His love that turns our hearts to good, not our striving."

Glancing over at Todd, David saw his friend staring out the window, picking at the upholstery on the door.

David focused on the road again. "Sharon, we're going to have to drop you off soon, but I have a friend nearby you might want to talk to. Her name is Pam. We went to school together and she recently moved to Cabrillo Bay. She can answer a lot of questions for you."

After a thoughtful silence, Sharon said, "Okay, I'll see her."

They arrived at Pam's and, after a short introduction, the two girls hit it off well. Gyra remained in the Blazer, out of sight.

As David climbed back into the car, Todd said, "We need to find a place to hide for a while. The police are gonna pounce on every blue Blazer they see."

"I've got just the spot to lay low," David announced as he started up the car.

Todd eyed David. "Where's that?"

"Marine World."

10. The Chelra of Marine World

"Marine World?" Todd's hazel eyes scowled. "I thought you didn't want to go there. Why the change?"

"What better place to get lost?" David cast a glance at Todd. "Do you have a better idea?"

"I don't know this town like you do. I guess it'd be a good place to hide the Blazer, get it off the road. What about Gyra?"

"We'll all just stay in the car."

Wrinkling his nose, Todd said, "Wonderful. Well, I suppose it's better to be stuck in a car for a few hours than in a jail cell for a few months."

They paid for parking and entered a large lot half full of cars. A small picnic area abutted the wall surrounding the theme park. Pulling up to the picnic area, David cut the engine. "Too bad there isn't a shady place to park. It's going to get hot in here."

"Yeah, I'm already starting to roast," Todd grumbled as he rolled down his window.

A security car cruised by. "I hope this isn't a bad spot," David whispered.

Gyra pulled out his book and continued to write with swift sure strokes.

Over the next hour, the security car made three passes down the perimeter road. The last time the driver's eyes seemed to scrutinize David with keen interest. Gyra cocked his head. "David, the man in that car thinks we might be part of a gang that steals car stereos. He said if we're still here when he makes his next sweep, he's going to question us."

"Great," David whispered.

Todd tugged rapidly at his shirt collar, fanning himself. "Whatta we gonna do? It's too soon to get back on the road. The police will nab us for sure."

Releasing a long sigh through his teeth, David said, "Time to turn Gyra into Sam the Seagull."

"You're kidding."

"If you have a better idea, I'm all ears!"

The transformation was much more difficult than David anticipated. Adding the seagull bill and webbed feet were easy enough, but when they tried to spray Gyra's wings, the gray paint beaded up and ran onto the seats and floor.

"Your Aunt Alice is gonna kill us," Todd warned.

"She's the least of my worries right now. I'll find some way to make it up to her." David pulled out the black spray paint. "Maybe this will work."

It didn't. Now black spots decorated the upholstery as well. With a moan, Todd said, "Gyra must be part duck!"

"I hope this washes out," David whispered as he wiped the beaded paint off the phantera's back.

"Well, at least we can use it on ourselves."

David stared at the can. "That's not a bad idea. Then we won't look like the suspects they're searching for. Here, give me a hand."

Todd added a little gray to David's dark hair.

David turned Todd's blond head jet black. They laughed at each other and admired their work in the car's mirrors.

"Okay, here's the plan…" David began.

Passing his ticket to the man at the turnstile, David received a fluorescent stamp on his hand in the shape of a dolphin.

Todd followed.

They both took a brochure and wandered over to a place where flamingos roamed a manicured lawn.

Todd opened his brochure. "I still can't believe you paid for Gyra."

"We may have to sneak him in, but that doesn't mean we don't pay admission. That would be stealing," answered David in a low voice.

Todd rolled his eyes, then looked around. "For all the cars I thought it'd be more crowded. Where is everybody?"

"Most of the people are at the dolphin show. It's one of the main attractions."

"The coast looks clear," Todd whispered.

David whistled "Amazing Grace." Swooping over the wall, Gyra landed on the lawn. The flamingos flapped their wings and squawked, but since they were always squawking, no one seemed to notice. Gyra hopped off the lawn and joined them.

"Let's go cruisin'," Todd said with a smile. "Now remember, Gyra, you're Sam the Seagull, so be extra friendly to kids."

The phantera nodded and they set out. In spite of it being the off-season, there were still quite a few families with children visiting the area. Gyra posed for several photos.

A crowd of kids gathered around the phantera. David and Todd were used to the small stir they created when Gyra was with them, but children were the most unpredictable. The more unruly ones tried to pull Gyra's tail, but Todd put a stop to that. Whenever some kids looked suspicious, Todd would take his stand behind Gyra, fold his arms, and stare down any would-be attackers.

A food peddler called to a woman working a gift wagon. "Hey, Shelly, take a look at the new character we've got. Sure looks a lot better than Ben's whale costume."

Peering out from between her hanging T-shirts and inflatable whales, Shelly said, "I wonder why they brought him on now? Usually they start their new gimmicks in early summer. It *is* a good costume, but I wouldn't have given him arms *and* wings. The guy's got six limbs!"

David glanced at Todd, who looked worried too.

"Six limbs?" answered the food peddler. "What are you talking about?" He took another look at Gyra. "Well, yeah, that *is* kind of weird, but the rest of the costume is first rate. The kids don't seem to notice. They love the guy."

David and his friends moved on and sat in on several shows.

Seeing his first sea lion, Gyra got excited and whispered, "They look like the haranda on my planet, only smaller and with a split tail."

David smiled wistfully. "I wish I could see one."

Once the sea lion show was over, Todd glanced around at the exiting crowd. "Now what?"

David read his brochure. "There's a film called *The Rising Tide* about grunion. Want to see it?"

"Nah." Finishing off his bag of popcorn, Todd took David's brochure and scrutinized it. "I've never seen a killer whale. Next show is in three hours. Let's see them now while there's no crowd."

"Okay, I always like watching the orcas." David led the way. He had visited Marine World frequently as a child. Some parts had been updated or removed, but a few things never changed. Pausing in front of an old machine, David savored a peculiar, plastic aroma. He remembered his father slipping quarters into this same machine. It had hummed as the metal halves of the mold came together. After a few minutes, the mold opened, revealing a blue plastic dolphin. The toy tumbled into a compartment where David's eager, small hands had retrieved his warm prize.

Heat, pressure, and a mold. David felt heat and pressure, but what was he being molded into?

"Come on, David," Todd called. David tore himself away and joined his friends. They reached the orca tank and found it was deserted—except for two orcas. One was much larger than the other.

"My gosh, I didn't know they were so humongous!" Todd exclaimed.

The half-circle tank contained a wall of glass that faced the enormous grandstand. The audience could view the whales from above and below the waterline at the same time.

Gliding silently by the glass, two orcas surfaced to breathe. The noise of their explosive exhalation made Todd jump. "Hey, I thought they spouted water!"

David grinned. "They're mammals like you and me."

"I knew that," Todd said under his breath.

"Sometimes water pools on top of their blowhole. When the whale exhales it blasts the water up into the air, creating a mist. It's more obvious on the bigger whales."

"*Bigger* whales?" Todd looked at David out of the corner of his eye.

"Yeah. The old whalers could tell what type of whale they saw in the distance by the way it spouted. Orcas are among the smallest of whales. They're really more like big dolphins."

"Big dolphins," Todd muttered. "Really big dolphins."

Todd waited in line to purchase a hot dog and fries. A security guard strolled by. He smiled at Shelly seated behind her dangling inflatable whales and fish.

"Hey, Chuck!" Shelly called. "That new Sam the Seagull character is really cute. The kids love him."

Chuck came over to her cart. "What seagull character?"

Todd cringed.

"You mean you haven't seen him? Oh, he's great. His costume really looks like a bird, except for the fact that he's got six limbs, but other than that he's *really* cute."

"I wasn't informed about a new costume character. Ted forgot to tell me. I'll have to speak with him." He pulled out his radio. "Ted, this is Chuck."

"This is Ted, what's up?" the radio crackled.

"Hey, why didn't you tell me there's a new costume character? I should know these things."

"Wait a minute, Chuck, what are you talking about?"

"I'm talking about the new character, Sam the Seagull."

"We don't have any seagull characters. We haven't hired

anyone since summer. We even had to let a few people go. I know we definitely don't have any Sam the Seagull."

"Well, then who—"

"Uh oh!" Ted answered. "I'll bet it's one of those animal-rights activists. It could be the Free the Whales group. Bring that seagull impostor to me, but do it without creating a stir. We don't want him to get any publicity if we can help it. I'll contact the other security personnel and let them know what's going on."

"Yes sir!" Chuck placed his radio back in its holster and walked briskly down the path.

Todd abandoned his place in line and hurried off to the dolphin tank.

David leaned over the concrete four-foot wall of the dolphin petting tank. He stared at the dark, turbulent waters churned by dorsal fins and flukes. Sixty feet in diameter, the circular petting tank held half a dozen dolphins.

When he was a child, his dad used to buy fish for him to feed the dolphins. The sleek creatures never came unless David offered them a fish and he always lamented how quickly the smelly herring disappeared.

"He is coming," Gyra announced.

Todd walked so fast he was almost running. "We've got trouble! The security guards are looking for Gyra and they think he's some animal-rights activist!"

Glancing around, David said, "It won't take them long to comb the place. Where can we hide Gyra?"

"I hear them coming." Gyra snapped his bill. "And I have an idea!" Hopping onto the wall, the phantera dove into the green water. Unlike the pristine show tanks, this water was a bit murky.

Todd flashed David a wide-eyed look. "You don't think the dolphins will hurt—"

"Shhh," David cautioned.

A security guard sauntered into the area and strolled around the circular tank.

David watched the water. He glanced at his watch. Why did the guard have to take his time? Surely Gyra couldn't hold his breath much longer!

The guard reached the far side and paused. He looked at the cluster of surfacing dolphins, glanced at Todd and David, and resumed his ponderously slow pace. David realized he was holding his breath. He exhaled slowly. The guard came around to David and Todd.

David bowed his head. *Lord help us. Lord protect us. Lord...what happened to Gyra?*

Picking up his radio, the guard moved on. "This is Chuck. I'm at the dolphin petting tank. No joy." He left the area.

Todd turned to David with an expression that seemed to say "Now what?"

The dolphins in the tank floated placidly in front of David, eyeing him. Leaning over the concrete wall, David hung his hands in the water—the way he had done when he was a boy. He was startled by a nudge to his hands.

A dolphin grinned up at him. David took in a breath. Here was a dolphin staring up at him. Would it let him touch it? Stretching out his hand, David felt the smooth skin of its football-shaped forehead. It breathed, spraying him with warm moist air. Opening its mouth, the dolphin rinsed out a piece of orange rubber, picked it up with its snout, and pushed it into David's hand.

David dropped it but the dolphin patiently repeated the process until David caught the flimsy object. The dolphin sank, disappearing into the dark water.

Examining the piece of colored latex, David noticed a message scratched into its surface: *How long until I can come out?* He recognized Gyra's fake webbing. "Todd, look!"

After showing Todd the message, David shoved the plastic into his pocket and looked around. The place was still deserted. Plunging his arm into the cold water, David waved for Gyra to come.

A white feathered head broke surface.

"Gyra, are you all right?" asked Todd in a harsh whisper.

"I take it you got my message," Gyra responded. "I suppose I should tell you phantera can breathe under water."

He rubbed his pink beak. "Sorry, but the elastic broke on my seagull bill and all the fake webbing fell off. By the way, these dolphins are the first *chelra* I have met on your planet."

David frowned. "What's a chelra?"

A dolphin surfaced beside the phantera.

Gyra placed a hand on the animal's sleek back. "You don't have a word for chelra in your language. They are a level below the naharam, able to communicate with primitive speech. Chelra are between naharam and dalam."

"What's a dalam?" David asked.

"Animals with no real speech. A dog is a dalam. Chelra are more intelligent."

Frowning, Todd said, "Wait, you're saying you can talk to dolphins, *these* dolphins?"

Gyra looked down at the placid dolphin. "Yes."

"Cool!" Todd exclaimed.

Gyra wagged his head. "The guard is returning...and bringing others with him!" The phantera sank out of sight.

Five security guards hustled into the area. One pulled a line across the entrance and hung a sign that read: Exhibit Closed.

David's pulse pounded in his ears. What could they do?

Chuck approached Todd. "All right, you've had your fun, now get your friend."

"He's right here," Todd answered, pointing to David.

Chuck folded his arms. "Don't get smart with me, buddy. We want your friend in the bird suit."

Spreading his hands, Todd replied, "I don't see him, do you?"

Chuck wore a smug smile. "You think we don't know where he is? Did it ever occur to you we might have surveillance cameras around this tank?"

"No," Todd said meekly.

A man in a wet suit arrived. "I got here as soon as I heard."

"We've got a crank in the tank," Chuck said with a jerk of his head. "See if you can flush him out, Gary."

Gary hauled himself onto the wall and sat on it. A wall of dolphins rose before him, squealing and thrashing the water. Turning in unison, they smacked the surface with their powerful flukes, hurling water at Gary.

The man swore and got off the wall. "What was that all about?"

"Beats me! You're the trainer, you tell me!" Chuck teased.

Gary tried to sneak over another portion of the wall. Again, a violent blast of water met him, forcing him to retreat.

"Man, I've never seen anything like this!" Gary sputtered. "One or two might get riled up, but they're all acting in unison to keep me out!"

Gary got some of the guards to distract the dolphins while he leaped into the tank. A moment later, his body burst out of the water as two dolphins shoved Gary over the tank wall. He flailed about on the ground, swearing under his breath.

"Are you all right?" Chuck asked.

Standing slowly, Gary rubbed his backside. "Yeah. They seem pretty determined to keep me out."

Chuck caught Todd smiling. "I wouldn't be so cocky if I were you. We can wait here until your friend runs out of air, but we'll go easier on you if you decide to cooperate *now*."

David stepped forward. "Please, sir, we didn't mean to cause a disturbance. Our friend is shy and, well, when he saw you coming, he panicked and jumped in the tank. If you want, I'll try to call him."

"We're not letting you in the tank as well," Chuck answered.

Nodding in agreement, David said, "I understand. I'd only stick my arm in the water."

"Let him try," Gary called. "I'd like to see someone else get wet for a change."

"Just your arm," Chuck warned. "And if they go crazy, you're to back off, understood?"

"Yes sir." David approached the undulating waters of the tank, bracing himself for an attack.

A dolphin eyed him from underwater and darted off. David thrust his arm into the water and waved. In the middle of the tank, the phantera's head popped to the surface. David toyed with the thought of telling Gyra to fly away, but promptly rejected it. Better to let people assume Gyra was a human than to really stir things up.

"They've caught us," David told Gyra. "I figure if we cooperate enough, they might not get *too* nasty. The last thing they want is publicity."

"I'll come," Gyra said. His body rose straight out of the water as two dolphins, one under each foot, swam him to the wall. Todd and the guards stared in awe. Gyra hopped onto the wall. The remaining dolphins leaped in unison, as if saluting, before crashing back into the water.

Holding up a pair of handcuffs, Chuck said, "All right, you've had your fun now, birdie."

"Um, those really won't be necessary," David sputtered. "He won't fight."

Chuck gave David an appraising look before hooking the handcuffs back on his belt. "If he does, I'll use them on all of you. Come with me, you three."

David glanced at Todd's white face. He was sorry he'd gotten Todd into this mess.

Picking up his radio, Chuck said, "Ted, this is Chuck. We have the visitors and are bringing them to you."

The guards escorted them through a door in the wall. It led to the back side of Marine World, where offices and isolation tanks remained hidden from the public eye.

"Where're we goin'?" Todd ventured to ask.

"To see Ted Bates, chief of security."

Entering a building, they were ushered into a plain office. A tall, lean man with very short brown hair rose from behind his desk. "I think you owe us a few answers." He leveled his firm dark eyes at Todd. "We'll begin with an explanation of what your friend was doing in the tank."

"Wasn't it obvious?" Todd blurted. "He was hiding!" He began to giggle, but David silenced him with a glare.

"I'd like to know how he got the dolphins to protect him and carry him," Gary muttered.

Chuck crossed his arms. "And I'd like to know how he stayed underwater so long."

David raised his hands in entreaty. "We weren't trying to cause any trouble. We just wanted to spend the day at Marine World and things got out of hand."

Ted folded his arms, matching Chuck's posture. "Oh?"

David kept his voice calm, controlled. "Please, just let us go and we can forget this whole thing happened."

An eyebrow lifted on Ted's serious face. "You are hardly in a position to bargain." He poured himself a cup of coffee and sat down behind his desk. "All right, boys, are you going to tell us what you were doing or will we have to turn you over to the authorities for trespassing, molesting marine mammals, and malicious mischief?"

"Please don't turn us over to the police!" Todd whined.

Ted leaned forward. "A little truth will go a long way. I was watching you from our cameras for quite a while." He stared at Gyra and smiled.

The phantera didn't move.

Sipping from his mug, Ted said, "Let's start from the

top. Why are you here?"

David drew a deep breath and let it out. "All right, I'll tell you. Before I begin, may I assume you want to avoid publicity?"

Ted raised both of his eyebrows. "Are you telling me you *weren't* planning an animal-rights publicity stunt, or a college prank?"

"We really didn't want to attract attention." David looked down at the worn rug.

"You *didn't* want to attract attention?" Ted asked in a skeptical tone. "Then why the bird suit?"

"It's a long story."

Ted leaned back in his chair. "We've got time."

David prayed silently, but felt like he was trying to move a brick wall. Ted had him completely intimidated. Looking at Gyra, David knew his friend's welfare depended on the answers he gave right now. What if he took all the blame so they would release Todd and Gyra? Nope, Ted wasn't going to bargain. What had he said? A little truth goes a long way? Not a bad philosophy.

Looking at the hard faces surrounding him, David said, "I'll tell you, but not in front of all these people. I can hardly breathe."

"Fair enough," Ted replied. He appeared pleased with himself for getting a confession so easily.

All the men left except Chuck and Gary.

"Is this good enough for you?" Ted asked.

"Yes."

Ted pulled out a compact tape recorder and turned it on. After readying a pen and large notepad, he looked up at David. "Go ahead."

11. A Hard Confession

David glanced at his friends. Todd's face mirrored anxiety and curiosity at the same time. Gyra's was unreadable.

"We came here to get away from the UFO convention," David began. "We were in town on a short vacation, saw the big tent and decided to check it out. We were just curious. My friend, Gyra, was talking with a girl when this lady came up and accused him of being a spy." David swallowed. He shouldn't have used Gyra's name! Now Ted could trace them. *God, forgive my blunder.*

He continued. "This woman, I think her name was Rose, she began screaming at us, calling us right-wing fundamentalist bigots, or something like that. The woman started a riot all on her own. We ran out of the tent, afraid they were going to kill us. The next thing we knew, the tent was falling down and the security police were after us. We got scared and fled. I drove here to hide in the parking lot for a while, but your security patrol made us nervous. We decided to sneak our friend in and pass him off as Sam the Seagull."

"Good try," Ted said as he eyed his notes. "But you left a few things unanswered. Why didn't your friend just ditch his outfit?"

"He's kind of stuck in it," Todd blundered in. "Just try to find the zipper. We couldn't."

Ted lowered his brows. "You mean he can't take it off?"

"Not unless you can take off your own skin," David said with smirk.

Scratching the back of his head with a pen, Ted asked, "Well, what was he doing with it on in the first place?"

Todd shrugged his shoulders. "It's just him. He goes around looking like that because it's the way he is."

"Are you saying he's a nut case?" Ted peered up from his notepad.

"Oh, no!" David reassured. "He's very, very bright...just a little eccentric. Geniuses often are, you know."

"Well, I like to see the faces of my suspects." Ted turned to Chuck. "See if you can figure a way to get that outfit off."

"Careful," Todd warned. "It fits skintight, and I do mean skintight. You wouldn't want to hurt him. It could bring a lawsuit."

Chuck looked all over Gyra, probing beneath the feathers. "I can't find any seam—nothing! This thing fits better than a glove."

"I did say that he was bright," David reiterated. "Maybe there's no way to get him out without hurting him."

Ted stared at David. "All right, Chuck, that's enough for now."

Frowning, Chuck drew back.

"So, tell me how your friend was able to get the dolphins to help him out." Ted's narrowed eyes bore into David.

"He...asked them to," David stumbled.

"Oh, good grief!" Ted exclaimed. "You *are* a bunch of whale worshipers, aren't you!"

"I do not worship whales," Gyra spoke.

Ted's eyebrows rose. "So, you do talk!"

"There is only one who is worthy to be worshipped. God alone." Gyra gazed at Ted.

"Are you some sort of religious nut?" asked Ted.

"I'm not a nut, I'm a Christian."

"He's a nut all right," Gary muttered.

Ted glared at the trainer. "Gary, my wife is a Christian."

"Sorry." Gary blushed and looked away.

"So, you say you talked to the dolphins?" Ted continued. Gyra nodded. "Yes."

Ted fingered his pen. "And what did they tell you?"

"Not much, I did most of the talking. A female is not feeling well. She's still sore from the needles that poked the skin near her pectoral fins."

Gary's head snapped around. "Who told you that?"

"She did." Gyra looked at Gary, then Ted.

"Is this true?" Ted asked Gary.

Scowling, Gary replied, "I don't know about the dolphin telling him—"

"No, was she poked with needles?" Ted flexed his pen between his fingers.

"Yes, we vaccinated a female yesterday. Only the trainers and the vet know."

Ted's face froze. He turned back to Gyra. "What else did they tell you?"

Scratching the back of his neck bird-style, Gyra said, "Another female in the tank is pregnant. An older male dolphin is in pain. You have an isolated tank behind a wall with a lone dolphin. She calls to the other dolphins and has trouble breathing."

Ted's eyes locked onto Gary.

Shaking his head, Gary said, "I don't know about the ones in the dolphin tank, their next physical is in three weeks, but we do have Kathy in isolation. She's got pneumonia—it's real bad too." Gary's pained eyes turned toward Gyra. "Are you a vet?"

"No. I can only tell you what they told me. I wish I could help you more."

Ted pressed a finger into his cheek. "So, they didn't tell you any words of wisdom, any revelations?"

Gyra balked. "No! Why should I go to them for wisdom? They're not as smart as people. Although they possess wonderful sonar and coordination, their language is crude, like their thought processes. Humans are on an entirely different level."

With a smirk, Ted said, "You're not from Free the

Whales, that's for sure!"

The door opened as a guard burst in. "Ted, sorry to interrupt you, but you've got to see the news! It has somethin' on your bird-man."

"Let's go," Ted ordered as he herded everyone down the hall to a room with a TV.

"And now the latest on channel six news," the newscaster announced. A sharply dressed woman in a red outfit stood before a deflated tent.

"Hello, I'm Gloria Greenfield at Cabrillo Bay. A UFO convention had its ups and downs this week, the biggest down being when the roof fell."

A video clip of a large woman came on. "I just thought I was going to die. It was the scariest thing I've ever been through. Someone screamed and then the thing fell. I wasn't hurt, but I could hardly move when the canvas landed on me. It was a good twenty minutes before they helped me out."

The woman reporter reappeared. "Just before the tent fell, witnesses claimed there was an altercation between Madam Rose Celeste and a group of fundamentalist Christians."

A clip of Rose Celeste flashed onto the screen. "I am appalled that these born-again bigots could come in here and disrupt a peaceful convention. They have no respect for those with different beliefs. Our rights were violated today and America had better wake up, or we'll find ourselves losing all the freedoms we cherish."

"Do you believe fundamentalist Christians sabotaged the tent?" the reporter asked.

Rose nodded emphatically. "Absolutely. The police chased them, but they escaped in a blue Blazer. There were two men, a girl, and someone dressed up as a bird. We hope that witnesses will come forward to help us catch these terrorists."

A prerecorded video showed the fallen tent as the reporter continued. "Fortunately, there were only minor injuries, a few cuts and scratches, caused by people pan-icking when the tent fell. It could have been a lot worse."

A man appeared on the screen. "One of the large sup-port poles fell over and demolished a bunch of booths. The destruction was awful. I would hate to think what would have happened if it had fallen on some people."

Another view of the flattened tent appeared as the news-woman resumed her report. "The owner of Mayan Rental Tents claims his tents are safe. He insists today's disaster was the result of sabotage."

A clip of Fred Mayan appeared. "Investigators found several of the cables disconnected from the top of the second pole. Someone would have to be on top of the tent to disconnect them. I personally don't know how they could climb up there, but evidently someone did. This is consis-tent with the testimony of several witnesses who claimed they saw someone's shadow on top of the tent."

The screen flashed back to Gloria Greenfield with a backdrop of flattened booths. "Who was that mystery person? Nobody really knows, but there is a lot of specula-tion. The four suspects who escaped may provide the strongest lead. For now, all anyone has seen of this fifth mystery person is his shadow.

"But the story doesn't end here." A shattered wind-shield flashed onto the TV. "This is the police car that was pursuing the suspects. Officer James was chasing them when his windshield mysteriously shattered."

A video of Officer James came up. "I was pursuing the suspects when my windshield went *bang*, like a fire-cracker. I didn't see anything hit it, but the glass shattered evenly into pieces the size of a pea—like it broke every-where at once. Fortunately, the windshield stayed in place. I slammed on the brakes and stopped. I've seen a lot of broken windshields, and usually you can determine where the point of impact was, but the fracture patterns on this one were totally different. I can't explain it."

The woman reporter returned. "While the police continue their investigation of the fallen tent, some of the convention delegates are considering filing suit against Mayan Rental Tents. And the police are asking the manufacturer of their vehicles to do a special investigation of their own. They are concerned that the windshield may have been defective. One thing we do know is that the untimely failure of this windshield prevented the apprehension of today's four suspects. This is Gloria Greenfield, and now back to you, Rusty."

David's cheeks burned as every eye in the room focused on them. This was a nightmare. No, he wished this *was* a nightmare; then he could hope to wake up in his own bed instead of ending up in a jail cell.

He remembered his friends. Todd stared at the television, his face as white as the walls around him, while Gyra seemed unaffected.

Turning to Ted, David engaged the eyes of his judge. What was the man thinking? David was afraid to know.

Finally, Ted broke the awful silence. "I want to see you, David, in my office. Alone."

As David followed Ted, no one spoke a word. Breathing in the stale hall air, David felt his pulse pounding in his ears.

Once they were inside the office, Ted shut the door and sat down. He motioned for David to take a seat as well. The chief of security gazed at him for a long time until David wondered if this was some sort of interrogation technique.

With a flick of his wrist, Ted turned on the tape recorder.

In a slow, measured voice, Ted asked, "Where are the other two people?"

"The only other person was the girl. I took her to a friend's house where she'd be safe." David stared at his clammy fingers.

"Who was up on the tent?"

Squeezing his hands, David said, "Sir, you mentioned that a little bit of truth would go a long way. I've been truthful with you, but I need to talk with you without the tape recorder."

Ted's features hardened. "Are you going to try to bribe me?"

"No," David said, shaking his head vigorously. "It's just that...what I say could put someone's life in danger if it fell into the wrong hands."

Ted stopped the recorder. "Does this have to do with the mob at the convention?"

"No, it has to do with a new form of intelligent life and the potential for abuse."

Ted tensed like a cat. "The dolphins?"

"Not the dolphins, not the whales." David leaned forward. *This is one whale of a risk, but I don't see any other options, Lord.* "Gyra," he whispered.

"The man in the bird suit?"

"Not a man, a phantera. He crash landed here."

"Sounds to me like you spent too much time at that convention," Ted responded with narrowed eyes.

"You say you want answers? You say you want the truth?" David baited. "Then listen closely. Gyra was the one on top of the tent. He undid the cables somehow and made the tent fall to save our lives. The mob was going to kill us. Gyra *flew* up onto the tent—his wings are real. I'll tell you how the windshield was broken too. Gyra leaned his head out our car and emitted a sonic blast. He found the frequency to shatter it. That's why the cracks were evenly distributed all over it.

"You want to know about the dolphins? Gyra can learn someone's language by merely touching their head. When I first met him two weeks ago, he didn't know a word of English. Now look at him. Know why you can't find a seam in his suit? It's because there isn't one. How did he stay submerged for so long? If he had a tank on him, there would have been bubbles when he exhaled. Even *I* didn't know he could breathe underwater until today."

"Enough!" Ted ordered. He rose and opened the door. "Send the bird-man in."

Gyra entered and waited before Ted. After shutting the door, Ted pointed to a glass paperweight on his desk. "Gyra, can you shatter this?"

David nodded his approval and the phantera said, "Yes."

"Do it!" Ted's eyes flicked between the paperweight and Gyra.

The phantera swept his head back and forth, faced the paperweight, and sang a note. The paperweight exploded, scattering bits of glass all over the desk.

"I don't believe it!" Ted exclaimed, jumping back. "I didn't think he'd really do it. What a mess!"

"I'm sorry." David picked up a piece of paper and began to sweep up the glass.

Wearing a chagrined expression, Ted mumbled, "I should have picked a less expensive object." He pointed to an aquarium in the corner of his office. "Gyra, can you shatter this?"

David balked. "Are you sure you want him to try?"

Crossing his arms, Ted said, "Absolutely."

Gyra wagged his head. "I'm sorry. It's not made of the same material."

David thought for sure Ted would accuse them of being fakes, but to his surprise, Ted answered, "That's right. It's not glass. It's acrylic." The chief of security almost smiled as he went to the door and called for someone named Rick.

Rick came in, saw David cleaning up the glass, and gave Ted a questioning look.

Pacing the room, Ted said, "Rick, you spent some time in Uganda right?"

"Yeah, before I decided to be a sea lion trainer." Rick stared warily at David.

"Are you game for an experiment?" Ted asked.

Rick shrugged. "Sure."

"Let's see if Gyra can speak some Ugandan." Ted winked at the phantera. "Gyra, touch Rick's head."

Gyra laid a hand on the trainer's head.

"Hey, you shocked me," Rick chuckled as he rubbed his scalp.

Ted stopped pacing. "Okay, Rick, say something in Ugandan. Nothing dirty either."

Grinning at Ted, Rick said, *"Nkoye. Njagala oku genda eka."*

"What'd he say?" Ted asked the phantera.

Gyra fingered a flight feather. "He said 'I'm tired and I want to go home.'"

"You know Luganda?" Rick asked with wide eyes. "I picked some up while on a two-year research assignment! You must have been in the same area of Uganda."

"Tell him something in Luganda," Ted ordered Gyra.

Gyra rattled off a few sentences as Rick listened, fascinated.

Playing with the pen in his hand, Ted asked, "What'd he say, Rick?"

Rick smirked. "He apologized for upsetting us. He was afraid we were going to hurt him and didn't know he wasn't allowed to swim with the dolphins."

Ted dismissed Rick before the trainer could ask any questions. After he shut the door, Ted resumed his pacing. "I'd be lying if I told you I believe everything I see on the news, especially tonight."

David glanced at his watch. It was getting late in the day. "Are you going to call the police?"

Ted stopped. "I haven't decided yet."

Well, they'd made *some* progress. David took a deep

breath and said, "Do you know what the authorities would do to Gyra? They might treat him like a lab specimen and run experiments on him. Maybe that's a little extreme, but it's not hard to see them caging him as ego-hungry scientists fight over how to study him. Maybe they'd just hide him away in the interests of 'national security' and who knows what they'd do to him then. He's not human, so legally they could treat him like an animal. Are you ready to condemn a fully sentient being to that kind of life?"

Ted stuck his pen between his teeth. "How do you know he's not dangerous?"

"He hasn't done anything violent so far. Gyra just wants to fix his ship and go home; he didn't want to land here in the first place."

"How do you know he's not just spying?"

David blew out his breath in exasperation. "I think his technology could leave us in the dust. It's *possible* Gyra's a spy, but isn't it our custom to give people the benefit of a doubt? Do we really believe in 'innocent until proven guilty'?"

Pulling the pen out of his mouth, Ted watched with a poker face. "I still say you're not in a position to bargain."

Ted sighed, leaned back, and set his pen down. "Why should I be lenient to some kids who sneak their friend inside my park and stir up trouble?"

David reached into his pocket and pulled out a whole ticket and two torn stubs. "I did pay his way, but I doubted the attendants would let him in as he is."

Ted picked up the unused ticket, eyeing it.

"Please, just let us go and we won't cause you any more trouble," David pleaded. "As security chief, I would think the smooth operation of Marine World would be your first priority."

"*Safety* is my first priority," Ted countered. His eyes locked onto Gyra.

"David was only trying to protect me," the phantera spoke in a soft voice. "Let the blame fall on me. I will not resist whatever punishment you deem necessary for my transgressions. What do you want me to do?"

Chuckling, Ted wagged his head. The stillness became stifling. Ted exhaled into the silence. "Give me one good reason why I should let you go."

David looked into Ted's brown eyes. "Sir, I have never been in trouble with the law until now. I have tried to do what I feel is right, even if the consequences are difficult. Contrary to the news, I am not a terrorist. Yes, I *am* a Christian, but the last time I checked, that wasn't a crime. I'm just trying to help a friend get home."

"And just what's preventing your friend from leaving?" Ted's tone of voice didn't give any indication of favor.

"He needs some titanium to repair his ship."

A wry expression crossed Ted's face. "That's all? No plutonium or uranium?"

"He's repairing a ship, not building a bomb!" David blurted in exasperation.

The corners of Ted's mouth softened. "What would you say if I told you I could get you some titanium?"

David's heart raced. Was this a joke? A trap?

The black pen scribbled on Ted's notepad. "We built a research boat out of titanium and kept a few scraps. Now, how much do you need?"

David was in such a state of shock that Gyra had to answer for him. Ted phoned down to maintenance. After he finished his request, he picked up the tape recorder and pulled out the cassette.

David's heart raced. "Why are you doing this?"

Ted stood and paced the worn path on his rug, eyeing the pen and cassette in one hand, and the ticket in the other. Stopping, he turned to David.

"I've dealt with a lot of criminals in my line of work.

I've also seen innocent people crucified by the system in the name of 'justice.' I don't want to see another victim."

He held up Gyra's ticket. "You and I have one thing in common: we're both people of principle."

"What about your staff?" David asked.

Ted gave the cassette tape to David. "I can only do so much to cover for you. As soon as it's dark, I'll arrange to have you escorted back to your car." Tearing off the notes from his pad, he said, "The later part of this interview did not take place. You'll have ten minutes from the time you reach your car to when I call the police. Will that be enough time?"

David thought for a moment. "It would if they didn't know what type of car to look for. If they search for a blue Chevy Blazer, we won't be hard to find."

Ted bit his pen. "I'll report one of the company cars as 'missing.' It will all be a mistake, but it should throw them off for a while. We'll 'find' it late tonight down on the beach."

Standing, David shook Ted's hand and said, "Thank you!" Ted's face finally warmed into a smile.

After the park officially closed, the titanium arrived, and Ted had David's friends brought in. Todd moaned when the three were handcuffed by security guards and escorted out. David winked at Todd to keep his friend from panicking.

Night had claimed the sky and a faint breeze blew from the sea. Entering the parking lot, they stopped beside the Blazer. Ted ordered the guards back to the office. After they'd left, he unlocked the handcuffs and handed the titanium sheets to David. "Quick!" he said in a low voice. "You've got ten minutes before all hell breaks loose. I've got to take a company car for a little 'drive.'"

"Thanks again," David whispered as he unlocked the Blazer's door.

Once they were all in the car, Todd's mouth flew into

action. "What happened? I thought for sure he was gonna use us for shark bait! What did you tell that guy?"

David started up the engine and roared out of the parking lot. "I told him the truth, Todd, and it was the hardest confession of my life!"

12. On the Run Again

"We've got just ten minutes before he calls the police," David explained as the car screeched around a corner.

Planting a hand on the dashboard, Todd braced himself. "So, did you strike some sort of bargain with him?"

"Not exactly. I'll explain later. Right now we have to make these ten minutes count. I need to think!"

They rode on in tense silence. David sped down the interstate hoping no police would see him speeding. The wheels squealed as he turned down a road leading to a state park.

"Whatta you thinking?" Todd asked, clinging to his door handle for support.

"There used to be an old dirt road running to the Inland Valley Freeway. I took it a couple of times as a short cut. Few people know it's there. It could save us a bundle of time and the police might not expect us to get that far so fast."

David slammed on his brakes.

"Dang it!" Todd exclaimed. The road ended at a parking lot. Todd read the sign. "'Day use only.' What a bummer! It looks like things have changed since you were here last. The gate arm is down and the other side says 'Do not enter. Severe tire damage.'"

"And there's the road," David added, pointing to a strip of dirt just within the range of his headlights.

"So close and yet so far," Todd fumed. "Now what?"

Looking around the park, David spied a partly built fence. Nearby, lay a stack of 2x6's.

"Quick, Todd, take the driver's seat and wait for me!" David leapt out of the car and ran toward the lumber. Snatching up a plank, he raced for the park exit and laid the wood on top of the sharp teeth. He made certain the board leaned toward the car to form a slight ramp.

Todd cruised up, saw what David was doing, and drove over the covered teeth. He grinned. "Great idea. Now let's get out of here!"

David shook his head. "Not yet." He picked up the board, ran back to the pile, and placed it face down so the deep grooves would not be noticed. Then he sprinted back to the car.

Todd had already moved to the passenger side. "You could've just put it in the car," he admonished as David drove on.

"That would be stealing. Besides, I didn't think of it. I sure didn't want to leave the board on the exit. It would have been a dead giveaway."

Chuckling, Todd slapped David's back. "Where did you get such a devious idea if you're such a moral guy?"

David glanced at Todd out of the corner of his eye. "Just because I don't do all the mischievous things you do doesn't mean I don't think about them."

The Blazer jumped the curb and rumbled down the dirt strip. Todd gripped his seatbelt. "I hope this still goes through." He placed a hand on the dash again as the car bucked and rolled on the rough road. "Was it this bad last time you drove it?"

"No. I think they stopped maintaining it when they closed it off."

Fortunately, the road was only bad in a few spots and soon they were closing in on the Inland Valley Freeway.

David glanced at his watch. Nine minutes—perfect!

He slammed on the brakes.

"Shoot!" yelled Todd.

A gate spanned the road.

"It's not locked," came Gyra's calm voice. "I can see the empty rings from here."

"Thank you, Jesus!" David whispered as Todd got out and ran to the yellow pipe. It wasn't locked, but it was rusty and required a lot of grunting and sweating from Todd before it opened.

Driving through, David waited while Todd battled with the gate to close it again. "Working out in the gym this summer paid off," Todd said, panting as he collapsed in his seat. He didn't need a reminder to buckle his seatbelt before David accelerated onto the freeway.

David glanced at his watch. Ten and a half minutes—time to be extra vigilant. At least they had a good start. Placing a hand on his forehead, David muttered, "Oh, no."

Todd gave him a wide-eyed look. "What now?"

Chuckling at his friend's fright, David said, "Nothing really big. I just need to call Steve and find out if Mom left any messages."

"Do you think they did anything to her?"

David flinched. He hadn't thought about the trouble she might be in. "I sure hope not."

David ran back from the pay phone and opened the door as Todd started up the engine.

Todd moved over to the passenger's side and asked, "So, what's up?"

Hopping inside, David shut the door. "Apparently, running from the police is becoming a family thing. Do you know what my mom did after we left?"

Todd wagged his head.

David pulled onto the street. "She took Debbie and

drove my car to the Valley Mall to shop. Afterwards, they went to church for an all-night prayer meeting. They didn't stop her until she was on her way home. Mom told them we left her the car to use while we went on vacation. They were a little annoyed."

"Did she say who 'they' were?" Todd picked at a spot on the window.

"All my information came through Steve. It's too risky to call Mom direct." David turned onto the freeway, joining the river of white headlights and red taillights. "Steve said a police officer pulled her over, but the man who really questioned her was from the federal government. His name was Darius Blackwell, and he gave her the creeps. Mr. Blackwell made a few veiled threats to intimidate her, but good ol' Mom stood her ground. She tried to find out why they wanted Gyra, but he wasn't too keen on sharing. Mr. Blackwell was more interested in getting answers. While Mom was on the run, she called Dad at work and told him everything before the police got her. He was extremely skeptical, I'd be disappointed if he hadn't been, but when he listened to Mr. Blackwell, it convinced Dad that something really fishy was going on. Mom and Dad were unnerved by how much Mr. Blackwell knew about our family. He's been investigating you too."

"*Me?* Oh boy, that's scary." Todd grimaced and rubbed his scalp. "If they dig through all the dumb things I've done, they'll find plenty of blackmail material."

"Well, it's a little late to turn back now."

"Yeah, we're sort of into it up to here." Todd held his hand above his head. "I gotta confess, sometimes I wish we hadn't stopped to look for that spaceship."

"And leave Gyra to Mr. Blackwell, a man who thinks nothing of digging into people's private affairs and flaunting it? I doubt if the man has a moral bone in his body."

"Sorry I mentioned it!" Folding his arms, Todd stuck out his lower lip.

David sighed. "I'm sorry, Todd, we've both been through a lot the last few days."

"Weeks!" Todd snapped.

"Weeks," David conceded. "You've done far better than I'd expected."

"Hmmph!" Todd grunted, but one corner of his mouth began to turn up.

David went on. "You've handled an incredible amount of responsibility with maturity, and I don't mean in comparison to what you did in high school, or even last year. You hung in there with Gyra when most people would have bailed." David knew Todd always admired loyal people.

Todd smiled. "Do you really mean that?"

"I wouldn't lie to you, Todd."

Todd threw back his head, filling the car with loud laughter. "You better not be lying! If you can tell the truth to that Ted dude back at Marine World, you'd better tell me!"

David chuckled. "Well, it sure wasn't much fun when I told the truth to Ted."

"Tell me about it!" Todd pleaded.

Darius Blackwell glared in anger at the man before him. He hated unwanted interruptions. They were an affront to his sense of order, his sense of control.

But the worker simply held up a note and said, "David Decker just left Marine World. The police are searching the area."

Snatching the note, Darius scrutinized it. "But what direction did he go?"

"They don't know, sir."

"First the fiasco at the UFO convention and now this. You're getting sloppy, Mr. Decker. Where will you go? You can't hide a space alien forever." Darius looked up at the man waiting before him. "Inform me immediately if you get any more sightings."

Gyra wrote while the car whizzed down the dark highway. Sometimes the vehicle lurched, but the phantera continued his work relentlessly.

David finished his story about Ted long before they stopped at a small motel. The men climbed into their beds and dropped off to sleep.

Gyra used the time to write in his book, filling many pages. As the men slept, he stood in the moonlight, methodically translating the New Testament into Ramatera.

He wished he had time and space to translate the entire Bible. A sense of urgency bore down on him like never before. *Yavana, I feel the dark hard presence of the enemy closing in on us like the jaws of a shadook. If I am killed, my work might remain, but how will it get back to my people?*

Turning the page, Gyra wrote furiously in Ramatera script.

"We've been stuck here for three days," Todd whined. "I'm bored out of my gourd. I say we go for it. We can't wait here forever."

David's scalp itched from the cheap, motel shampoo. "We're almost out of cash. Okay, we'll leave this afternoon, but I don't want to arrive at Gyra's ship until after dark. That way we'll be more hidden."

At twilight, David drove down the old farm road. He was afraid they'd miss it in the dark, but he recognized the intersection when he saw it.

Gyra sat in Todd's place, his tail resting on David's lap. Hanging his head out the window, the phantera scanned for any people.

David parked on the roadside and turned off the car's

headlights. Each of them carried some of the scrap metal. Gyra clutched his book as well.

"Let's make this fast," David whispered, feeling vulnerable. Gyra might be able to see in the dark, but he couldn't. They didn't even have a flashlight.

Gyra guided them to a cluster of trees and looked up. *"Delah charane teayoo sa Panagyra,"* the phantera commanded. Releasing its grip on the trees, the ship descended to the ground. *"Toorah barune,"* came Gyra's voice in the darkness. A door slid open and the interior light blinded David's eyes momentarily. "Come in," Gyra offered. "It's safe inside."

David entered and Todd followed cautiously. As his eyes adjusted, David found the cabin more spacious than he expected. A U-shaped seat stood before the instrument panel, its padded concave shape ideal for a phantera's belly. Two T-shaped pedals rose from the floor, perfect for Gyra's grasping feet. Out of the instrument panel protruded what looked like a control yoke and another T-shaped lever.

"Set the metal down on the floor over here," the phantera instructed as he slid his book into a compartment.

Looking around, Todd gave a low whistle.

Gyra approached a rectangular wall panel and pressed a button. A deep drawer slid out with a cylindrical container. Opening a smaller panel, he grabbed an object the size of a standard flashlight. Its tapered point was bent at a 45-degree angle.

"What's that?" Todd asked nervously.

Gyra held up the odd tool. "It's a laser." The phantera used it to cut the metal scraps into smaller pieces. After weighing some of the scraps, he dropped them into a few silvery cylinders.

The phantera refined and mixed the metals, adding a few mystery ingredients. Although he kept the containers' lids on most of the time, the moment he popped one off, the temperature rose a little higher in the cabin.

"This will take some time," Gyra said as he busied himself with gauges and gadgets.

David examined the ship while the phantera continued his work. Several large secured containers rested in the rear. What was in them? He saw no beds, but then he'd never seen Gyra sleep.

None of the gauges were labeled on the instrument panel. He smirked. Why should he expect them to be? A phantera wouldn't forget what they were. Even the gauges in cars and planes weren't always labeled.

A few instruments were analog. "It's nice to know everything's not digital," David said under his breath. A screen lay flush with the panel's surface, displaying a map of the surrounding region. Some areas glowed orange, red, and yellow. Pointing to the screen, he asked, "Gyra, what's this?"

The phantera didn't even look up. "It's what you'd call a topo map with different metals highlighted. I used it to determine if your planet had the materials I needed." Gyra typed the keys on another computer and bobbed his head. "The mixture looks good." He opened another panel in the wall, revealing a storage space for several curious-looking tools. He grabbed a small box.

"What's that?" Todd asked.

"A repair kit to help me bond the metal into place. Would you like to observe?"

Todd shifted his weight. "Sure."

"I'll stay here for now," David offered, peering into an opened floor panel. What a mess. He examined the twisted levers, damaged when the wings were forced open. It was amazing Gyra got them to work at all.

Sitting on the floor he took in the whole interior. Where had this *delah* been? What was Gyra's planet like? If only these walls could speak! David's thoughts were interrupted by the return of Todd and Gyra.

"Boy, you missed a really cool sight," Todd boasted. "It was like watching someone pave a sidewalk with lava. Gyra heated up the damaged part then spread the molten stuff on as if he were icing a cake!"

"It wasn't a smooth job," Gyra added, "But it's sound enough. It's just a temporary patch until I get home."

David stood. "Well, it sure didn't take you very long. What now?"

Gyra pointed to the opened panel in the floor. "I have to repair my wing extenders. After that, I'll fix the *trelemar* equipment and navigational guidance. The weapons will have to wait until I get home."

"Uh, weapons?" Todd eyed the phantera.

"To defend myself against the mel-hanor. Hopefully, I won't need them." Gyra took the laser and crouched near the tangled levers. He looked at Todd. "Can you go on top and tell me when the metal is cool enough to touch?"

"Sure." Todd bounded out the door.

Turning on the laser, Gyra moved its beam over the twisted metal until the levers glowed. His deft bare hands bent the levers back in place.

"I didn't want Todd to see this," Gyra whispered. "The fewer of your people who know about my resistance to heat, the better." Pulling off another floor panel, Gyra worked on the damaged wing deployment motor. Todd's feet stomped on the roof above.

When Gyra finished, he typed in a command on the instrument panel. On the screen, a silhouette of the ship appeared, its wings pivoting back and forth. The phantera swung the wings until they pointed straight out from the fuselage and tested the control surfaces. Seeming satisfied, Gyra folded the wings back completely.

"Impressive," David whispered.

"Hey!" came a voice from outside. "I can't get down! I don't have a wing to stand on. I can't reach them when

they're way back there...unless you want me to melt my
shoes on that hot-spot!"

Gyra swung the wing forward. "Thanks!" Todd
plopped loudly onto a wing. "It's still hot enough to fry a
pancake up there."

Gyra went out to inspect and returned promptly. "It
appears to have bonded well." The phantera opened a panel
on the rear bulkhead. "My trelemar and navigation equipment must be fixed or it'll be a long trip home." After rear-
ranging an odd assortment of tubes and checking gauges, he
returned to the cockpit and popped off another panel
beneath the computer.

Todd bent over the instrument panel. "Hey, check out
the screen. It's got those same weird little characters Gyra
writes with." He drummed his fingers on the glossy panel.

"Careful!" David warned. "You might make something
go off!"

Todd yanked his hand back as if it had been burned.

"Don't worry. It won't do anything without my command." Gyra pulled his head out from under the panel. "I
am ready to go, but I have a request: could I get a Bible in
the original Greek and Hebrew?"

"You want a *what*?" Todd exclaimed.

Gyra's red eyes gazed at David. "Perhaps it was for this
reason that Yavana had me crash here. I've been thinking
about that a lot. I know your Bible was translated, so I
would like to have it in the original languages, along with
reference books on those languages."

"I understand." David looked over at Todd. "As a
Christian, it's important to him."

Todd raised both his hands. "All right, all right. Just
make it quick. I'd like to get back to living a normal life—
whatever normal is!"

Rubbing his chin, David said, "Let's see...the main
library is too near the police station." He glanced at his

watch. "And the smaller libraries would be closed."

"Can't we buy them at a bookstore?" Todd asked.

"All the Christian bookstores will be closed." David looked through his wallet. "Besides, we're about out of money. I could go back to the apartment and get my study books. I'd be happy to give them to you, Gyra. They'd go to a great cause."

"No!" Todd vetoed. "The apartment is too dangerous. There're probably spies crawling all over the place. The feds know where we live."

Blowing out his breath, David said, "It's been days! No one would be there now. We didn't keep any valuables in the place, so why should they expect us to return?"

A chime rang from the instrument panel. "There is a car coming down the road," Gyra whispered. They watched in tense silence as a position light crept on the screen. Todd and David sighed when it continued down the highway and out of range.

"I have an idea," David said. "We'll call Rhoda and find out if it's safe. If it is, we'll sneak in, get the books, and race back here."

Todd frowned. "Forget about calling Rhoda. Relative or no relative, she'd be the first to turn us in. She always sides with 'law and order.' I still think we should wait and go to a bookstore in the morning."

"I don't know if we've got that much time," David pressed. "And I don't like the idea of leaving Gyra with the ship. If we take him with us, he'll be able to see and hear things we can't. He can tell us if it's safe."

Todd's worried look almost made David reconsider. Almost.

13. A Disastrous Escape

David drove into an alley and stopped.

"I still don't like it," Todd grumbled. "Shoot, are you sure you want to risk this, Gyra? What if you get killed?"

"It would be a noble death," Gyra replied.

"Oh, brother!" Todd opened the door. "Do your super ears and eyes tell you anything?"

Wagging his head, Gyra scanned the area. "It's clear." They stepped out into the dark dank alley. It smelled of old trashcans.

David turned to the phantera. "Gyra, see if you can fly to the roof and wait for one of us."

The phantera eyed the walls and phone lines hemming him in. "I can't fly straight up, but I can climb to the top of this building and fly from there."

"Go for it," David said.

Gazing up at the narrow space above him, the phantera used his wings to scale the brick walls. The rush of wind was noisier than David had expected, but the dull roar of traffic from a nearby street nearly covered it. Upon reaching the top, Gyra leapt into the air and flew away.

David peered around the corner. Seeing no one, he led Todd across the street and into the tall building's entrance.

They entered the deserted lobby and found the elevator open, waiting for them. David breathed a prayer of thanks on the way up. When they reached the fifth floor, he hurried to their room.

David unlocked the door and stepped into chaos. Every piece of furniture was overturned. Books, clothes, and other objects lay strewn across the floor.

Todd looked around. "Man, what a mess! It's going to take a little time to find your books. They really tore the place up!" Placing his hands on his hips, he said, "We better find your stuff before we get Gyra."

Darius Blackwell beamed as he read the latest report. At last his patience was paying off. David had led him right to the ship and soon the alien would be his as well.

After a token knock, a man entered the office. "We have another report, sir. It appears that David and Todd have returned to the apartment."

Standing, Darius received the report. "Why would they do that? Those kids are getting dumber by the hour. Where's Gyra?"

"No word on him yet, sir."

"I want Gyra captured, even if it means using extreme force—yes, that's right. I'd prefer him alive, but we don't know how dangerous he is. If the only way we can catch him is to kill him, so be it. Tell the reinforcements to move in—and get my car ready."

Gyra couldn't land on the roof because two men with binoculars were on it. They appeared preoccupied watching the ground below and didn't see Gyra circling above them. The stairwell door was propped open.

"No sign of birdie yet," a man spoke into his radio.

Gyra glided down to the roof. His feet and legs cushioned the landing, making it almost silent.

Before either man could notice, the phantera darted down the stairs. His bare purple toes hurried down the steps to David's level. Voices echoed off the hall walls. Gyra waited in the stairwell, listening. Rhoda Stearns was berating a tenant for being late on his rent...again. She finally left and the tenant closed his door.

Gyra dashed from the stairwell to David's apartment door, listened for a moment, and burst in.

David spun around and faced the door, heart racing.

"Gyra!" Todd hissed and promptly shut the door.

"They're on the roof," the phantera stated.

"I told you this was too risky," Todd growled at David.

David slipped three books into his daypack. "Here's one book on Hebrew and Aramaic, one on Greek, and a Hebrew–Greek Bible. Let's get out of here!"

Grabbing David's arm gently but firmly, Gyra kept him from opening the door. "The floor above and the floor below have people who are watching for you. You were seen entering the building. They know you are here."

"Oh sh–oot." Todd muttered. "I told you this was a lame-brain idea. What do we do now, Einstein?"

David sat on the overturned couch. "God, help us!"

"They're coming," the phantera spoke in an urgent voice.

Skidding tires screamed from the streets below.

Peering out the window, Todd cried, "Dang! It looks like the whole police force is out there! And the military!"

"I can take one of you and fly out the window," Gyra offered.

David stared at him. Was that a sad look on Gyra's face? Sad that he could only save one? "I'll stay," David said with resignation.

Todd flinched. "No, wait! I have a plan!" He beamed. "There's no time to explain. Just get on Gyra and go!"

David looked at Todd in shock, but he had no time to question his friend. "Okay, take care of yourself, Todd!"

"You too!" Todd shoved the bulging book bag into his friend's chest. "Pray for me!"

Opening the window, David yanked out the screen. He followed Gyra out onto the ledge.

The rising rumble of many boots thundered down the hall.

David tried to climb onto the phantera's back, but Gyra resisted. "No!" the phantera said in a desperate voice. "I can't fly with you that way! Turn away from me." David didn't understand, but he obeyed, clutching the bag to his chest. "I have to hold *you*," Gyra whispered in his ear.

Someone pounded on the door. "FBI! Open up!"

Before David had a chance to speak, the strong fingers of the phantera wrapped around his shoulders. Gyra leaped into the air and grabbed David's calves with his powerful toes.

David didn't even have time to scream. He was in the air staring down at a sea of flashing lights.

The door burst off its hinges and Todd held up his hands as he faced the barrel of a gun. This time he uttered a real swear word.

A dark-clothed man grabbed him by the shoulder and slammed him into the wall, yelling, "Spread 'em!"

Todd remained still while the man patted him down. He heard others searching the apartment. A radio buzzed with words he couldn't discern.

"They jumped out the window," a man yelled. "Let's go!"

Todd's captor pulled him away from the wall. The open window faced Todd, blowing a slight breeze into the stale room. "Godspeed," Todd whispered as he felt the cold handcuffs wrap around his wrists. Did they have to put them on so tight?

As they dragged him into the hallway, Todd wore a slight smile. His plan had worked. He had tricked his best friend into escaping.

And he had done it without lying.

Darius squeezed the cellular phone until his fingers ached. "They flew out the *window?*" He lowered the phone and shouted to his driver. "Turn around! Take us to the ship—now!"

"There are men on some of the roofs beneath us," Gyra shouted above the cool wind.

A gunshot cracked from a building below.

Gyra screamed—a long inhuman wail that made every muscle in David's body stiffen. The phantera faltered and dropped. Gradually, his wings returned to their steady rhythm and they resumed their pace.

Liquid ran down David's neck, cooling rapidly in the wind. He knew what it was. "Gyra, how bad are you hurt?"

"It is a noble thing to die for."

"Gyra, no!" David stared at the lighted streets below. *Lord, help us! If he faints, we'll both end up splattered all over the ground. Don't let Gyra die!*

The great wings kept going and soon the confusion of the city was behind them.

David didn't want to sap his friend's strength with questions, so he just prayed in silence. The moon lit up the rolling hills, turning ponds and lakes into bright silver. Although the scenery was beautiful, David was too terrified to really enjoy it.

"I can't make it," Gyra said in a weak voice. "If I don't land now, we'll crash. My mind is...fading." He glided to a hill several miles from the ship's hiding place. His approach was smooth, but the moment his feet touched down, he tumbled.

David got up. He was okay aside from a few scratches. "Come on. I'll carry you."

"No." Gyra's voice was emphatic. "They have found the ship."

"Oh Lord, *please!*" David hung his head. He felt Gyra's hand upon his arm.

"There is still hope," the phantera wheezed. "Listen carefully if you want to save my life. I will call my ship. When it comes, I won't have enough strength to command it. You must get me inside and find a blue button under a clear shield beside the door. Push it. You'll have a four-second delay to get out before the ship's autopilot takes it home."

Two helicopters droned from up the valley.

Gyra clutched a clasp on his cloak and closed his eyes.

Darius watched the ship from his hiding place on a low hill. A row of bushes concealed most of his blind.

"The scouts report they should be here any minute," a soldier whispered.

Darius nodded. "So, the sniper didn't kill him."

"It's moving!" a man screamed.

The delah rose up through the trees, snapping off branches in the process.

"What the..." Darius ran out of the blind. "Hit it with the lights!"

Five searchlights lit up the silver and white craft.

"Stop it!" Darius bellowed.

"How?" asked the man beside him.

The ship shot away like an arrow from a bow.

"Track it! Get the helicopters to track it!" Darius shouted.

David watched as the delah raced toward them. The ship descended and landed beside them on the field.

The helicopters altered course and followed.

"Come on, Gyra! Let's go!" The phantera was limp. David dragged his friend to the delah, but the door wouldn't budge. Thumping rotor blades drowned out his pounding heartbeat as searchlights sliced through the darkness like knives. The helicopters were almost upon them.

Throwing his weight against the door, David shouted, "Open up!"

"Toorah barune," Gyra whispered, his voice barely heard over the racket of the roaring blades.

The door slid open and David shoved the phantera inside as a searchlight found the field. Throwing his book bag into the cabin, David climbed inside. He spied the blue button and pulled back the clear shield.

"Come out with your hands up and you will not be harmed," shouted a voice from a loudspeaker. "We have you surrounded. You cannot escape. Again, you will not be harmed if you give yourself up."

In the light of the delah, David saw the wound in Gyra's chest. A trickle of blue-purple liquid ran down the white feathers. The phantera's eyes were shut.

"Come out and you will not be harmed," the loudspeaker blared again.

"Yeah right, and I'm a terrorist!" David muttered with anger. *Lord, I'm tired of running. I'm willing to surrender, but what about Gyra? How can I make sure someone will take care of him back on Arana? It's my fault he got hurt. Todd was right. We should never have gone back to the apartment.* David set his face like flint. *It's my responsibility to take care of Gyra. I must see him through.*

"You have five minutes to give yourself up," the helicopter warned.

David hit the button. *Besides, everyone here wants to barbecue my hide.*

Soldiers crept near the end of the field. They weren't going to wait any five minutes.

The door slammed shut and the delah shot forward and rose steeply. Thrown on his back, David clawed for the chair as the g's increased, finally grabbing the chair's support post. "Gyra, I hope you fixed your ship," he said through clenched teeth.

The great bird tumbled across the deck until his skull struck the rear bulkhead with a crack, but David was unable to move to see if he was all right.

Clinging to the chair post as the ship nosed up still higher, David's mind became spacey. How many g's could a human take? How many could a phantera take? His vision darkened and he passed out. When he awoke, he was still clinging to the post.

The g's gradually decreased, but the floor remained too steep to climb. Stars glimmered in the darkening sky outside the windshield. After many agonizing minutes, the delah lowered its nose.

David got up easily, his body significantly lighter. He sat awkwardly in Gyra's U-shaped seat. The windshield wrapped around, allowing excellent visibility. Below him hung the great curved surface of Earth, its eastern edge glowing from the distant sunrise. "Mighty are Your works, O Lord," he quoted in awe.

A faint movement among the stars caught his eyes. A computer voice spoke in a foreign language. Strange characters whirled by on the screen. The silhouette of a black ray-shaped ship flashed onto the screen. Was it a crullah?

The dark ship fired at him.

"Jesus, help!"

The computer spoke again. A strange humming built up behind the back wall of the delah. David stared at the shimmering stars as laser beams streaked by. Would this be his last view before death?

The view in front exploded into light.

"I'm sorry, sir. They're gone."

Darius flinched. Control, he had to maintain control. He wanted to slam the phone against his car, to smash it into a thousand pieces, but his men were watching him. It would never do to appear out of control.

Turning off his cell phone, Darius gazed up at the stars. *If you ever come back, David Decker, I'll be ready for you.*

You've stolen my prize—not a wise thing to do. Until you return, I'll be busy, very busy, finding out everything I can about you. I'll know your next move before you do. And after I catch you, you'll tell me all you know about Gyra— you can count on it!

14. Across the Milky Way

David was certain the delah had been hit, but there was no sound or force of impact. When the white flash cleared, the stars were different. Perhaps the delah had turned during the explosion.

But when the delah really did turn, the truth hit him. The great, curved mass of a planet crept into view—Arana. Clinging to the instrument panel, David watched as the delah oriented itself for the descent.

Rugged mountains, wiggling rivers, emerald lakes, and golden deserts graced the continent below. Multicolored patches blanketed parts of the landmass. Vegetation? Like veiled dancers, clouds swirled over blue seas. David guessed the white mass he saw near the curved horizon was a polar ice cap, but he didn't know if it was north or south.

The nose of the ship slowly rose, obscuring part of the view.

He glanced at his watch. It was midnight back home, but he was still wide-awake from the adrenaline coursing through his body. How was Todd? What had been his last-minute plan? *Lord, please take care of Todd. May he come to know You.*

Descending in a nose-high position, the delah quivered as it fell through the thickening atmosphere. A profile of the ship appeared on the screen. Did the bright colors represent surface temperatures on the delah? The monitored areas corresponded to the shiny metal covering the ship's nose, wings, tail, and underside. Perhaps the silver stuff acted like a heat shield.

Peering down at the approaching planet again, a growing dread seized him. Now he'd done it. He didn't even know if this place could support human life! What if the atmosphere contained poisonous gases? What if the gravity was so strong it crushed him? He couldn't even drink untreated water on Earth without risking giardia. David rubbed his stomach. And what would he eat?

He walked over to Gyra. The phantera had not stirred. Was he dead? Kneeling beside the body, David tried to move one of Gyra's arms. It was rigid. David closed his eyes and wept. *Oh, Jesus, please! I'm going to a planet I know nothing about and my only guide appears to be...dead.*

As the atmosphere thickened, the delah shook violently. Its wings rotated forward for increased control. Squeaks, rattles, and groans echoed ominously through the cabin.

David opened the book bag he'd brought for Gyra. What was this? There were not three books, but *four*. His personal Bible was in the bag. "Todd, you rascal," David said in a choked voice. Tears ran down his face, blurring his vision as he clutched the beloved book to his chest.

Remembering Gyra's book, David wiped his eyes and took the phantera's book out of its compartment. With a sigh, he slid it into the book bag, along with his Bible.

The delah's angle of attack changed as it entered the thicker atmosphere. David could see better now that the nose was lower. A great expanse of tan desert stretched to his right as far as he could see. To his left jutted enormous mountains, and straight ahead glimmered a distant body of water.

The control surfaces of the wing made minor corrections to keep the delah on course as the speed of the space-ship decreased.

An enormous white bird the size of a plane flapped its wings above the foothills. It fell behind before David could get a good look at it.

The delah headed for a circular dirt landing site. A cluster of gray and white objects crept along the back side of a nearby hill. Once the delah reached the landing site, it descended vertically like a harrier jet and came to rest on the desert sand. The humming engines died.

Before David had a chance to act, the door opened. He made a futile attempt to hold his breath. If the atmosphere wouldn't sustain him, there was absolutely no way he could fight it. *Lord, I'm yours.*

David exhaled slowly and sipped the air. At least it didn't contain any painful gases. He drew in more. Maybe it was okay. The warm dry air caressed his face. Standing up, David stepped out of the ship.

The steep hill obscured his view of the mysterious gray and white objects, but a strange melodic noise came from that direction. Something was coming.

A hooded figure appeared on the crest of the hill. It stopped and wagged its head from side to side, the way Gyra did when he scanned with sonar. Emitting a quick series of notes, the figure glided down the hill toward the ship.

Several dozen phantera came flying after the first. Their cries reminded David of a flock of songbirds. Gathering around the delah, the phantera bobbed their heads, eyeing him.

David would have laughed if his situation wasn't so desperate. He stumbled forward. "Help! My friend is hurt!"

The phantera went silent.

"My friend Gyra...Panagyra is hurt." David pointed to the delah where Gyra lay.

"Panagyra," one of the closer phantera repeated.

A large phantera stepped forward. "Ramatera," the bird announced in a loud voice.

David watched, amazed, as the entire group began speaking in an obvious language, presumably Ramatera. He figured the big phantera must be their leader. Several phantera pressed forward, jabbering eagerly to David.

Blushing, David realized he couldn't even say "I don't understand" in Ramatera.

One of the birds peered into the ship. Releasing a cry, he hopped inside. Five others joined him. Carrying out Gyra's stiff body, they ran over the hill, creating a stir.

The big phantera pointed to the side of David's neck and babbled. David touched his neck and felt caked blood, Gyra's blood, on his skin. He cringed. This wasn't the best way to impress an alien species, showing up with the blood of their comrade on your neck!

Another phantera went inside the delah. He popped back out and spoke with the leader. The only word David could catch was *Trenara*—Earth.

Turning to David, the leader said, "Trenara."

David nodded. He didn't even know the word for *yes*. "Naharam," David said, pointing to himself.

"Naharam," the leader repeated. He raised his hands and the crowd grew quiet. The big phantera addressed his flock. They shifted uneasily when he spoke the word "Trenara."

David was desperate; he had to tell them what happened. "Rhutaram," he said, reaching for the leader's hand.

The phantera drew back before David could touch him.

"Rhutaram," David pleaded stepping forward. They had to learn his language!

The large bird leaped back. "*Myute!*"

"Well, I can guess what *myute* means," David said in frustration.

The leader spoke again. "Talnar charane."

A small phantera approached him.

"Talnar salan," the leader ordered.

The little bird turned and walked away.

The leader raised a hand. "Talnar *bot*."

The small phantera stood still.

David figured *Talnar* must be the little phantera's name.

"Talnar nal naharam tor Trenara charane," said the leader. Turning around, he strode toward the hill.

Talnar followed. It was obvious to David that the big phantera expected him to follow as well. Reluctantly, he hurried after Talnar. The whole gathering marched beside him at a safe distance, jabbering in Ramatera as they bobbed and cocked their heads.

The group crested the sandy hill. Before them lay a small valley divided by a creek weaving from the foothills. The creek emptied into a shallow lake whose shores glittered white with mineral deposits. On the far side of the valley, a large rock formation rose with a cave at its base.

They came to the creek. Although the waters were shallow, they were too wide to leap across. David wished he'd worn his hiking boots as his feet got soaked. At least the water was warm.

When they arrived at the entrance to the cave, the leader turned to face David. "Talnar nal naharam tor Trenara bot."

Talnar stopped. So did David. The cave entrance was just large enough for a phantera to enter without stooping.

"Mojar," called the leader.

A slender phantera emerged from the cave with a belt full of instruments around its waist. The two phantera talked and David caught the words "Panagyra" and "Trenara" a few times.

Unlike Gyra or the large phantera, the slender phantera had blue eye-rings. David gazed at the flock around him. Half the birds had red eye-rings; half had blue. The phantera with blue eye-rings tended to be smaller and more slender. Could they be females?

Wagging her head, the slender phantera walked around

David. He couldn't feel it, but he knew he was being scanned. Was this a phantera doctor or scientist?

"Barune," the slender phantera said. She opened her bill wide. David imitated her. Placing a slender instrument into his mouth, the phantera collected a saliva sample. "*Steen,*" the slender bird said. Her bill snapped shut. David closed his mouth and listened while the two phantera conversed again.

Once more, he examined the crowd around him. The small phantera had pale pink feet and blue eyes. The bigger ones' feet were red or purple. The feet and eyes appeared to grow darker as the birds matured. Seeing that the leader's feet were deep purple, David reasoned he might be some kind of village elder.

The two birds paused in their conversation.

Taking advantage of the lull, David pointed to the phantera child and said, "Naharam phantera Talnar." He pointed to himself. "Naharam human David."

The leader placed a purple hand on his feathered chest. "Naharam phantera Daphema." He pointed to the slender phantera. "Naharam phantera Mojar."

David nodded. The two phantera conversed again. When they finished, they bobbed heads. Then Daphema addressed the rest of the flock. David would have given his eyeteeth to know what he was saying. When the phantera finished, the entire group bobbed their heads, but not in unison.

Daphema spoke to three large phantera and they took up positions around the cave's entrance. He walked away and Mojar disappeared back into the cave. The crowd wandered off and David felt as if he'd become invisible. Was he to be shunned? Ignored? Left to his fate in the desert?

But not all the phantera had gone. The little ones remained. Staying just out of reach, they eyed him with the curiosity of children. Since he did not appear to be under guard, David decided to wander around. He walked toward the creek. The children followed, babbling constantly.

When David reached the water, he realized he was thirsty, very thirsty. Was the water safe to drink? He didn't have the means to make a fire and boil the stuff. By the time he figured out the words for *fire, water,* and *boil,* he'd be dead from thirst!

Squatting, he scooped the liquid up in his hands. It was warm. "Thank you for this water, Lord. Please keep me from getting sick." *Here goes.* He took a sip. It tasted bitter, but was just drinkable. Grimacing, he drank some more, muttering, "I can't imagine anything growing in that."

David wet his hair and washed the blood off his neck. Weariness slowed his stride as he wandered back to the landing site. The delah was gone. Now he was really stuck—not that he would have known how to fly the thing home anyway.

Although it was near noon, the air was warm, but not hot. How cold did it get at night? He'd worry about that later.

Fatigued, David stretched out on the warm sand and sank into a deep sleep.

Whispers. Soft strange whispers. Definitely not English. David opened one eye. The phantera children stood beside him. Moaning, he rolled over. They were on that side too. With a heavy sigh, he sat up. The sun hung closer to the horizon and the temperature had dropped. He hadn't eaten in hours. Rubbing his stomach, David caught the attention of one of the birds. "Hungry."

The child cocked his head and babbled.

"Hungry, food," David repeated. He put his hand to his mouth and pantomimed eating.

Another child jabbered, but none of them moved.

"I must have food or I will starve!" David grabbed his stomach and cried out as if in pain.

One of the children ran off and returned with Mojar. David was still doing his routine when the adult phantera strode up.

Mojar scanned him. "David charane." Turning, she walked toward the creek. David followed. He was surprised when she led him to the cave.

Mojar spoke to the guards and they escorted David inside, two in front and one behind. Running his fingers along the cool walls, David marveled at the cave's glassy surface. They reached a fork and one of the guards stepped aside to block the left path. Once David passed it, the guard dropped in behind them.

The outside light grew so dim David stumbled. "I can't walk if I can't see!" Frustrated, he sat down. His stomach growled in the darkness.

Mojar spoke with the guard behind David. He heard the guard's retreating patter. Why didn't they just lead him by the hand? They seemed unwilling to even touch him. Welcome to Arana!

A warm light filled the passage behind him. The guard returned holding a stick crowned with a small glowing orb. David stood and they continued. The air grew cooler and mustier the farther they traveled. Were they taking him to a dungeon?

Mojar turned into a room. "*Aireah*," she commanded and the room blazed with light. David squinted in the brilliant glare. When his eyes adjusted, he saw Mojar staring into his face. Once he stopped blinking, Mojar pointed to a latticework of metal against the wall. By her gestures, David understood he was to raise his arms and stand with his back to the lattice. Warily, he complied.

Two of the guards approached him with cables in their hands. As they wrapped the smooth cool cords around his wrists and ankles, he fervently hoped this wasn't a prelude to torture.

Mojar spoke to him again. David could have sworn it was an apology.

The guards drew back.

Wearing a glove on her hand, Mojar approached David. She held something small, like a piece of bread, between her covered fingers. *"Sarena, sarena,"* she soothed. Something cool dabbed the skin on David's neck.

The slender phantera pulled out a clear cylinder with an odd handle at one end. She snapped a needle onto it. David knew what that meant! "Sarena, sarena," she cooed again. *"Yavana dee David sarena."*

He held still as the needle stung his neck. The pain persisted for a few moments until Mojar withdrew the needle. *"David shalar Mojar,"* the phantera said, backing away. Was she asking for forgiveness? She sent a guard out and slipped the blood sample into a narrow slot in the wall.

As he waited, David examined the strange round room. It was about thirty feet across and twelve feet high with circular lights covering the ceiling. Silvery panels, like the ones in the delah, lined the walls. Off to one side of the room was a collection of strange instruments and elaborate machines. The hard blue-green floor shone smooth like polished marble. No dust or dirt marred the immaculate surface.

Mojar activated a screen on the wall. Strange writing appeared in rows, highlighted in different colors. She spoke a few words and more rows of characters appeared.

The guard returned holding a large bowl piled high with bizarre vegetables. David couldn't help comparing them with Earth's produce. Purple ginger roots, tan sponges, blue broccoli, indigo carrots, and orange-spotted potatoes were just some of the exotic fare. His mouth watered as the vegetables were placed on a small table, but he forgot about them when Mojar approached him again. This time both of her hands were gloved.

"Sarena," she repeated.

David felt a cool dabbing again, this time on the inside of his forearm. Lifting an instrument with a flat head, Mojar eyed David and turned it on. It buzzed as she drew it across David's forearm. The buzzing tickled. She stopped, adjusted a knob, and returned to David's forearm. This time it burned. The pain was not unbearable, but it was irritating. When she finished, tiny beads of blood oozed from the surface of his forearm.

"David shalar Mojar," the phantera whispered as he winced. Walking over to a different panel, Mojar removed two disc-like containers from the back of her instrument and inserted them into a slot. She returned to the monitor.

Pictures of David's skin cells flashed onto the screen, accompanied by text. Mojar talked to the screen as it magnified various areas. She rubbed a finger against her opposing thumb and sent out another guard.

Turning to the bowl, Mojar separated the vegetables into three piles. From the larger group she held up what looked like a yellow coral formation. "*Horlah,*" she said. Mojar broke off a piece and swallowed it. Turning to David, she snapped off another piece and held it up. Opening his mouth, he received it. The horlah tasted chalky, but he could swallow it. Mojar avoided touching David and seemed content to observe him for now.

The guard returned with a large transparent bowl containing a clear liquid and some kind of fish. The bluish creature darted around the bowl as its golden eyes rotated back and forth. Fine scales glittered in the light, and only three fins adorned its six-inch body. After setting the bowl beside the vegetables, the guard returned to his place by the door.

Mojar's long deft fingers pounced on the fish. She held the wriggling, dripping creature out to David and said, "*Loomar.*"

"No thanks, I'm not that hungry yet." What was that

stupid word for "no"? David turned his face away and kept his mouth shut.

Mojar cocked her head and withdrew. She dropped the fish back into the bowl and brought samples of the other vegetables for David to taste. Some plants were too bitter for him to swallow, others too spicy. In the end, they found a variety he could stomach, and a few he enjoyed.

David's body began to ache. "Do I have to stay bound like this? It's really uncomfortable." Straining at the cables, he gave Mojar a mournful look.

She spoke a few words and the guards untied him from the lattice. Mojar called David to the table where the bulbs and roots lay sorted into three piles. She gestured to the pile he had eaten from and liked. "David *caleah*," she said. Her purple finger pointed at the pile he never tasted. "David myute caleah."

David reached for one of the bulbs.

"Myute!" Mojar cried, grabbing his wrist with a gloved hand.

David stopped. "Myute?"

"Myute caleah!"

"*Caleah?*" David asked.

Mojar picked up the horlah David had eaten from earlier. "Caleah." She dropped a piece into her mouth.

"*Caleah* is 'eat,' and *myute* is 'no.' Okay." David nodded. He pointed to the third pile.

"Yuck," Mojar said, imitating David's response to some of the items.

"So, those won't hurt me, but I didn't like them," David reasoned. Was this all the variety of food Arana had to offer?

Daphema appeared in the doorway and talked with Mojar. David heard his own name mentioned several times. When they finished, Daphema called David to follow.

The two guards led the way ahead again with the one

guard staying at the fork to protect it as they went by. Leaving was much easier with the orb stick to light the way.

When they came out, it was dark. Brilliant stars winked in the clear sky like exploded fragments of fireworks. A large crowd of phantera stood forty feet from the entrance, illuminated by the bright orb stick.

Daphema addressed the silent crowd. Even the little ones were still. When he finished his short announcement, he bobbed his head. "Philoah," he spoke out into the night.

An averaged-sized phantera stepped forward. His arms were not as purple as Gyra's, so David guessed this phantera was younger. Philoah came and stood beside David.

Daphema raised his hands and looked up. The rest of the phantera imitated him except Philoah, who raised his hands but bowed his head. Daphema appeared to speak a pronouncement upon Philoah. David recognized the word *Yavana*, but he was clueless about the rest of the speech. Daphema finished with the phrase *"Ramara Yavana!"*

"Ramara Yavana!" the flock echoed back. Then they wandered off into the darkness, leaving David alone with Philoah.

The guards returned to their place in front of the cave. David had a feeling they would not let him in again and now he had another pressing need.

He was getting cold.

15. The Dalaphar

The temperature dropped rapidly and David shivered. A chill wind stirred. Resting beside him, the orb stick stood upright on its three retractable legs. He picked it up and, with a little patience, figured out how to fold and unfold the legs. Philoah's keen red eyes watched him. David put a hand on the bright globe but felt no warmth. The light illuminated a large area but he could not see anything that would serve as a decent shelter.

Wandering to the creek, David squatted down and touched the water. It was barely warm. Philoah followed him as faithfully as the children had. Cocking his head he asked, "David caleah?"

David struggled to remember the word for *no*. "Myute," he finally said. "David is *cold*." He shivered again. "Cold," he repeated, wrapping his arms around himself to get warm. If only he'd brought a jacket!

"Manar ta 'cold'?" Philoah inquired. David bounced in place to keep warm. Philoah imitated his movement. "Cold."

David groaned. He'd be a human popsicle before he could explain his problem! He got an idea. "Mojar charane sa David."

"David salan sa Mojar," Philoah amended. He turned toward the cave and David followed. Reaching the entrance, Philoah spoke to one of the guards who turned and disappeared into the tunnel.

David stomped his feet to keep them from going numb. *Please let me inside!*

Mojar appeared and watched David as he rubbed his bare arms and shivered. Pulling an instrument off her belt, she persuaded David to raise an arm. The phantera placed a disk on his bare skin. A line ran from the disk to a small box on her belt.

Mojar removed the disk and glanced at the readings on the main unit. She spoke rapidly to one of the guards, who darted into the cave and returned with a familiar looking instrument—a laser just like the one Gyra used. Mojar adjusted a knob on the laser and aimed it at a nearby portion of sheer rock. A brilliant, yellow beam struck the wall of rock. Keeping the beam moving over a three-foot area, she heated the rock until it radiated heat like a furnace. Mojar cut the beam and, much to David's surprise, handed him the instrument. His stiff fingers took it. After showing him the button to turn it on, Mojar promptly disappeared back into the cave.

David drew back from the hot wall as his chill gave way to perspiration. Finally, he was warm!

Philoah hugged himself. "Cold?"

"Myute," David responded, smiling. "Warm."

"*Cold* lar *jarune*." Philoah hugged himself. "Jarune." Pointing to the heated rock he said, "*Awal*."

Cold and hot? It must be. David sighed. His sleep cycle was all messed up. Lying down on the ground, he resolved to at least *try* to rest. His front side was warm, but his back was freezing. That wouldn't do!

Sitting up, he looked around. No other place offered a windbreak. David fired the laser at the ground. After heating a strip of sand, he bedded down between the wall and the heated ground. Now he was warm on both sides. The heat made him drowsy.

Lord, watch over me in this place, David prayed silently. He would have prayed longer but he was too tired.

Singing. The voice was rich, the words foreign.

David opened his eyes. It was before dawn. The air was freezing as the cold stars burned overhead. Where was he?

Singing. A lone voice carried aloft on a faint breeze.

David sat up, stiff and cold. The orb was still on, so he found the laser and blasted the rock and ground. He nursed his sore limbs in the penetrating heat. Nearby, Philoah crouched bird-style on the ground, watching him.

The singing continued from the direction of the foothills. The melody wove its way through the canyons and echoed off the hard walls. Picking up the orb stick, David made his way to the small stream for a drink. Philoah followed.

After wiping his mouth, David stood and listened. The sky grew lighter and the singing continued, but now another voice joined in. The second voice came from nearby, just across the stream, and wove around the first in a light countermelody.

David crossed the stream, following the second voice. He found most of the flock assembled on a small hill. None of the phantera stirred, except a few children who glanced at him. The flock was so still David decided it would be better not to ask Philoah questions.

The second voice belonged to a slender phantera standing by herself to the east of the group. She sang back to the voice in the hills. High above, the feathery clouds glowed a soft pink. The first voice grew bolder. David could hear the words clearly even though he did not understand them.

Gradually, the sun ignited the clouds with gilded gold and brilliant orange. Its beams touched the first of the peaks, setting them aflame with color. As the rays reached the foothills, the first singer soared out from the mountains, a phantera, basking in the golden light. His voice was as rich as the colors of dawn. The white bird circled and rolled, dancing through the air in graceful aerobatics, never breaking the flow of his song.

The moment the sun's rays lit up the ground, the first singer descended in a spiral glide and landed beside the female. The song ended with their voices blending in unison.

Breaking into loud jubilation, the flock encircled the couple.

"What is this?" David asked.

"*Dalaphar,*" Philoah answered. He held his two hands out and clasped them together for emphasis before adding his own voice to the celebration.

"Thanks, that explains everything," David mumbled. He rubbed his arms in the warmth of the sun.

The flock made way for the two phantera. Based on the reddish shade of their feet, David concluded they were a young couple, but how young was young for a phantera? The crowd followed the couple back to the valley and David trailed behind. A great long table had been set up. Large blue bowls laden with many vegetables ran down the middle of the table while smaller bowls lined the rim.

Philoah pointed to a place between himself and Mojar for David to stand. There were no chairs.

When all had gathered around the table, a hush fell upon the flock. The male singer stood at one end of the long table and the female at the other.

Lifting high a piece of vegetable, the male looked across to the female and addressed her solemnly. He raised a small silvery bowl and spoke to her again. Then he passed the vegetable down one side and the bowl down the other.

David's side had the bowl. As Philoah gave it to him, David noticed the blue-purple liquid swirling in the silvery basin. Mojar took the bowl from him and passed it on.

When the two objects arrived at the other end, the female singer held them in each hand. Looking back at the male singer, she gave what appeared to be an acceptance speech. Then she ate the food and drank daintily from the bowl. After she finished, the male raised his bowl. The rest of the flock held up their bowls in response. Not wanting to offend, David mimicked them. His indigo bowl had the grain and texture of polished wood.

The male singer spoke a few sentences and ended with, "Ramara nal harana sa Yavana."

Repeating the words in a thunderous reply, the crowd lowered their bowls and filled them with food. The large serving bowls were passed around the table while the white birds jabbered and feasted.

Mojar spoke to Philoah.

David picked out a few of the vegetables he remembered

liking, but he could not remember all of them. He reached for one that looked familiar.

"Myute, David," Mojar cried, snatching the vegetable away. "Myute caleah!" she placed it back into the pile, grabbed another similar-looking vegetable and set it in his bowl.

Feeling like a little child, David sighed. There were no utensils, so he picked up his vegetable and munched on it. By pointing and asking, he learned that the male singer was Ranjar and the female was Layan.

A most wonderful aroma filled his nostrils. He stopped eating and looked up as a bowl of steaming food made its way down the table.

His look of longing was not lost on Mojar. When the bowl reached her she pointed to the contents and asked, "Caleah loomar?"

It was fish, but this time it was cooked. David burned his fingers as he helped himself to a piece and blew on the fish to cool it. He finally sampled it. He tasted a second piece. It was delicious! "David caleah loomar," he said, turning to Mojar.

Mojar's eye-rings blushed a deeper blue. Was she embarrassed? Perhaps she hadn't realized David only disliked *raw* fish. When the serving bowl came around a second time, she dropped a load of the cooked fish into David's bowl.

The flock consumed an enormous amount of food in twenty minutes. When David was through gorging himself, he looked around. The phantera turned their bowls upside down as they finished eating. David did the same. The serving bowls began to disappear.

With the flipping of the last bowl, Daphema pounded a simple rhythm on the bottom of his bowl. The rest followed until even David was drumming.

Daphema burst into song. The rest joined in on the

chorus. Ranjar leaped onto the table and ran down its length. When he reached the end, he took hold of Layan's hand. Together they leapt into the air. Ten males and ten females joined them. As the couple flew, their escorts did wild choreographed aerobatics, dancing through the air as they sang.

Those who remained at the table also sang along. The wild dance lasted for hours as different phantera displayed their flying skills in individual and group dances.

David wished he could fly. He had never guessed the skill and grace these wonderful naharam possessed. "Gyra, why didn't you tell me?" he whispered. Immediately he felt a pang of grief.

Philoah and Mojar turned toward him.

"Panagyra charane?" he asked Mojar.

"Myute," her soft voice replied.

David bowed his head in sorrow. Even the wonder of the dance could not remove the ache he felt inside. "Jesus, please be with Gyra. If he's still alive, don't let him die. I know I should have listened to Todd and waited. Forgive me!" Hot tears rolled down his cheeks.

Mojar gave an exclamation and spoke rapidly to Philoah.

If only there was someone David could talk to in English! Turning to Mojar, he pleaded, "Mojar rhutaram David?"

Mojar snapped her jaw, and the feathers on her scalp rose. "Myute!"

Hanging his head, David berated himself. Why hadn't he learned more Ramatera from Gyra when he had the chance? All that time he spent teaching Gyra, David had learned so little about the phantera's world. Now he'd have to learn Ramatera if he was ever to communicate with anyone, and he didn't have Gyra's wonder brain. This was a nasty predicament! *Lord, is there any other way? No, I suppose not.*

Well, he wouldn't have to worry about college for a while. He'd be able to devote his full attention to learning the language.

As their glorious song reached a crescendo, the dancers descended from the sky. The couple glided to a spot near the table, dancers following.

During a lull, a group of phantera brought a strange variety of rhythm and stringed instruments. An elaborate beat rose as the birds formed a great circle. They began a complex dance involving their heads, arms, legs, and wings. The white birds leaped in graceful arcs and whirled in unison.

The celebration lasted all day and everyone participated except Philoah and David. Toward evening, the crowd returned to the table. This time it was set with small bowls and a few vessels shaped like ducks with strange crests on their heads.

Pointing to one of the vessels, David asked Philoah what it was.

"*Duca,*" the phantera replied. David didn't know if *duca* was the name of the vessel or the strange bird until he remembered Gyra saying the word upon seeing his first duck.

When all the phantera were at their places, Daphema lifted his bowl and gave a short speech. He ended with the familiar, "Ramara nal harana sa Yavana."

Again the flock roared the words back in response. Taking up the vessels, each phantera poured for the person next to them.

Philoah poured for David.

David turned toward Mojar and pointed to the blue liquid. "Is this okay? Uh, David caleah?"

"*Dala,*" Mojar said, bobbing her head bird-fashion. David had never tasted this liquid, yet Mojar did not appear worried. Perhaps it came from one of the plants he'd eaten.

When all the bowls were poured, the flock began to drink. The happy babbling lifted David's spirits. Raising the bowl to his lips, he took a sip. It had a light fruity flavor. "What is this?" he asked Philoah, pointing to the purple juice.

Philoah bobbed his head. *"Falatirah."*

David drank more and bobbed his head in response. Finishing off his drink, he turned his bowl over.

All the male phantera fled the table, except Philoah. "Where did they go?" David asked in amazement. Philoah only cocked his head.

As the sun began to set, a great cry came from the sky. The males flew in two interlocking circles with Ranjar hovering in the interlocked space. They burst into jubilant song as the formation descended.

All the females scurried away. A moment later, a formation of females rose from the earth to meet the males. It, too, was made of intertwined circles with Layan in the overlapping space. The groups merged into one formation of two interlocking rings. Ranjar and Layan hovered together as the overlapping space expanded into one great ring of male and female phantera.

The couple circled higher and higher, leaving the ring behind, and flew off together to the foothills.

The great turning ring descended as the phantera released a loud joyful cry. Once they landed, the flock dispersed.

David turned to Philoah. "Ranjar and Layan?"

"Dalaphar," Philoah said, clasping his hands together again.

David finally understood. He'd just witnessed a phantera wedding!

16. Into the Wilderness

Later that night, David returned to his previous resting spot. He unfolded his light stand, heated the area around him with his laser, and lay down. Philoah called the lighted orb stick a *dowel* and the laser a *caruk*.

Turning off the dowel, David gazed up at the stars. The constellations were entirely foreign, but a cloudy, white-ish band crossed the sky. The Milky Way? Did Gyra live in the same galaxy?

He released a deep breath and let his mind wander among the stars. Which way to Earth? Would he ever see her skies again? Smell her pines? Feel the caress of her breezes?

And what happened to Todd? Was he safe? What had his crazy plan been, and had it worked?

David shuddered and moved closer to the glowing, rock wall. What a mess he'd left behind on Earth; his parents must be worried sick. He'd end up dying here, alone. No one would ever know what happened to him.

Tears spilled down his temples.

Philoah leaned toward him. "David?"

"I'm okay, Philoah. I'm just a little scared and homesick."

Philoah couldn't understand, but he appeared to be reassured by David's voice.

"Father God, please watch over my parents and Todd," David prayed. Wiping his eyes, he rolled over and sighed. Soon, sleep mercifully claimed him.

The next few days, David threw himself into learning Ramatera and Philoah eagerly helped him.

Using a bag of small, assorted objects, Philoah taught the Ramatera words for colors, shapes, numbers, over, under, inside, and other elementary concepts. When David tried to scrawl the words into the sand using English letters, the phantera became very interested. Bending over, Philoah wrote a stream of bizarre characters into the dirt. He pointed to each character and made a sound.

David quickly grasped the Ramatera alphabet. Each vowel's name was the sound it made. Consonants were named by their sound with an "ah" behind it. Hence, the character for a *b* sound was called "bah," *d* was "dah," and so on. As Gyra had said, the entire alphabet was phonetic.

The following day, Philoah brought a leather bag and gave it to David.

Reaching inside, David pulled out a leather-bound book and opened it.

It was blank. He fingered the rugged parchment-like pages. Peering back in the bag, David found a curious-looking stick.

Philoah took the stick and removed a cap from one end to reveal a stiff blue brush. Taking David's book, the phantera wrote out the Ramatera alphabet in cobalt-blue ink. Then he uncapped the opposite end and rubbed a black brush over a character, erasing it. After rewriting the character, Philoah passed the book and writing brush back to David.

"Ramara," David said with a nod.

The book became his English–Ramatera dictionary and journal. He listed all the Ramatera words he knew with their definitions in English, using Ramatera script and Latin letters to aid his learning.

The next day he got an idea. "Philoah!" David pointed to the book. "*Patu* [mine]." The phantera bobbed his head. David pointed at the book again. "*Patu pinnah* [mine five]!" He pointed to the bag. "*Patu pinnah!*"

Philoah cocked his head. "Myute, *tren* [one]." He tapped David's book.

"I'm not asking for five blank books, I want my own books back!" David grumbled in frustration. He drew a picture of a delah and of a bag with five books. "Patu," David said, pointing to the drawing of the bag.

Philoah cooed and bobbed his head. He told David to wait and pattered off for the cave. Clutching David's book bag, he strolled back.

As soon as David saw it, his eyes watered. With eager hands, he took it, opened it, and saw that all five books were still there. Hugging the bag, he cried, "Thank You, Jesus! I have my Bible! Oh Lord, thank You, thank You, thank You! I thought I'd never see it again after the delah disappeared."

David sat on the ground, brush in hand, and wrote in his journal.

The phantera don't eat every day, so I have to ask for food. Mojar sees me from time to time, speaking with Philoah or drawing my blood. Now she swabs my neck with a numbing solution before she jabs me with a needle.

Ranjar and Layan have not returned. Philoah said they're getting ready for nachel—*children.*

I can't figure out why this village is located in such a barren spot. Where does all the food come from? I have yet to see a plant growing anywhere.

Philoah brought me a computer board with maps and pictures of plants and animals. Along with learning the words for Arana's geographical features, I've picked up a few customs. I raise my bowl before I eat, bob my head, and use the same sandy hill to bury my waste.

Every morning a phantera greets the dawn with singing, but there haven't been any elaborate displays like on my first morning.

The months march on and I've heard nothing about Gyra. I pray for him every day.

Philoah called David to the cave entrance where Daphema and Mojar waited. Mojar held up a belt with a few instruments hanging from it.

David recognized his laser, light, and small shovel, but the fourth object was new.

Mojar pointed to the cylindrical instrument while explaining something to Philoah. After Philoah bobbed his head, Mojar took two bowls from a guard. One was full of water, the other empty.

The phantera doctor unclipped the cylindrical instrument. A flexible tube drooped from one end. Placing the tube into the bowl of water, she held the instrument over the empty bowl as her purple finger pressed a switch. Water flowed through the cylinder from the first bowl into the second. Turning the machine off, Mojar lifted the second bowl and said, "Caleah." She drank the water. Pointing to the first bowl, she said, "Myute caleah."

David figured it was a water filter. He bobbed his head to show he understood.

After clipping the instrument back in place, Mojar passed the belt to David. He fastened it around his waist. "Thank you, ramara, Mojar."

Mojar nodded bird-style. "Yavana *hamoth* David."

Daphema stepped up with a folded gray cloth. Shaking it open, he revealed a cloak similar to Gyra's. The phantera elder offered it to David. Bobbing his head, David took the cloak. Lifting his purple hands, Daphema declared, "Yavana dee David sarena." Once more David bobbed his head.

"David charane," Philoah called, walking toward the creek. Figuring they would be traveling, David donned the cloak and joined his guide.

They followed the creek down to the shallow lake where a small gathering of phantera waited. The group greeted Philoah and David with bobbing heads. What were they all waiting for? Several trunk-sized containers rested nearby on the warm sand.

David scratched his growing beard. The sun had warmed the air to a pleasant temperature, so he sat on the soft sand and gazed off toward the foothills.

What was *that*? He sprang to his feet. An enormous white bird, far bigger than a phantera, soared above the foothills. "What is that?" he asked Philoah before catching himself. "Manar ta?" he inquired in broken Ramatera.

Philoah sighted down David's arm. "Duca," he announced with a phantera smile. Even though their beaks were hard, the phantera could smile with the fleshy corners of their mouths. A subtle shift of their feathered brows conveyed mood as well. David hadn't really noticed Gyra's facial expressions, but now that he was stranded on Arana, he paid close attention to details.

The duca glided toward them. This must be what everyone was waiting for. Like a great bird of prey, the creature folded its wings to lose altitude, plummeting toward the gathering.

"Now I know how a rabbit feels when it sees an eagle," David whispered as the hair on the back of his neck rose up. The duca was huge—big enough to carry a horse! It wore a brown vest around its chest and a phantera sat on its back.

The muscles around David's stomach tightened as the duca came in low and fast, but the villagers remained casual in their speech and posture. The duca flared, braking with its wings, tail feathers, and webbed feet. Rearing up, the creature beat the air with its enormous wings and plopped to the ground. Sand flew everywhere from the turbulence.

David used his cloak to shield his face. As the dust settled, he peered out from behind the fabric and almost laughed. The duca looked like a gigantic duck with its broad yellow bill and webbed feet. David remembered the Pekin duck he'd rescued at Whitefield Park. Hadn't Gyra said it looked like a duca?

But the creature before him was monstrous. Raising its head, it watched David with blue eyes five inches in diameter. A low rumble resonated from its chest. The duck-like head turned, viewing him with one eye, and then the other. A long bony tube covered with hairlike feathers protruded from the back of its skull, curving slightly downward.

After hopping off, the rider called to his mount with a melodic warble. The duca lowered its head and backed away, leaving the huge bulging vest on the sand. It proceeded to preen its ruffled chest feathers.

Several phantera scrambled to help the rider. Climbing the brown leathery vest, they opened a large pouch. Vegetables and leather bags were lowered to eager hands below. The rider opened the second pouch on the giant vest, and more vegetables appeared, along with some strange instruments.

Philoah!" the rider called out.

Philoah ran forward and received a leather bag full of food. He strode back to David.

"We're going on a long trip, aren't we?" David worried aloud. Would they take the duca? That might be fun. It would sure beat traveling on foot.

The phantera workers loaded the strange containers into the pouches on the vest.

Philoah turned to David. "Charane," he called, walking west toward the wastelands.

"Where are you going? Uh, *Philoah salan marana?*" David asked as he caught up.

Philoah didn't break his pace. "*Sa pendaram.*"

David frowned. To pendaram? Was pendaram a person or a place? *Maha* meant "who" and *marana* meant "where." David carefully formed the question in his mind before speaking. "*Maha ab marana ta pendaram* [who or where is pendaram]?"

"*Maha*," Philoah replied. So, pendaram was a "who." Philoah continued, "*Pendaram ta Ariphema.*"

"So, Pendaram is Ariphema. Well, that helps a lot!" David fumed in English. One of the words might be a title, the other a name, but which was which? Glancing back at the diminishing view of the duca, David said, "Philoah?" The phantera stopped and turned. David pointed back to the duck-like creature. "David nal Philoah nal duca salan pendaram?" Could they take the duca? His Ramatera was rough but he could get the message across.

"Myute," Philoah answered, blinking his red eyes.

Why? "Balute?"

"David *rusoph* Ramatera." Philoah turned and resumed walking.

"'David learn Ramatera.' Great," David grumbled. They were going to wander in the desert as he studied. There had to be a nicer environment to learn in. David guessed the phantera was in no hurry for him to meet the pendaram. Perhaps it was for the best. David could hardly understand questions in Ramatera, let alone answer them.

He ran to catch up with Philoah.

Sand, sand, and more sand! David was tired of it before he finished his first day in the desert. Toward the end of the third day it was almost intolerable. Philoah kept him well fed and watered, and the temperature was comfortable during the day, but David wondered if the monotonous trip was some sort of punishment.

They continued west, parallel to the foothills. The steep arid ridges were the only landforms in the flat, monotonous landscape. David plodded on as the sun set. At least there were few distractions out here. Philoah had been patient in teaching him Ramatera, but David wished he could question the phantera in English! Still, David was learning a lot.

Gyra's Ramatera New Testament was a tremendous asset, worth more than its weight in gold. The title of each book was still phonetically the same and each chapter and verse was numbered. Combined with his English Bible, David could unlock the words for difficult concepts like grief, joy, justice, soul, mind, and spirit.

But David was afraid to share Gyra's New Testament. He didn't know how Philoah would respond and wanted to be ready to answer his guide's inevitable questions. When the time was right, David would introduce the book.

On the fourth day, a duca found them. Philoah took on fresh supplies and exchanged a few words with the rider. David watched, fascinated when the creature prepared to depart. Facing the wind, the duca spread its wings. The great neck lowered as the bird accelerated from a waddle to a trot. It ran faster than David expected. The large wings beat in slow, labored movements until the huge bird simply dropped its feet back against its tail and the duca rose like a heavily loaded bomber.

David followed the duca with his eyes, longing to be onboard.

"David charane," Philoah called.

Another day, another march. David plodded after his guide.

In the cool of dawn, David awoke. This was the fifth day since they'd started traveling. How much longer? Sitting up, he looked around. The flat salt wastes had given way to undulating sand dunes. Where was Philoah?

David rose and walked around the low dunes, but couldn't see his guide. The provisions rested on the ground where they'd been dropped the night before. Finding his friend's tracks, David followed them.

The footprints stopped, the final impression deeper than the rest. He knelt down. The sand ahead was smooth, void of any other marks. Philoah must have flown from this point. Now what?

Shielding his eyes, David stared up at the brightening sky. Philoah's white wings flashed in the morning light as he circled high above the desert. "I guess even he longs to get away from all this dirt!" David muttered.

When Philoah landed, David asked the phantera why he had been flying.

"I was looking for *melcat* and *shartara*," Philoah answered slowly in Ramatera. He never showed any interest in learning English. The phantera picked up his burdens. Because his stamina was greater than David's, Philoah carried the provisions.

"Who are *Melcat* and *Shartara*?" David asked, racking his brain. His Ramatera vocabulary was growing fast out of necessity.

"Not who, but what," answered his guide. "Melcat are dangerous dalam found in the sand dunes." David remembered that *dalam* was the word for animals that had no ability for true language. They were a level below *chelra*.

"Can you not guess what a shartara is?" Philoah prodded his student.

"*Shartara*," David mumbled. "It has the word *tara* in it." Grimacing, he knew what *tara* meant—sand! "*Shar* means to mix...mix with what?"

Reaching down, Philoah flung sand into the air.

"Yuck! Stop!" David yelled out of impulse as the sand covered his hair and clothes. He finally regained his Ramatera mind. "*Bot! Bot Philoah!*"

Philoah ceased and cocked his head. "Does the sand bother you?"

"I'd rather not wear it!" complained David as he dusted off his clothes. "I wish I could take a bath. I've been walking around for days and I stink like a pig."

"I do not know what *bath* and *pig* mean." Philoah gave his feathers a shake and most of the dust slid harmlessly to the ground.

David spent a moment explaining what a bath was. He didn't even attempt the word *pig*.

Eyeing the horizon, Philoah said, "Today I will show you where you can get wet." David kept scratching his head, shaking out the loose sand. His scalp wasn't as rough as his beard, but it sure itched.

That afternoon, the phantera bobbed his head and ran to the crest of a large sand dune. "Here, David, you will find plenty of water to get wet."

David scaled the sand dune with eager legs. The thought of a real bath raised his spirits tremendously. Panting and sweating, he reached the top. "Where is it?" he cried in disappointment, seeing only barren dune upon dune. This must be a phantera form of torture!

"Why does your face look so strange?" Philoah commented. "Are you unhappy?"

"Yes! *Dala!* I am very unhappy! I do not see water!" David kicked at the sand.

Philoah eyed him. "You do not *smell* the water?"

"Myute! I can't smell water. I'm not a phantera!"

"I will show you." Philoah hopped down the dune. Curiosity replacing his anger, David followed. Philoah paused beside a great tan rock jutting from the slope.

David rounded the rock and stared into a gaping entrance. He unclipped the dowel from his belt and turned it on. "What do you call this?"

"An entrance to the doloom," Philoah said from behind. "Follow the path down to the water."

David took a cautious step inside. "Is it safe?"

"Safe from the melcat and the shartara."

David moved down the steep sloping shaft, enjoying the

cool dank air. After about eighty feet, the path leveled off and ended in an oval-shaped landing surrounded by dark water. The vast flooded cavern snaked off in several directions. Who knew how far it went?

Philoah spread his scaly arms. "See? Here is water."

Opening the stand of his dowel, David set the light down. He knelt beside the water's edge and stuck a finger in. It was warmer than he expected.

Unclipping his filter, he pumped a sample into a small bowl Philoah provided. The water didn't have the salty taste of the creek in the village. David stripped off his outer clothes and dangled his legs in the black lake. Then he wondered if that was such a good idea. "Philoah, are there any dalam in the water?"

"Many."

"Any dangerous ones?"

"A few." Crouching down, the phantera plunged his head into the water as if searching for something. Philoah drew back, shook the drops from his head, and asked. "Do you want to get wet or not?"

Protect me, Lord. David slid into the water, his toes reaching for the bottom in vain. He floated, listening to the eerie stillness of the doloom. The only sound was his splashing.

"I will join you," Philoah announced. He removed his own cloak and dove into the dark water.

David dunked his head and face, working the sand out of his scalp. While his ears were submerged, he heard a strange grunting sound from somewhere below.

Philoah still hadn't surfaced. What if something happened to him? What if there was something in the—

"Ahh! Help! *Elah!*" David cried as something brushed his calf. He clawed the stone landing, hauled himself onto it, and scrambled away from the edge. Panting, David crouched down and watched.

The surface stirred and Philoah's head burst through. He held a fish in his mouth and two more finny captives in his hands. "*Hoowah!*" the phantera cried joyfully as he threw the writhing fish onto the landing. "Loomar! We will eat well tonight." Reaching down, he removed two more fish from his grasping feet before diving again.

David examined the five squirming fish. Their aqua luminescent markings shone in the dark. Grunting and wiggling, the fish attempted to return to the water. Remembering the tasty fish at the dalaphar banquet, David made sure none of his captives escaped.

Surfacing again, Philoah added five more fish to their bootie and resubmerged.

As David waited, he washed his filthy clothes, beat them against the stone ledge, and wrung them out. All the while he kept an eye on the fish.

The water boiled, but Philoah's head did not rise like before. "Elah David!" he cried for help. "It's a big one! Elah!" His head sank, but not before David caught sight of an enormous tail with a spread of at least twelve inches.

David leaned over the water. How could he help Philoah? The caruk! He unfastened the laser from his belt, but the water was so dark, he could not see his prey. Feeling rather vulnerable, David set the caruk down, put on his soggy clothes, and leapt into the water.

The thrashing fish surfaced with Philoah. "What am I supposed to do?" David hollered in English. He saw the tail and grabbed it. The slippery fin wiggled free and smacked him in the face. "Oww! You slimy monster! I've got just one word for you—*dinner!*"

Lunging toward the fish, David searched wildly for anything to grab. Fortunately, the loomar had no spines. One hand found a fin. He grasped its base and held on while his other hand groped in the turbulent waters. Whoops, that was Philoah. The fish tired as David found a second fin. Philoah was wrapped around the fish's back holding on with his four limbs. Grasping the rock ledge with a hand, he drew himself up while one hand and foot remained on the fish. David released his grip, exited the water, and seized the fish's tail.

Together, they hauled the prized loomar onto the platform. The fish slapped the stone floor with renewed vigor, scattering some of the smaller fish. The great loomar inched its way closer to the edge with every flop. Leaping onto the fish, David straddled it. He had a wild ride for a few moments, but the loomar was soon resigned to its fate.

"Hoowah!" Philoah whooped. "This loomar will last us a long time!"

"A few of the smaller ones were knocked in," David observed.

"They won't matter. This loomar will give us more meat and fewer bones." The monster fish slapped its tail in response.

For the first time David noticed the smell coming from his clothes. "Yuck! I've been slimed!"

17. The Shartara

After the fish were cleaned, David washed his clothes again. Then he and Philoah bathed. "So, this is a doloom," David stated as he treaded water.

"Doloom," Philoah confirmed, raising his hand to indicate the vast dark cavern. He slapped the water. "This is *Adrana Sarena*. Much *drea* makes an *adrana*."

"So, if you have a lot of water, you get a sea or a lake," David muttered in English. This body of water was the Sea of Peace.

Leaping onto the stone platform, Philoah shook the

excess water from his feathers. He fired his caruk at a flat table-sized rock resting on one end of the platform. Once the slab was hot, Philoah took a flask out of his pack and poured an oily substance onto the rock.

The smaller fish soon sizzled on the simple stove. When they were done, Philoah heated the rock again and burned off the oil.

"What about the big fish?" David pointed to the large raw fillets stacked to one side.

"We do that differently. Help me carry it up to the entrance." Philoah retrieved a silvery stake and a roll of wire from his pack. Wrapping the raw meat in a cloth, they carried up the bundle and hung it on a hook near the entrance.

Philoah looped one end of the wire onto another hook above the doorway. Paying out wire as he walked, the phantera climbed halfway up the next sand dune. He stuck the stake into the sand and fastened the wire to it.

That's not going to hold very well. The sand is too soft, David mused. *What's he doing?*

Using his caruk, Philoah fused the sand around the stake. It didn't take long to cool in a large solid mass. Philoah hung the meat on the line.

"After this dries, we will travel again. Today we eat what was cooked."

David pulled the last piece of dried fish out of the provisions bag. On Earth he'd never touched the stuff, but now he was developing a taste for it.

Slinging the bag over his shoulder, Philoah resumed his steady pace. The dunes had grown in size and the air was getting warmer. David wiped his damp forehead as he followed his guide. He'd seen a lot more of those doloom tunnels and they all looked the same.

"Philoah, were the doloom entrances...made?"

"Dala, the doors to the doloom were made for the

haranda. They enjoy exploring the desert and sunning themselves on the warm sand. Phantera enjoy drinking, bathing, and fishing in the doloom."

David remembered that the haranda were another naharam species. They inhabited Arana, but he'd yet to see any of them. "Do they come here very often?"

"Myute, but it was a popular resting place in the past. Now many travel to other water planets for pleasure."

David now knew the doloom entrances didn't lead to isolated caves but to a vast network of enormous caverns. The convoluted chambers extended for many miles to the west. Water from the mountains flowed through subterranean rivers to reach the giant caverns. From there, it emptied through underwater tunnels into the great sea in the west.

West. They were wandering west now. Did Pendaram Ariphema live by the sea?

A duca gave a trumpeting call from above, bringing the usual load of supplies. Passing low, it circled back and landed. The great bird did a little dance—digging up the hot surface—and buried its feet in the cooler sand below.

Philoah bobbed his head. "The ground is getting hot for your duca, Gilyen."

"Dala!" The rider leaped down. "Soon, I'll have to do air drops or fly down myself."

As he retrieved their ration of food, Philoah jabbered with Gilyen about the latest wedding in some far-off village. David sat down to record his latest lesson.

Finishing his business, the rider mounted his duca. "Yavana hamoth Philoah nal David," Gilyen called to them. Because the sand was getting hot, the duca leapt straight into the air, beating hard with its wings.

David slammed his book shut and capped his pen just before the flying sand blasted him. "Great! I'm going to need another bath!"

*   *   *

In the warm light of dawn, David wrote in the journal section of his book.

The days are now very hot. Every morning Philoah takes to the sky and lands before the sun reaches me. I still haven't seen a shartara or a melcat, but from what he's told me, neither is pleasant.

I found out yesterday that Gilyen's duca is a male. They brought us some delicious fala fruit. It was purple and sweet.

"Ready for another lesson while we walk?" asked Philoah.

"Dala." David put the book away and stood.

As he began his steady leisurely stroll, Philoah said, "Today I will tell you about phantera government. There are twelve leaders of the phantera, one per planet."

"So, the phantera live on twelve planets?"

Philoah smiled. "They live on many more than that, but twelve planets have large populations of phantera. Each of the twelve leaders is responsible for the well-being of their planet's phantera. In matters that concern all phantera, they will meet together."

"Do they vote on issues?"

"On occasion."

"What if there is a tie, six to six?"

Philoah released a laughing coo. "That is rare indeed! When it happens, the leader of our home world decides the outcome."

"And Arana is your home world?"

"Myute! It is home to the haranda. We only share Arana with them. The phantera and ducas are from Dalena. Arana is one of the twelve planets with a large phantera population. Now, the twelve leaders are called *pendaram*. Our pendaram is Ariphema."

Shifting the book bag to his other shoulder, David asked, "Isn't he the one we're supposed to meet?"

"You remembered! Dala, when you speak better, we will see him. The pendaram is over the *delaram*. The delaram oversee large areas of a planet, traveling across their territories to stay in contact with the villages. Under the delaram are the *talaram*, who take care of the villages. You have met a talaram already."

"Daphema!"

"Very good. Under the talaram are the *yarama*."

"The village fathers." David recognized the word for "father."

Philoah nodded bird-style. "And the yarama protects the *yatala*."

"The families," David said in English.

They discussed the phantera family unit and social responsibilities until noon. After David ate lunch, they resumed their trek.

"What about orphans and widows?" David asked.

"Orphans are given to an older phantera. The elder will cover them with his wings."

"Cover them with his wings?"

Looking back at David, Philoah remarked, "It is a saying we have. It means to protect, nourish, and teach. As for the widows, the talaram covers them with his wings." Stopping, he stared beyond David, toward the east.

David followed his gaze to a brown haze creeping along the horizon. "What's that? Looks like L.A. on a smoggy day," he muttered in English.

Launching himself into the air, the phantera circled above for a few minutes. "Shartara!" he bellowed as he swooped down.

"What's a shartara?"

Bending down, the phantera flung sand into the air.

"Stop! Bot Philoah! Bot!" David cried as he covered his face.

"We must move quickly. Come!" Philoah commanded. He raced up the next dune like a roadrunner. David paused and looked back. A low cloud of golden brown billowed upward as it spread along the eastern horizon. The warm morning air began to stir.

"Hurry, no time to look back!" Philoah called.

After they crossed several dunes, the wind rose dramatically. Bits of dirt flew through the air. David ran with his back hunched over to protect his eyes and nose from the sand.

"We made it! This is the last hill," Philoah yelled above the strong winds.

David wished he could turn around and see the storm, but he'd only get an eye full of sand. At the bottom of the dune yawned the familiar doorway to the doloom. He couldn't wait to get out of the stinging sand! About ten feet from the door, the sky went dark. A deluge of dirt fell on him and he thought he was being buried alive. The stinging sand had only been the edge of the storm.

This was the shartara. *This* was scary!

Coughing and gagging on the dust, he threw his cloak over his head. Even under the material, he dared not open his eyes. The sand penetrated everything. David staggered in the direction of the door...at least where he thought the door was...somewhere around here....

Stooping, David reached out and felt the rising slope of the dune. How far off was he? Should he move to the right or the left? He could die inches from the door and not know it. The air was nearly impossible to breath! How long did these storms last? Minutes? Hours? Days?

Something tugged on his cloak—Philoah!

David stumbled as he followed the strong tugging. The ground beneath his feet grew firm and the wind diminished to a cool draft. Cautiously, he unwrapped his face in the dark cave.

"So *that's* a shartara!" he croaked and spat the sand out of his mouth. "Ramara, Philoah, for saving me." Unclipping his dowel, he turned it on.

Philoah walked further into the cave. "I wish I had seen the shartara sooner. Are you all right?"

"Dala, but I have sand in my hair, sand in my ears...even sand in my nose. *Gross!*"

"*Boosah*," Philoah commented.

"What does *boosah* mean?" David asked, shaking out his clothes and hair.

"I believe your words *yuck* and *gross* are similar to our word *boosah*. It means something that is not enjoyable."

Scratching his gritty scalp, David declared, "You got that right! I'm going down to take a bath."

As he bathed, David also washed his clothes. "How long does a shartara last?" he asked.

"It depends on how big it is." Philoah floated in the calm water like a swan. "Some only last a few hours. A big one like this may last a few days. They usually end as quickly as they begin."

The constant rumble of the storm echoed in the doloom.

David paced the platform beside the inky waters. *It's been three days and I'm going crazy, Lord. This shartara won't quit! I'm tired of Philoah's lessons and I'm sick of this constant darkness. What I'd give to see the sky again, even a cloudy one!*

He walked up the incline to stretch his legs. The wind roared non-stop over the dark entrance. "Go away!" he shouted at the hissing rumbling storm. Doing an about-face, David marched back down to the platform.

Philoah crouched beside the lit dowel. "It is hard for you to wait here."

"Dala!" David snapped, flinging an arm. In frustration, he broke into English. "This place is so oppressive! The eternal darkness of the doloom isn't much better than the deadly howling night above."

Philoah cocked his feathered head.

David decided it would be better to walk before he said something that might offend his guide. It was only the fifth time he'd checked the storm in the last hour. He stomped up the ramp.

The shartara raged as fiercely as before. Fuming, David headed back down the tunnel. Halfway to the bottom, he stopped. Something was different. Running back to the entrance, he stopped and watched in awe as the wind diminished. The sky faded from black to dark brown to reddish tan and, finally, to a pale blue.

Whooping for joy, David raced out of the tunnel and into the glorious light. He danced in the soft sand and ran up the next dune. The great storm could be safely viewed from behind and David was amazed at its height. He sprinted down the dune and over the next one, ecstatic in his freedom. He didn't care where he went, so long as it was away from that gloomy doloom!

Cresting the next dune, David stared down at a perfectly round, sandy crater a hundred feet in diameter. He hadn't seen one of these before. Did the shartara cause this? It reminded David of something he had seen long ago, something on Earth. What was it?

David casually descended into the crater, but halfway down he stopped. Something didn't feel right. The sand was much looser here than on the dunes. Turning, he tried to climb back up, but the dirt moved under his feet. He stepped faster, but could only hold his place. He stopped. The sliding sand stilled. Puzzled, he resumed walking. Again, the sand fell away from around his feet, sliding down to the center of the crater. This was definitely wrong.

David carefully watched the center of the crater while he struggled to ascend the slope. Sweat wet his brow.

Something moved under the sand at the bottom of the crater.

David's heart beat wildly.

Ant lion! That was where he had seen a crater like this! An ant lion dug a pit, buried itself at the bottom, and waited for some hapless bug to stumble in. If the bug tried to escape, the ant lion dug away at the dirt, creating a treadmill effect. When the bug finally tired and fell down…. "Lord, help me!" David cried. "I'm sorry I complained about the shartara. Please don't let that…thing get me!"

"David!" Philoah called from the sky. "Stop running! The melcat will only find you quicker!"

David froze in place but the sand still slid down. Raising a loud cry, Philoah landed on the crater's opposite side. The phantera leaped and stomped on the soft sand, sending down an avalanche. Flitting to another spot, he continued his disturbance. The sand stopped sliding beneath David, but the floor in the center of the crater stirred. Wailing, Philoah sent another load of sand cascading into the pit. He walked almost to the bottom, stomping as he went.

The whole floor of the crater shifted. Two antennae with searching yellow eyes broke through the sand, followed by an enormous pair of claws.

Philoah fluttered halfway up the crater wall, taunting the melcat. Large enough to rival a car, the great lobster-like creature emerged. Two serrated limbs unfolded from its head, like the forelegs of a preying mantis. With a loud crack, the vertically slit mouth opened and snapped shut.

The creature's tan and brown exoskeleton gleamed in the sunlight. Dark jointed legs spread out from under the thorax, their paddle-shaped feet perfect for digging sand. Behind the thorax hung a large cigar-shaped abdomen.

David remembered seeing the creature on Philoah's computer board, but he hadn't realized the monster's true size.

The melcat lunged for Philoah. David tried to climb out of the crater, but the melcat spun around and faced him again.

Fluttering off to David's right, Philoah screamed and threw sand. "David, don't move. The melcat can feel it. Wait until it's turned away from you, then shoot it in the back with the caruk!" The phantera recaptured the melcat's attention.

As soon as the creature turned its back, David unclipped his caruk, aimed, and fired. The beam grazed the melcat's back. Flinging sand like an enraged bull, the creature turned toward David. David struggled to shield his eyes. The caruk slipped from his sweaty grasp and slid down the slope.

"Myute, David!" Philoah yelled. "Not that back, the other back!" Screaming and beating the sand with his wings, he ran up to the melcat. But the furious monster would not be distracted so easily. Philoah flew over the melcat and scratched a tubular eye with his foot. Stopping, the creature swiped back with a claw.

The phantera darted back and forth in front of the melcat. Then he landed on the crater wall and limped up the slope. Dragging his left wing, he wailed. The melcat charged Philoah, sending up an explosion of sand.

Creeping down the slope, David retrieved his caruk.

"Shoot him now, David!" Philoah hollered.

"What did he mean by the 'other back'?" David muttered. The melcat's bulging abdomen faced him. "Maybe he meant that 'back'!" David fired into the soft abdomen. The beast recoiled as the laser breached its skin and a yellowish goo poured from the wound. The beam sliced open the deflating section. Steam rose as the liquid-filled innards boiled and burst. Flailing wildly as it turned, the melcat dragged its smoldering carcass toward David. Its jointed legs swiped away the sand below David's feet.

David lost his footing in the sliding sand. Dropping his caruk, he dug into the dune with all four limbs. The monster was dying but it was going to get revenge before it was through! David struggled to climb the crater wall, but the melcat dug after him like a relentless machine. Sweaty and exhausted, David collapsed. He turned to face his enemy, whispering, "Jesus, please don't let me die this way!"

The melcat's vertical mouth opened and rows of black teeth glistened on the walls of its mouth. The mantis-like legs extended toward him. Closing his eyes, David covered his head. Claws grasped his shoulders, snatching him off the sand. He screamed with all his might.

"Sarena!" Philoah called. Opening his eyes, David saw the melcat far below, sinking to the ground in defeat. Philoah held David by the shoulders and legs as he flew.

David's vision darkened and went black.

18. Phantera Theology 101

The fog in David's mind slowly cleared. Where was he? "Mom?"

A voice answered, a strange voice using a strange language.

Opening his eyes to a squint, he shut them again against the bright daylight. "Where am I? What happened?" he mumbled.

The strange voice repeated its questions. David listened carefully.

"David, are you all right? Are you sick? Can you understand me?"

Like a stormy wind, the memories rushed back. With a shuddering gasp, David sat up. Someone gripped his arm.

Blinking, David saw sunlight streaming through the entrance to the doloom. A scaly hand steadied his arm.

"Philoah, you're touching me!"

"Dala."

"You wouldn't touch me before. You carried me away from the melcat too. Why?"

Snapping his bill, Philoah replied, "He would have killed you. I had hoped you would escape his pit or kill him faster. When I saw that was not to be, I was forced to rescue you." He cocked his pigeon-like head. "Is it normal for you to sleep when you are in danger?"

Rubbing his sweaty curls, David said, "It's called *fainting*. Sometimes humans faint when they get really scared. I'll be all right."

"It doesn't seem like an effective way to deal with fear. How do you survive if you faint in dangerous situations?"

"We don't always faint," David said defensively. "Some people never faint. This is the first time it's happened to me. I've never been so scared in my entire life!" As the cool air of the doloom's entrance revived him, David stood. "So, tell me why you couldn't touch me before, but now you can."

Philoah slung the provision bag over his shoulder, his signal it was time to move on. "When you first arrived on Arana, we did not know if you were good or mel. Were you trying to save Panagyra or kill him? Daphema commanded us to avoid all physical contact. We didn't know if Panagyra's brain was damaged from attempting rhutaram on you, or if it was just an injury."

David remembered Gyra's head had been injured during the delah's escape from Earth.

Philoah continued his leisurely stroll. "I offered to teach you Ramatera and take you to Pendaram Ariphema. Daphema solemnly charged me not to use rhutaram on you or touch you unless a life was endangered."

"But why couldn't I have stayed in the village to finish learning Ramatera?" David asked.

"Pendaram Ariphema was worried you might harm us. He allowed you to stay in the village to acquire a basic understanding of Ramatera. Further instruction was to be done in isolation. You must be able to accurately answer the pendaram's questions."

"Do you think I tried to kill Gyra...I mean Panagyra?" Halting, David stared at Philoah.

"I was not there. I do not know." Philoah continued a few paces and looked back. "I do not think you are dangerous now."

"Do you think using rhutaram would harm you?"

"It does not matter what I think. I am under a vow. If Pendaram Ariphema believes it is safe to do rhutaram, he can release me from my vow."

With a tight throat, David asked, "Is Panagyra going to be all right?"

Philoah gazed off toward the mountains. "I don't know. He lost much blood. The swelling has gone down in his head, but he is still sleeping. Mojar worked very hard to save him. Now, all we can do is wait."

Turning, the phantera eyed David. "Why does drea flow from your eyes?"

David bowed his head as the tears dropped to the dry sand. "Panagyra is my friend. I tried hard to cover him with my wings, to protect him from the mel-humans who hurt him."

"Your eyes leak water when you are sad? It is similar with us." Philoah put a hand on David's shoulder. "Yavana dee David sarena."

The simple prayer moved David. "Ramara Yavana," he responded. "And ramara for giving me a friend like Philoah."

"That is the first time I have heard you really speak to Yavana," the phantera commented. "Do you follow Him?"

"Yes, but He is not known as Yavana on my planet. I've spoken with Him many times since arriving on Arana, but I didn't use Ramatera."

Philoah nodded. "I would like to hear what Trenara knows of Yavana and how she faired after the Great Disaster."

David's mind took a tangent. *Tren* meant *one* or *first* in Ramatera. The first what? "Philoah, why is my planet named *Trenara*?"

"You do not know?" The phantera lowered his feathered brows. "Have you lost all knowledge of time and major events? Incredible! Every naharam in this starry disk knows of Trenara's role, her glory, her shame—the Great Disaster!"

"Everyone but us, apparently. Please, tell me!"

Philoah eyed him in silence before continuing. "Trenara was the first of all living worlds. Her plants the first plants, her animals the first animals, her naharam the first naharam. Yavana made the other worlds and naharam, but Trenara was the first.

"Then Trenara spurned Yavana, joining herself with the mel-aradelah [demons]. Like an unfaithful wife, she turned her glory into shame. The light around her gave way to darkness and the Great Disaster spread through the universe like a mighty shartara. Naharam died, dalam and chelra killed one another, wicked thoughts corrupted minds, eggs went bad, and children died. Males and females fought each other and abandoned their vows. Pain entered every naharam. Pain of flesh, pain of shredded soul, pain of longing, pain of despair.

"As the storm exploded out from Trenara, whole planets succumbed to her wickedness, each taking an element of her evil and magnifying it. Other planets were buffeted and battered. Their naharam became divided about serving Yavana. No place in the universe remained untouched from the decaying influence of Trenara. Every world lost naharam to the mel-aradelah; every planet but Dalena!"

"The home world of the phantera?" David asked in awe.

"We suffer the effects of Trenara's disease, but there have been no mel-phantera."

"You mean you do no evil—ever?" Did the phantera think they were sinless creatures?

"We are not without evil!" Philoah amended shaking his head as his eye-rings paled. "The phantera cry out for the day when we will no longer be plagued with dark thoughts and desires. We are not as Yavana first made us, but we look to Him for help. The difference is that none of us *completely* abandoned Yavana for the mel-aradelah."

"You mean you don't have a choice?"

Philoah's feathers rose on his head. "Of course we have a choice! We just find the thought of totally rejecting Yavana repulsive. We may argue, quarrel, and resist His desires at times, but we are bound to Him like a male and female in a dalaphar. We still choose to love Him."

David was stunned. Here was an entire species that, of their own free will, followed God!

"What else do you know about Trenara?"

Staring off toward the mountains, Philoah said, "Trenara grew in her wickedness. She filled her bowl of wrath to the brim, so Yavana washed her like a dirty bowl and started over with a few naharam. These grew quickly in their knowledge and wickedness. They wished to spread their influence beyond Trenara, so Yavana shattered their voices." Philoah eyed David again. "You have never heard of this?"

"I have," David confessed, "but most people on Trenara do not believe it."

"How strange that Trenara's own children should reject their history! When Trenara lost her voice, we were forbidden to touch her. We may only observe her at a distance. Whatever happens to Trenara affects all of us to a certain degree. Yavana gave each naharam species a new language, and many lost the ability to speak Ramatera. It created serious communication problems later when different species began to visit other planets."

"So, is that all you know about my home world?" David hoped Philoah would go on.

Philoah resumed walking. "There are some mysterious sayings from Yavana's servants, but their meanings are hidden at this time."

"Tell me some." David drew closer to the phantera.

Looking up, Philoah drew in a breath.

> *Trenara is first*
> *First to be made*
> *First to rebel*
> *First to die*
> *First to revive*
> *First to bring healing to others!*

The phantera raised his hands and cried:

> *Trenara, Trenara!*
> *You who brought death shall bring forth life.*
> *You who brought shame shall blaze in glory.*
> *Yavana Himself shall touch your face.*

Lowering his hands, Philoah closed his eyes.

> *Who knows the mind of Yavana?*
> *Yaram is our father*
> *Vashua is our provision*
> *Naphema is our counselor*

> *Who knows the plans of Yavana?*
> *Yaram will send*
> *Vashua will bleed*

Naphema will enable

You ask, "Where will all this take place?"
On Trenara!

David stopped and stood still.
Turning toward him, Philoah continued:

> *The ancients told us long ago of Trenara and the*
> *Great Disaster, but I tell you the glory and honor she*
> *will receive will overcome her shame. For it is on*
> *Trenara that Yavana will do His mighty work, and out*
> *of Trenara will flow the healing balm of the universe.*

> *Vashua the hidden shall be revealed*
> *Vashua the mystery shall be proclaimed*
> *Vashua the Provided One shall be poured out,*
> *Like a bowl of falatirah upon the ground,*
> *Upon Trenara's ground.*

Breaking in, David said, "I know who Vashua is and
what He did."

The feathers undulated on Philoah's head. "You do? We
know about Yaram the Father, and Naphema the True
Spirit, but Vashua is a great mystery!"

"Do you believe Vashua is a part of Yavana?" David
asked.

"That is a primitive way of putting it." Philoah smiled.
"Yaram, Vashua, and Naphema are all 'a part of' Yavana.
They are three, yet they are one. They are Yavana. Hand me
your notebook."

Taking the book and writing brush from David, Philoah
opened it to the next blank page and wrote *Yavana.*
Underneath, he wrote *Yaram, Vashua,* and *Naphema.*

"Now, look at the first two characters of the three

titles," the phantera instructed. "What does it say?"

"Ya-va-na, Yavana!" David cried. A phantera concept of the Trinity!

Eyes sparkling, Philoah said, "You know what *phema* means, don't you?"

"It means *spirit*, that part of a naharam that separates him from a chelra or a dalam, but what does the *Na* mean?"

"*Na* is short for *najaran*."

"So, *Naphema* means "True Spirit?" David blinked. The Spirit of Truth—the Holy Spirit!

Philoah nodded. "Many of our names have words within them."

"Like *shartara*," David added. "*Shar* is *to stir up*, and *tara* is—hey!" He failed to dodge the handful of sand Philoah tossed at him. "I don't need to see it!" David protested.

Turning toward the mountains again, Philoah said, "So, humans know about Yavana and the Three?"

"Some do," David replied, shaking the sand off his clothes. "When I talked to Panagyra, he told me the phantera know little about Vashua."

"Dala." Philoah dropped his gaze. "We know something mysterious happened on Trenara, something involving Vashua, but beyond that we have only His servants' veiled sayings."

Opening his book bag, David removed his Bible. "Yavana had special servants called *prophets* on Trenara. Some of them recorded words from Naphema. They, too, spoke of Vashua and predicted His coming to Trenara. This book contains their writings along with the testimonies of some later humans who met Vashua. They describe the mighty things He did."

"So, He went to Trenara!" Philoah said in a hushed voice. Taking David's Bible, he flipped through it. "I would like to know this book."

"You will have to learn my language first and that

would take a while—unless you did rhutaram."

Philoah's eyebrows lowered into a determined expression. "Long time or short, I will learn what Vashua has done."

"When you had my bag, didn't you examine my books?" David asked.

"We did open one book. When Talaram Daphema saw its strange writing, he figured the bag belonged to you. It is not our custom to search a naharam's property without permission. Daphema was going to hold the books until your trial, but returned them at your request. He thought they might bring you some comfort."

"Dala, they did bring me comfort," David replied.

Eyeing him, Philoah asked, "Do you understand the words of Yavana's servants, the phantera prophecies I recited to you?"

A sudden joy flooded David. "Dala! It is time you read Gyra's book."

Philoah snapped his bill. "*Gyra's* book?"

Removing the Ramatera New Testament from his bag, David gave it to his guide. "Gyra was translating some of Trenara's Scriptures. It's not complete, but I think you'll find it interesting. Before you read it, let me tell you what I know of Vashua and His visit to Trenara...."

David had never seen Philoah so excited.

Dancing over the dunes, the phantera sang as if he were doing his own dalaphar. He cradled Gyra's New Testament, yellow tears running down his neck.

"Oh, David, my *crealin* is so full of joy it is about to burst!" Philoah spread his wings and snapped them, spinning his body like a top a few feet off the sand. Turning, David shielded his face from the resulting spray of sand. While David knew little about the mysterious crealin organ, he did know it was strongly affected by emotions.

Philoah dropped back onto his feet, panting. "My mind

is whirling with questions. Pendaram Ariphema will be overwhelmed when he hears about this book. I'm certain he will send for you as soon as he returns from his meeting on Dalena."

When they stopped on a dune to rest for the night, Philoah did not cease his questioning. Taxed to the point of desperation, David begged Philoah to let him sleep. He appeased the phantera by letting him look through the rest of his books.

Early the next morning, David opened his eyes to see Philoah paging through his Bible. "What are you doing?" he asked in a groggy voice.

Continuing his examination without looking up, the phantera answered, "Studying. I've gone through the other books and now I'm on the last one."

"But you don't know English. How can you read it?" Sitting up, David rubbed his eyes. The soft sand made a superior bed compared to the hard rock landing of a doloom.

"I am not reading," Philoah replied. "You are right, I can't understand your language. I'm memorizing the characters so I can read it later in my mind. Once I learn your language, I will read it in my memory."

The phantera finally looked at David. "Should anything happen to your books, what they contain will not be lost."

"Sounds good to me." Yawning, David stretched his arms and stood.

"Can I ask you some questions now?"

"Not until after breakfast!" David's voice was firm but he smiled.

Philoah gave his subtle phantera smile. "You humans seem to eat all the time. Don't you tire of eating?"

David chuckled. "Not when we're hungry."

"Since I may not ask you questions, I will tell you more of the phantera." Closing the book, Philoah began his story.

When Trenara rebelled, the parents of all
naharam followed. Some were sorry later, but
others continued in their rebellion and became
mel-naharam.

As the evil overcame Dalena, Yal, our father, covered Doiyal, our mother, with his wings. He wept
into Dalena's fair soil, now corrupted with decay.
"Yavana," he cried, "what will happen now to Your
great Name? The mel-aradelah have destroyed Your
work, they have turned Your children against You,
and the glory of Your worlds is gone.

"Now take my life, for I cannot bear to see Your
Name disgraced. Do not let me live to see my children become mel-naharam. If you will not kill us,
then give us shalar [forgiveness]."

Yavana spoke to Yal and said, "Because you did
not justify your rebellion, but were concerned for
my Name, I will grant you this: none of your
descendants will become mel-phantera. Yet they will
suffer much. They will wrestle with evil from within
and without.

"You shall die, but your life will be a thousand
circuits of Dalena's path. Only a few of those who
come after you will live beyond five hundred, and
none will reach six hundred.

"And I will use your children to unite the
naharam who follow me. The phantera will be my
servants. They will be hunted by the mel-naharam,
yet they will be blessed.

"From out of Trenara, I will bring you a hope.
It will take root among the phantera and spread to
the other naharam, crushing the schemes of the
mel-aradelah."

Then Yavana gave special gifts to the phantera.
He gave us rhutaram and falarn. He made us able to

*live in hot and cold climates, to sleep when in pain
and to live in or out of water.*

Philoah's fiery-red eyes turned to David. "That is why
we can talk with naharam on every planet. It is also why the
mel-naharam fear us and kill us."

Frowning, David said, "I still don't understand why
they fear you."

Fingering the strap on the provision bag, Philoah said,
"If the mel-naharam can destroy the phantera, many of
our diverse allies will have no way to communicate. We
are the cords holding the Naharam Alliance together.
Without us, the mels would crush the remaining naharam
worlds. The mel-naharam hate the naharam, especially
the phantera."

Picking up his burden, Philoah prepared to walk. David
finished his last piece of dried fish and stood. "All right, I'll
do my best now to answer your questions."

After a long hot march, David spied a large rock jutting
from a dune. "Let's stop over there for lunch," he said.
Philoah altered course for the rock. David brushed the
sweaty curls off his forehead. How much longer could he
travel in this heat?

Leaning at an angle, the great slab cast a slim shadow
across the sand. David took refuge in the shade and ate his
lunch. "It's getting too hot. Maybe we should start traveling
at night," he suggested.

Bobbing his head in agreement, Philoah said, "Dilari
will be up. You can see by her light."

David bit into a plum-sized fala fruit. Dilari was the
smaller of Arana's two moons. Too bad Agaria, the larger
moon, had just set.

"I'm so tired, all I want to do is sleep." Rolling his cloak
into a pillow, David reclined on the sand.

"You want to sleep *again*? Are you well?" The bird's scarlet eyes stared down at him.

David sighed. "I just didn't get *enough* sleep last night."

"Then may I finish memorizing your book?"

"Go ahead." David rolled over. His mind drifted off in the oppressive heat.

Suddenly, Philoah bellowed, "Shartara, shartara!"

19. The Mel-Naharam

They scrambled safely inside a doloom entrance before the storm hit. David went swimming, relishing the cool waters of the doloom while Philoah studied the Bible. Rolling onto his back, David floated. *Ah, this is better than a nap in that heat!* It felt so good to just lie there, listening to the stillness.

The phantera carefully placed the book into David's book bag. "I am finished. If Panagyra recovers, he can teach me your language, and I will understand your books!"

Pulling himself upright, David treaded water. "Do you think Gyra will recover?"

With scrutinizing eyes, Philoah cocked his head. "You asked me that before. Did you forget my answer?"

"No, I guess it's a human thing. I want someone to reassure me, to tell me he will be all right."

"To desire reassurance is not a *human* thing, it's a *naharam* thing. I don't understand how asking a question repeatedly can bring reassurance." Philoah's eyes softened. "I speak to Yavana often about Panagyra."

Hoisting himself onto the landing, David said, "Did you know Gyra well?"

"He didn't tell you about his family?"

"I never asked him." David rubbed the excess water

from his curls. "I should have asked him a lot of things, but I didn't."

"I am Panagyra's brother."

David's head snapped up. "His *brother*! Why didn't you tell me?"

"You didn't ask."

"Is that why you offered to take me to the pendaram?"

"As his closest relative, it's my duty to see that you are brought to justice if you harmed him, and protected if you didn't."

"What if Gyra dies? How will you determine my guilt or innocence?"

"That is not for me to determine. Pendaram Ariphema will do that."

"And if Gyra recovers?" David didn't relish the idea of a trial.

"Then he will testify of your guilt or innocence."

David shivered. "I hope he wakes up soon."

"So do I."

"Do you think I'm guilty, Philoah?"

"You already asked me that. Are you seeking reassurance?"

"In a way, but I'm also wondering what you think about me. If you had to judge me today, what would you say?"

Shaking his head, Philoah replied, "I don't even know your defense. I am not fit to judge you."

"I understand, but if you had to...*darn*," David said, switching to English, "I don't know the word for *guess*."

The two stared at each other in awkward silence.

"I hope that you didn't try to harm my brother," Philoah spoke in a soft voice.

"Ramara, Philoah. That's good enough for now. While we're waiting for the shartara to pass, I'll try to explain what happened to Gyra on Trenara...."

*   *   *

The shartara finished before David did.

Philoah snapped his jaw and raised his scalp feathers many times, but didn't question David until he finished.

"This is very disturbing," Philoah declared, scratching the feathers on his neck. "So, Panagyra was attacked by a mel-naharam near Trenara's moon. Did he say which species?"

"He did, but I can't remember what it was."

"Mel-balahrane?"

"Myute."

"Mel-dijetara?"

"Myute."

"Mel-hanor?"

"That's it! He said it was a mel-hanor."

Philoah snapped his jaw. "The mel-hanor are fierce and reckless, but what would they be doing near Trenara? Perhaps the mel-balahrane are involved in this—the mel-dijetara too."

"Why do you think that?"

"They are the Dark Three, the leaders of the mel-naharam alliance. When Trenara fell, their planets rebelled to the point where all their naharam went mel. That is why they are called the Dark Three."

"Not one of them ever sought Yavana?" David asked in amazement.

"Not one."

Rubbing his scalp, David asked, "Why didn't Yavana wipe them out?"

"We don't know. Since they united, they have persistently attacked our planets. Even Arana has seen battle. The mel-balahrane seek the mel-aradelah, eager to spread their influence. Theirs is the dark worship. The mel-dijetara pursue power through weapons and machines. They care not for Yavana or the mel-aradelah, believing only what they can see and study. Skillful builders and brilliant inventors, they fashion terrifying weapons like the crullah.

Theirs is the empty knowledge. The mel-hanor indulge their basest desires, delighting in the suffering of others. Their children are taught to torture dalam before devouring them. Among them the dalaphar is unheard of, faithfulness is a vice, loyalty a weakness. They derive their greatest joy from killing naharam—especially phantera. Theirs is the false freedom."

David shivered, his wet clothes offering no comfort. "Why would the mel-hanor want to visit Trenara?"

Philoah was silent for a long time before he spoke. "I do not think the mel-hanor are interested in Trenara, except to steal her dalam to kill and eat." Eyeing David, he remarked, "I doubt they'd be interested in hunting humans. You're too slow. They like a challenge."

"I don't know whether to be happy or offended," David replied with a nervous laugh.

"I think the mel-hanor are working for the mel-balahrane."

David rubbed his rough beard. "Why not the mel-dijetara?"

"The mel-dijetara may not care for spiritual things, but they know from history that Trenara affects everyone. They have nothing to gain from Trenara's knowledge or inventions. From what you've told me, the mel-dijetara are better builders then humans."

"So, you think it's the mel-balahrane," David concluded. "What would they have to gain?"

"I'm not certain." Philoah's head twitched. "Perhaps the mel-balahrane think they can influence Trenara by re-introducing their dark worship, strengthening the power of the mel-aradelah."

David blew out his breath. "We already have a lot of dark worship on my planet. How would they increase it?"

"I thought you might know." Sighing, Philoah closed his eyes. The silence of the doloom became almost tangible.

David ran his fingers through his growing hair. How would the mel-balahrane influence Earth? His mind wandered to the federal agents, the military, the UFO convention…. He blinked. "Philoah, if the mel-naharam landed on Trenara, some humans would worship them."

Philoah red eyes snapped open. "Worship a mel-naharam? That would be terrible!"

"A visit from a mel-naharam could encourage the mel-humans to resist Yavana and those who serve Yavana would be severely ridiculed."

Philoah's feathered eyebrows lowered. "Why?"

Blushing, David answered, "Most of Yavana's servants have given little thought to alien naharam because His Scriptures don't mention you, but many mel-humans believe alien naharam exist."

Philoah's scowl deepened. "Why should that matter? Yavana doesn't reveal everything at once! Our existence doesn't mean what you believe is false."

"I know that now, but a mel-naharam would still do a lot of damage."

Picking up the provision bag, Philoah announced, "We should resume our travel." They left the doloom and plodded through the dunes in the cool of evening. Philoah continued his lessons as the stars appeared, one by one.

The small moon, Dilari, shone from the lavender sky. She wasn't quite full, but she was waxing.

"Some questions have puzzled me since I came to Arana," David stated as the sun sank behind the dark dunes. "Why did Gyra's delah land at Daphema's village?"

"It's Gyra's home."

"Why is the village in such a wasteland? I know you have plants, we eat them every day, but I've never seen any growing…locally."

With an amused smile, Philoah said, "I can see why you would be confused, especially since you eat so often. Our food is grown in less arid regions and imported. The village was established because of a large *marza* deposit formed where the creek washes into the shallow lake."

David nodded. "I remember the lake."

"The water in the lake evaporates, leaving behind minerals. After mining the minerals, we extract the marza. A duca takes it to another village where it is combined with certain metals. Marza is prized because it greatly increases the strength of those metals. We trade with it on other planets. The phantera work in the Marza Village during the dry season. When the great rains come, we leave for a mine on the southern continent and return after the rains cease."

"Why don't you build any...caves to live in?"

Glancing toward David, Philoah replied, "We can all fit into the one cave."

"Is that what you do when a shartara comes?"

"Myute." Philoah observed the fading ribbon of pink in the darkening sky.

"What do you do?" David prodded.

"We don cloaks to protect our feathers and close our *hamjea*."

David halted. "Your *what*?"

"Turn on your dowel," the phantera instructed. David did and Philoah bent close to the light. "Now, watch my eye." A clear third eyelid slid across Philoah's red eye.

Straightening up, the phantera resumed walking. "The hamjea lets us see with protected eyes. We use it when we swim. We do not see with our eyes in a shartara, but the hamjea combined with our outer eyelids keeps the sand out."

David remembered that birds on earth had a third eyelid. "How do you see in a shartara?"

"With our ears."

"Oh yeah," David breathed in English.

They traveled for most of the night until David was

weary. Finding the next doloom entrance, they bedded down inside the great cavern.

"When we get close to the sea, the air will be cooler," Philoah said.

David could hardly wait. He longed for daylight without heat.

The next two weeks they traveled southwest by starlight, resting in the doloom by day. One night David smelled the ocean and felt its cooling breeze. It heralded the welcome end of his nocturnal schedule.

On the morning of David's first day back in the sunshine, Philoah spotted the duca searching the eastern dunes. "Wait here while I speak with Gilyen," he instructed before flying off to meet the duca. The duca set down several hundred yards away and his rider dismounted.

David reclined on the slope to watch as Philoah and Gilyen greeted each other. Sand tickled David's neck. He brushed it off. More peppered him. Leaning forward, he shook his collar and wiped his neck. He turned. A small hissing avalanche slid from the top of the dune as a serrated leg clawed the ridge. David had seen one of those before! Abandoning his bag, he leaped down the dune, yelling. Then he realized his mistake. His commotion would only draw the melcat!

The creature's massive hulk charged over the top. Scrambling up the next dune, David screamed, "Philoah!" He raced down into the hollow, out of Philoah's sight. David realized the melcat was probably hidden from view as well. Would the phantera see David's peril in time? Panting and sweating, David crested the next sandy hill. It was hard to run uphill in the soft sand. "Philoah, help!" he wailed.

Philoah's white head snapped around. "Yavana elah! It's a melcat!"

The great dark legs of the monster clutched the top of

the dune behind David. Realizing the phantera could never reach him in time, David despaired. *I'm dead.*

Then he saw it—just beyond that odd boulder lay a door to the doloom!

"Thank you, Jesus!" he wheezed. Racing for the entrance, David glanced back at his pursuer's tank-sized bulk. This melcat was much larger than the last! Screaming in terror, he sprinted for the doorway.

The unusual "boulder" sat up and roared at him. David stumbled to a stop. A seal-like creature the size of a walrus faced him with large brown eyes. Protruding from the base of its skull was a long bony horn with a stretchy membrane. "You'd better hurry for the door!" it said in a husky voice. Turning, the creature inchwormed rapidly through the entrance, its spade-like tail trailing behind.

David followed, plunging into the tunnel until he could hardly see. He turned on his dowel.

The great "seal" watched him, eyes reflecting green. "The melcat cannot follow us here. She's too big."

"How can you tell it's a she?"

Wiggling the whiskers on its brown furry face, the creature replied, "By the size." It turned its head toward the door and the horn's elastic membrane stretched to the back of its neck like a sail.

Watching the bright doorway, David said, "I'm not from around here."

"I can see that!" his companion barked. The rough voice was harder to understand. "What are you?"

"I'm a human. I come from Trenara."

"Trenara!" The glistening brown eyes widened.

David leaned closer. "You're a haranda, aren't you?"

"Dala." Releasing a series of snorts, the haranda asked, "What brings you to Arana?"

The outside light diminished as the melcat scratched at the entrance, trying to enlarge it. "A phantera crash-landed on my planet and I helped him get home." David kept his eyes on the searching, prying legs. "Now I'm stuck here for a while."

"The phantera could send you home. They must be holding you for a reason."

"Dala, they want me to learn Ramatera so I can speak to the pendaram." David backed away as a claw reached toward him.

"I think you speak Ramatera well enough," the haranda noted.

"Ramara."

Shoving its face in the doorway, the melcat watched David with its tubular eyes. A pair of two-foot fangs extended from its vertical mouth.

"She's near egg-laying time," the haranda observed.

"How can you tell?" A chill traveled down David's spine as he stared at the fangs.

"She wants to suck our fluids with her sharp hollow tubes. Females need water to lay their eggs." The haranda released another snort. "She can drain us both easily."

"How do you know she's not just hungry?"

Twitching his whiskers, the haranda replied, "Hungry melcats chomp their teeth. Fangs are only used to suck fluids, and the only time they suck fluids is right before they lay!"

The melcat flinched. Lurching back, it showered the tunnel with sand. A great bellow echoed from outside. "Is she trying to lure us out?" David asked. "I've never heard such strange sounds."

"Melcats have no voices. That is a duca you hear!" Arching its back, the haranda wiggled toward the door. David followed, joining the haranda in the sunlight.

Nearby, Philoah and Gilyen whooped and cheered in their birdsong language. The melcat's back was turned toward David, its enormous claws raised in defense, as the bellowing duca charged. Grabbing a massive pincher with his beak, the duca snapped it off at the base and tossed it aside. With opened mouth, the duca faced the second pincher, but the great claw seized his upper bill.

The duca rumbled ominously as the two behemoths wrestled. Like a vise, the pincher gripped the bill and the great bird couldn't pull away. Creeping forward, the melcat extended its fangs. Gilyen sang a few notes. In response, the duca rolled onto his back with the melcat on top. The nails on his webbed toes grasped his enemy. Like a spider, the giant arachnid's fangs reached for the bird's exposed belly. Arching his back, the duca beat the melcat furiously with both wings. Sand and segments of legs exploded into the air. When the mighty bird ceased, only two legs remained on the stunned monster.

With the disabled melcat grasped firmly in his nails, the duca pulled with his powerful neck, straining to remove the lone pincher locked on his bill. Philoah and Gilyen whooped and warbled encouragement. The jointed limb crackled and popped as the pincher broke away from the body.

"*Hoowah!*" Philoah cried.

Raising a fist, David shouted. "Yes!"

"Run melcat—if you can!" the haranda barked. "Soon you'll be duca food!"

The melcat tried to run, lurching across the sand with its two remaining legs. The duca tossed his head to remove the massive pincher from his beak, but the stubborn claws held fast. His blue eyes spied the fleeing melcat. With a muffled roar, he charged. Gilyen warbled instructions and the duca leaped onto the melcat. The great bird threw his head against the melcat's hard back, pounding the severed pincher until it shattered. Gilyen cheered.

The duca shook his head and worked his jaw. Lifting his neck, he trumpeted in triumph and hopped off the melcat. Yanking violently, the lethal yellow bill tore open the bulging abdomen and the duca proceeded to gorge himself.

"*Gross,*" David said as he turned away.

"*Gross?*" the haranda asked.

"It means *boosah!*" David ran to join Philoah and Gilyen.

Grinning, Philoah said, "We will eat well tonight! The vest on Gilyen's duca will hold enough water for cooking. The meat must be properly boiled."

David watched as the phantera took hold of a broken melcat leg. "Philoah, don't tell me we're going to eat *that*! Boosah!"

Philoah blinked. "Why not? And why do you call it boosah when you've never tasted it?"

"It's the thought." David's eyes wandered toward the duca. No, the bird wasn't finished yet. Cringing, he looked back at Philoah.

"I do not understand." Philoah dragged his prize toward the doloom entrance. "You eat loomar, yet it is boosah to you before it's prepared. Why not wait until the melcat is cooked before you call it *boosah*?"

Sighing, David raised his hands in surrender. "All right, but don't ask me to help prepare it. I'm too exhausted. I need to lie down and rest somewhere."

20. Traveling by Duca

David stirred on the warm sand. The shade had deserted him and the sun glared down mercilessly. He rolled over. No shade there either. A delicious aroma wafted by. Drifting back to sleep, he dreamed he was in a restaurant with a plate of lobster. The legs grew until they were three feet long. David snapped a leg in two. The white steaming meat gave off a tantalizing fragrance. Jabbing the meat with a fork, he raised it to his mouth and...

"David, time to eat," called a distant voice.

He awoke. The seducing aroma did not leave as he sat up and blinked at Philoah. "What do I smell? It's making me hungry."

With a cocked head, Philoah said, "Really? The thought of eating a melcat makes you sick, yet the smell makes you hungry. I don't understand you!"

David winced. Well, perhaps melcat would taste as good as it smelled. Standing up, he stretched. The plump duca slept on the sand, his massive beak resting on a bulging chest. His large blue eye opened drowsily and closed again. Although his bill was cut and bruised from fighting, the duca appeared unconcerned.

Turning, David saw the duca's vest resting beside the doorway to the doloom. The great bird must have shed his burden before attacking the melcat. Supported by poles and lines, the vest's two pockets brimmed with boiling water.

Perched on top, Gilyen fired his caruk intermittently into the water while he prodded the cooking limbs. "Pendaram Ariphema will be holding council in three days," the phantera said to the haranda. "Pendaram Halora will also attend."

The haranda's long muzzle twitched. "Is that all? I'd think the council of the twelve would want to see him as well. A visitor from Trenara is of great importance. We haranda have our prophecies too."

Checking one of the support lines, Philoah replied, "I know, Hurc, and the prophecies belong to all naharam, but Pendaram Ariphema wishes to examine the human before he calls the council of the twelve."

"Gilyen, the meat is done!" Hurc barked, raising his flaring nostrils. "If it stays in any longer, the flesh will be too tough!"

Philoah and Gilyen calmly reached into the scalding water, retrieved the giant legs, and set them on the ground.

Gathering in a circle around one of the legs, the four raised their hands—and flippers—skyward.

"Ramara Yavana!" Gilyen exclaimed.

"Ramara Yavana!" three voices echoed back with enthusiasm.

Picking up a hammer, Philoah pounded the top of the leg. It cracked and steam rose as he pried off the top pieces of shell. The aroma from the snowy-white meat made David's mouth water. Gilyen tore off a slab of tender meat, placed it on a fragment of shell, and set it down in front of David. He did the same for Hurc, the haranda. The seal-like creature blew on the meat to cool it. David followed his example.

As the meat cooled, Gilyen tried his piece. He smiled. "You were right, Hurc, the meat is perfect."

Nosing the tantalizing meat, Hurc replied, "I always enjoy cooked melcat. It's a nice change from raw loomar."

David blew on his meat and sampled a morsel. In his mind, he pushed aside the hideous images of melcats. This was just a giant crab. Closing his eyes, he savored the beckoning scent. Yes, just a giant crab. He nibbled it. This was better than crab! What would people on Earth pay for this dish? Looking out of the corner of his eye, David caught his tutor watching.

"You like the melcat?" Philoah asked.

"Uh, dala." David's cheeks burned. "It's delicious."

The corners of Philoah's mouth curved up into a smile. "I have good news for you, David."

David's heart leaped. "Gyra? Is he all right?"

"No, not that good." Blinking, Philoah looked away.

David cringed. "Sorry."

"It's all right." The phantera put a hand on David's shoulder. "Our desires are the same."

"What were you going to tell me?"

"That you don't have to wander in the desert anymore. Tonight you will sleep in the Pendaram's City."

David drew in a sharp breath. "How will we get there so fast?"

"By duca."

Jumping about on the sand, David shouted in English, "Yes, yes, *yes!*" He switched to Ramatera. "No more shartaras and melcats! Ramara Yavana!"

"I didn't know you hated the desert so much," Philoah commented as he observed David's response. "I thought you'd be used to it by now."

"Philoah, the desert is...is...*boring!*" He exclaimed the last word in English.

"What is *boring*?" asked Gilyen.

David blew out his breath. "It's like singing a song with only one note, or eating horlah for every meal, or...or seeing the same thing every day. In the desert all I see is hills of tara, everywhere tara! No vegetables, no rivers, no dalam—"

"There are melcat," Philoah corrected.

"Melcat? Boosah!" cried David. "Except when you eat them."

A rasping cough came from Hurc and it took David a moment to realize the haranda was laughing. The creature's voice rose to a barking roar. David chuckled as he watched Hurc.

"I still don't understand," Gilyen stated before dumping a deluge of water from the duca's vest.

Philoah fingered a flight feather. "I think I do. I believe the word *boring* is similar to our word *myudel*."

Myudel? David knew the word. A rough translation would be "no message," but it really meant "no purpose." Did boredom come from a lack of purpose? The desert had bothered him most when they seemed to wander aimlessly, *without purpose*.

Gilyen and Philoah loaded the remaining melcat legs into the cavernous vest pockets. The leathery material still steamed as they strapped the flaps shut. Turning to his mount, Gilyen gave a melodic birdcall. The duca opened his eyes, stretched his neck, and yawned. Rising, he waddled toward his master. Gilyen sang another order. Threading his neck through the yoke, the enormous bird raised his head and the vest slid into place.

"I will see you in three days." Hurc pulled himself almost upright and raised his flippers. "May Yavana give you a swift safe journey."

The three returned the blessing and Gilyen ordered the duca to kneel. Philoah and Gilyen flew onto the top of the duca and waited.

"Don't forget your book bag," Philoah called. "I retrieved it while you were sleeping."

Finding the bag, David slipped it into the duca's vest. Then he grasped the leather straps and climbed up. Reaching the top, he asked, "Where do I sit?"

"In front where we can watch in case you fall," Gilyen instructed.

"Thanks," David muttered. He settled in at the base of the duca's neck. Gilyen fastened David in place with a leather strap and gave him a set of eye goggles.

"Humans are not as strong in their backs as we are," Philoah informed Gilyen.

The duca owner bobbed his head. "David, grab the straps in front of you and don't let go until we land."

Wrapping the leather straps around his hands, David squeezed them for good measure. Gilyen spoke to the duca and the mighty bird lowered his head, climbed a dune, and spread his wings. Flapping with increasing speed, the duca ran along the dune's crest. The rolling motion of the duck-like gait stopped as they rose into the air.

Looking back, David spied the haranda inchworming his way back to the doloom.

"Hurc will swim to the Pendaram's City," Philoah yelled in the rushing wind.

The higher they rose, the more rolling sandy waves spread out before them. Mountains and foothills loomed in the south and to the west lay a vast shimmering body of water—*Agera Adrana,* the Great Sea.

The flowing air cooled David and he reveled in the speed of his mount. This beat crawling around in the hot dusty sand any day! Under the clear sky, a shartara brewed in the far north. David relaxed when he realized it wasn't headed their way.

A large number of chocolate-brown objects dotted the dunes. They bolted, long legs kicking up a cloud of sand. "What are those?" David yelled as he pointed to the stampeding elk-sized animals.

"Lampars," Philoah shouted. "They're what the melcats usually eat. After the lampars fatten themselves on plants in the mountains, they come down to the desert. They're very shy."

Gilyen had the duca descend so David could get a better look. David now recognized the animals from Philoah's computer board. The creatures sprang like great deer, their graceful legs hardly stirring the sand with their two-toed feet. Long faces bobbed up and down on slender arched necks. A few flicked their rabbit ears, but most kept them laid back. The glossy muscular bodies gleamed like bronze and copper in the light.

David had observed many tracks in the desert, but few animals. "Why do the lampar come to the desert?" David hollered back. "There is nothing here to eat!"

"Now there isn't, but just after the rains, there are plenty of plants. The lampars come down from the northern hills to graze on the desert plants. When the plants die, the lampars migrate south and climb the mountains to feast on fala vines. When the fala vines lose their leaves, the lampars return, living off their fat until they reach the northern hills. There, they graze on horlah plants until the wet season is over. Each circuit they migrate back and forth."

David gazed at the rumbling herd. *And in between are the melcats waiting to devour them.* The herd dropped behind. He squeezed the riding straps as the duca banked, turning southwest toward the ocean. The great mountain range dove into the sea; its stubborn peaks reappeared as a series of islands before succumbing to a watery grave. Near the shore, strange vegetation covered the wrinkled foothills. The woolly stuff carpeted dells and valleys in lavender, pink, and green.

"*Tearel* [plant life]!" David exclaimed.

"Dala, David, the pendaram chose a location with plenty of food for his meeting city," shouted Philoah from behind.

On the shore, just before the foothills, rested an orderly collection of geometric buildings. This was where the barren desert and lush foothills met, where sea and land conversed. Lapping at the buildings, the water stirred up the sandy shores. A massive round building sat half in, half out of the water. Green waves crashed against a series of breakwaters protecting the building's immaculate white walls.

"What's that?" David asked, pointing to the round building.

"The council chambers," Philoah replied above the rushing wind. "We will appear there before Pendaram Ariphema in three days. If you wish, I can show it to you after we land."

Gilyen spoke to the duca. The great bird slowly spiraled down toward the city. Several delahs and other bizarre ships rested on a pink circular clearing. Pedestrians roved the streets, not all of them phantera. Large numbers of haranda moved among the buildings, basked on the beaches, and frolicked in the waves.

Gilyen warbled another command, and the duca drew in his wings, heading for the circular clearing in front of the council chambers. David's ears popped and his stomach leaped as the bird plummeted. The wind beat against his face and he was thankful for the goggles.

"Hoowah!" Philoah cried out. Raising his head, the duca trumpeted. As they swooped low over the surrounding buildings, some of the inhabitants looked up. The great bird stretched his wings and spread his tail feathers, slowing his speed.

A small gathering of phantera waited beside the landing area. Pink vegetation covered the ground, groomed to form a perfect circle.

The duca flared, raising his crested head as he bled off airspeed. When he was near stalling, the giant bird reared up and beat the air with his mighty wings, braking their forward momentum. Hunkering down, David gripped the riding straps. The massive bird plopped onto the pink lawn. Like a rooster, the duca raised his head and trumpeted again.

"It's Pendaram Ariphema!" Gilyen exclaimed.

"I thought I wasn't going to see him for three days, when he examines me!" David spoke in a panicked whisper. He wasn't ready to meet the ruler of Arana's phantera— especially after months in the desert. David stank of stale sweat and his hair had seen better days.

"Hurry up, David. You can see more ducas later," Philoah urged.

Looking around, David realized he was the only one left on the giant bird. He slid down the bird's vest, caught his foot on a strap, and did a face-plant on the lawn. At least it was soft. *I'm going to die. So much for first impressions.*

Philoah and Gilyen helped him to his feet.

"Is he ill?" a large phantera asked.

"No, Pendaram Ariphema, he is quite well, I think." Philoah eyed David. "Are you all right?"

"My body is all right." David brushed off the sand and

clinging vegetation. "But my soul is...full of shame." David couldn't remember the word for *embarrassed.*

"Why?" Ariphema asked. His deep purple hands revealed his great age.

Bowing his head, David said, "I wanted to clean myself and my clothes before I met you."

"Why? You just came from the desert. I would not expect you to be clean."

"It is the custom of my naharam to clean themselves before speaking to someone of importance."

"Are not all naharam important?" Ariphema cocked his head. "Perhaps you mean some *meetings* are more important than others."

"Dala."

Eyeing David, Ariphema said, "When I heard that the naharam from Trenara was arriving, I hurried to see you. It is our custom to value greetings over appearances. I apologize if this custom offends you."

David smiled. "I am not offended. It is a better custom than what we have on Trenara. Your words have removed my shame."

"Good." The pendaram bobbed his head, obviously pleased. "When we meet again, I will have many questions for you. Rest for now and enjoy the fruits of Arana. Brusaka will take you to a place where you can eat, sleep, and bathe." From out of the group stepped a phantera with black feathers.

"Philoah, I didn't know phantera come in black," David whispered.

"Do your naharam come in only one color?" Brusaka asked.

"No," David said, taken aback. He'd forgotten how futile it was to whisper around a phantera.

"Does my color disturb you in some way?"

Brusaka sure was observant. "I wasn't expecting it,"

David answered lamely. "You're the first black phantera I've seen. Do you come in other colors?"

Brusaka cocked his head and blinked.

A whooping laugh came from Philoah. "Shalar Philoah," he entreated David. "You forgot to use the plural form of *you* to include all phantera. Your *English* crept in on you."

Horrified, David realized he had asked if Brusaka came in other colors. "Shalar David!"

The black phantera watched him with orange eyes. "I took no offense."

Turning back to Philoah, David asked, "Are you sure my Ramatera is good enough?"

"Dala, David. Even the best *yaki* traders have made blunders. Don't you make mistakes using English on Trenara?"

David scratched his sandy scalp. "Dala, but humans have killed each other over errors as small as this."

The feathers on Ariphema's white head rose while the other phantera snapped their bills.

"I will explain all this and more in three days," David added hastily.

21. The Pendaram's City

Gazing up through the atrium's open roof, David relaxed on his back in the pool's warm water. Alamar blazed overhead, as fair as Earth's sun. He could really enjoy it here. The guesthouse was pretty nice—especially compared to the deep desert!

Large windows lit the white stone dwelling. From the pool, he could see into the sparse dining room. The whole place lacked furniture with the exception of a few tables and shelves. Turning his head, he gazed at the shelves piled high with vegetables, dried loomar, and bowls. A skin of falatirah hung from a peg. He wouldn't lack any good food here.

Dunking his head, David scrubbed his scalp to remove all the dirt. A little soap wouldn't hurt, if he could find any. Water poured into the pool from the carved snout of a marble sea creature. Four paddle-shaped limbs extended from its lithe body.

"Brusaka," David called. The black phantera was his only companion in the private dwelling since Philoah had left to visit a friend. Emerging from a room, Brusaka eyed him.

David pointed to the statue beside the pool. "What dalam is this?"

"It is not a dalam. It is a *nadrea*, the haranda's chelra. Nadreas assist the haranda like the ducas assist the phantera."

"Does every naharam have a chelra helper?" David asked.

"Most naharam do. Yavana gave them as helpers. Some of the mel-naharam exterminated their chelra."

David scratched his hairy chin. "When the naharam were first created, did they each have chelra on their planets?"

Cocking his black head, Brusaka said, "I do not know."

David hauled himself out of the water and checked his hanging clothes. They were still soggy. If only he had a towel. Was there even a *word* for towel in Ramatera? He got an idea. "Brusaka, are there any cloaks around here?"

"There is the one you brought. It is drying in the sun." The dark phantera pointed to the dripping garment.

Combing his wet curls with a hand, David said, "No, are there any other cloaks besides that one?"

The phantera scowled. "You need two?"

"It is uncomfortable for humans to wear wet clothes."

Brusaka disappeared and returned. "Here is a cloak, but it is a little big."

Taking the gray garment, David dried himself off with a corner and then put it on. Brusaka wasn't kidding. Two feet of extra material lay on the ground.

The black phantera watched with keen orange eyes. He bobbed his head. "Wait here." He scurried off and returned with a leathery cord. Gathering up the material, Brusaka wrapped the cord around David's waist.

David tied it in a knot. That was better! Slipping off his long neglected underwear, he washed it in the pool.

"Where do I sleep?" David asked.

The phantera led him to a nearby room. David spied a water pedestal identical to the one in the dining area. The carved head of a duca protruded from the wall, cool water pouring from its mouth into a basin. A drain near the rim kept the bowl from overflowing. The stone basin rested on a column three feet off the ground. There were no beds, only a thick pile of pink plants in one corner.

"We do not know what humans usually sleep on," Brusaka explained. "Philoah said you found hard rock uncomfortable, and you hate sand."

David lay down on the spongy *alawa* plants. The makeshift bed was soft but itchy. "Do you have another cloak?"

"Dala." Raising a feathered eyebrow, Brusaka left the room and returned with another cloak, larger than the last.

"Perfect!" David declared, rubbing his hands together. The phantera watched as David covered the bed with the enormous cloak. David lay down again and sighed with relief.

"Is it good?"

"It is very good," David answered with a smile. He closed his eyes. "It is the best sleeping spot I've had on Arana."

"I am glad you like it."

Opening his eyes, David sat up. "I feel like eating."

The dark phantera cocked his head. "Philoah said you slept a lot, but I did not realize your sleep was so short."

David laughed. "I didn't sleep! I was just making sure I had a comfortable bed. Usually, I don't sleep until after sunset."

"Ah, that is a relief. Come, I will get you something to eat."

After David ate heartily, Brusaka took him out to tour the city. The black phantera was a wonderful guide, enduring David's many questions without complaint. David found fountains spaced throughout the city. Fresh mountain water flowed from the duca statues while salty ocean water poured from the nadrea statues.

"The haranda prefer the taste of the adrana water to the taste of the mountain water," Brusaka explained. "But some naharam prefer the mountain water."

He took David "haranda watching" pointing out their variations in color, size, and shape. Brusaka gestured to a haranda sporting a long bony tube from his head. "Only the males have head crests. The females do not."

"Do they use them for fighting?"

The black phantera fingered his dark cloak. "They can if a mel or dangerous dalam attacks them."

David noticed the stone flagging beneath his feet. The smooth white stones fit perfectly together.

Three silver-colored phantera strolled by. Brusaka caught David staring. "I will tell you about the silver phantera. When a black phantera and a white phantera dalaphar, their children are silver. When a silver and silver dalaphar, half are silver, a quarter are black, and a quarter are white." David realized different colored phantera inter-married without social stress.

"The city is a meeting place for haranda and phantera," Brusaka continued. "Aliens from other worlds also visit the city to vacation or call on the phantera to mediate disputes."

"Are there any mel-naharam here?" David asked after a pearly feline creature passed by.

Brusaka eyed him. "Not that we know of...yet."

David stopped. He'd felt a wall of skepticism with Brusaka and now he understood. Looking the dark phantera square in the face, he said, "I will not attempt to defend my naharam. I know my planet affected all the others and I won't blame you for suspecting I'm a mel. Many of my kind are mel, but Yavana has done a wonderful work on Trenara. You will hear about it soon."

"You follow Yavana?" The feathers on Brusaka's head undulated.

"Dala, and in His name I ask you to treat me as a brother."

"Shalar Brusaka! Pendaram Ariphema said you would stand trial for Panagyra's injuries, but he did not say you claimed to be a naharam. I was warned to be cautious. Now I see I have overstepped, treating you as guilty before your trial."

David nodded. "I give you shalar." He noticed a cluster of haranda and phantera watching him. "Why are they staring?"

"They know you are from Trenara. Word spreads fast." The cluster snagged more passers-by.

"Does that make me an object of interest?" David whispered.

Brusaka's feathered head bobbed. "You are the most talked about naharam on Arana."

David winced. Great. He couldn't even sneeze without the whole world watching. Blushing, he bent over and scooped a drink from a duca fountain.

He felt a presence. Looking up, he was startled by an old black phantera in a hooded cloak. Brilliant orange eyes blazed from the beneath the raised hood. "You are the one," the phantera declared in a steady voice.

"What do you mean I'm 'the one'?" David turned to his guide. Brusaka stood trembling.

"I have been waiting to see you since Naphema called me." The intimidating form drew closer. "You are the *vadelah* and you have come at last."

"Rammar, are you sure?" Brusaka asked in a hushed voice.

"What's a *vadelah*?" David asked. A realization descended on him like a summer rain. "Vashua's messenger?"

"Dala, Trenara's child," Rammar answered. "You will bring Vashua's message to many worlds." David reeled back. He was here by chance, just an accidental visitor, wasn't he? No, there were no "accidents" in God's plan.

"Long ago, Naphema gave me words for you." The old phantera's fiery eyes bore into David's soul. "I will tell you when the time is right. You *are* the vadelah." A shudder traveled through David.

Raising his blue-purple hands, Rammar said, "May Yavana grant you sarena to accept your calling." The old phantera turned and wandered off.

Feeling numb, David walked aimlessly down the street. The great crowd, which had gathered during Rammar's pronouncement, followed.

"I am honored to serve the vadelah," Brusaka spoke softly, bobbing his head.

David flinched. Was he really chosen for some great task? "Who is Rammar?"

Trembling once more, Brusaka said, "Rammar is a highly respected prophet. He has lived over five hundred of Trenara's circuits. Yavana has spoken through him more than any other phantera in recent times. What he declares *will* happen."

David wanted to run, but where could one hide from God? Now he knew how Jonah felt!

Brusaka's sharp eyes watched him. "Perhaps you would like to see the council chambers, without this crowd?"

"Dala."

Transformed from a skeptic into David's staunchest advocate, Brusaka shouted to the crowd to disperse, staring down the more stubborn gawkers. He was so successful that David didn't see anyone by the time they entered the council chambers.

David stared up inside the great structure. The empty building proved a place of refuge for his troubled soul. Walking down the silent hall, he lost himself in the stately columns, intricate ceiling lights, and circular windows. The stately structure was a wonderful distraction. Colorful inlaid stones adorned the smooth floor, bursting with scenes of land and sea creatures.

Brusaka led him to the end of the great hall. "Here is where the large meetings are held," he said in a soft voice. The phantera pulled open one of the towering double doors. Passing through the peaked doorway, David drew in a deep breath. The main council room was large enough to hold two thousand phantera. White arches vaulted toward the top of the domed ceiling. From the center of the roof, a round window set in a triangle illuminated the chamber. A colonnade ringed the outer perimeter of the room.

The soft squeak of his shoes echoed off the polished surfaces. David was drawn to the center of the solemn room. A modest platform with a podium rose from the heart of the chamber. Mounting the platform, David examined the odd podium. Switches and gauges covered its face. What did they control?

The floor sloped into a large pool at the far end of the chambers. Pointing to it he asked, "What's that for?"

"The water naharam. It has an underwater passage leading to the sea," the black phantera replied.

"I guess that keeps the haranda happy."

"And other water naharam," Brusaka added. "Not all

of Arana's visitors come to see the dry half of the Pendaram's City."

"You mean the other half is *underwater*?"

"Dala. The council chambers are in the center of the city, not the edge. I can show you the other half sometime, but I think you will need some help. Philoah doesn't believe you can live underwater for very long."

"He's right," David confessed. "I need to breath air...and I can't endure cold temperatures."

"We can take care of that," the phantera reassured.

Looking around the room, David wondered what it would be like in three days when the place was full of haranda and phantera. He crept over to a window and gazed out at the placid blue waters. "Yavana give me sarena. I'm really going to need it!"

David awoke while it was still early. He drank in the aroma of dried alawa, the fibers of his mattress. The past three nights he had slept wonderfully on the soft spongy bed. But today was *the* day and David was restless. Walking over to the water pedestal, he plucked a large bowl from a shelf and drew water from the basin. As the duca fountain refilled the stone basin, he smiled.

Yesterday morning he'd made the mistake of plunging his head into the basin. Brusaka's gentle rebuke was still fresh in his memory. *One does not wash in the basin. It is for drawing water. We use the bowls for drinking and washing so the basin remains clean.* It was only one of the many social blunders David had made on Arana, but his latest mistake only reinforced his feelings of inadequacy.

David splashed his face, wet his hair, and rubbed his head vigorously with a spare cloak. After donning his clean, but worn, clothes, he combed his fingers through his lengthening hair. If only he had a mirror. His fingers wandered to his beard. Who on Arana would have a razor? Oh well. At least there weren't any other humans for the natives to compare him with.

"I've never seen you take so long grooming yourself."

David spun around. "You startled me, Philoah. I didn't hear you come in."

"Will you be ready soon? The meeting will begin after you've eaten."

Flipping the curls off his forehead, David said, "I guess I'm as ready as I'll ever be, but I'd like to speak to Yavana before I go."

Philoah's bird head nodded. "Brusaka will cook you some fresh loomar. Hurc arrived last night and sent it for you. Come when you're ready." Philoah's nails clattered softly on the stone floor as he left.

Sitting down, David faced the still pool. Today the phantera would examine him to determine if he'd attacked Gyra. What would they do if they found him guilty? David was too afraid to ask how the phantera and haranda treated mel-naharam. Shuddering, he remembered that the haranda did use the death penalty on occasion.

"Jesus help me. I'm scared!" he poured out. "Rammar believes I'm the vadelah, destined to tell others about You, but I'm not the courageous type. I'm a chicken! There're plenty of pastors better trained to preach. Why not use one of them?" Sighing, David reined in his frantic tongue. "Yeah, I know. Your strength is made perfect in our weaknesses, but I don't even know if I'll be alive tomorrow."

His mind returned to his pending trial. "Rammar might believe I'm special, but he could be a kook for all I know. Gyra's the only one who can establish my innocence. I have a feeling the phantera aren't lenient in their punishment. If they're eager for vengeance, no one will be able to save me."

A dark cloud of shame overwhelmed David and he prostrated himself on the floor. "Lord, forgive me. You've watched over me since I was born. Help me to trust You. I want to do Your will, but I feel so inadequate. I'm shy and clumsy, but if You spare my life, I will go wherever You send me. My life is Yours."

Closing his eyes, David drank in the silence of the guest-house. Deep in his inner being, he felt a sweet peace as he let go of his anxieties, his need to control, and his desire to impress others. The stone floor cooled his burning cheeks.

It was time.

Rising, David walked into the dining room. Philoah and Brusaka were conversing in low tones. "The whole city has heard what Rammar proclaimed to him," Philoah said. "The chambers will be crammed with naharam."

"David, are you ready to eat?" Brusaka asked.

Standing before the table, David raised his bowl of loomar. "Ramara Yavana." He picked up a piece of fish and began his breakfast.

"We are eagerly looking forward to the meeting," Brusaka began. "I'm sure it will be remembered for generations to come."

David felt a twinge in his stomach. He knew Brusaka meant well, but it wasn't the type of encouragement he needed. Turning to the black phantera, he asked, "Can you help me?"

"I would be honored to help the vadelah!"

"Good. Please ask Yavana to give me sarena during the meeting, and that I might communicate clearly."

With bobbing head, Brusaka said, "I will speak to Him on your behalf the entire time."

Philoah spoke to David in English. "I want you to know I found you an interesting student. In my time working with you, I've grown to care for you. While I am not the one to determine your guilt or innocence, I pray that God will have mercy on you."

David stopped chewing. He forced down his food so he could respond. "Philoah! You know English?"

Smiling, the phantera continued in Ramatera. "Only what I've been able to pick up from comparing your book to Gyra's New Testament—along with your mutterings. I didn't want to spoil you out in the desert. If you knew what I understood, you would have been tempted to use English instead of relying on Ramatera. I couldn't let that happen."

David finished his meal and the three set out for the council chambers. Philoah offered to carry David's book bag. "Where is everyone?" David asked as they strolled the empty streets.

"They're all in the council chambers, waiting for us," Philoah answered.

David's stomach turned to stone. "Don't tell me I've kept an entire city waiting! How long have they been there?"

"Not long. Only since sunrise," Brusaka replied.

Stopping in his tracks, David cradled his forehead. They'd been waiting for three hours!

Brusaka eyed him. "Perhaps I should begin speaking to Yavana now?"

David broke into a trot. "That would be a good idea."

"Yavana, giver of sarena, director of our paths—"

"I meant silently!" David snapped.

The black phantera raised a feathered eyebrow. "As you wish."

They reached the building and David clipped down the hall walking as fast as he could without running. Voices rumbled from behind the doors guarding the council chambers.

Hesitating before the towering doors, David stared at the duca-shaped handle on his left, and the nadrea-shaped handle on his right.

Philoah grasped the silver duca, Brusaka the golden nadrea.

Drawing in a deep breath, David whispered, "Jesus be with me!"

22. Arana's Council

The great doors parted silently as Philoah and Brusaka pulled them open. A bell rang and the murmuring voices fell silent. David couldn't believe so many naharam could be crowded into the hall. His feet were glued to the ground. Every eye—for those creatures that had eyes—stared at him. His cheeks burned and his heart raced as he surveyed the surrealistic scene. Even his feet perspired.

Stretching before him, a path of white inlaid stone led straight to the center platform. Somehow David got his legs to move. He walked through the crowd, a lone human in a sea of aliens. Not a foot, tail, or tentacle touched the white line as the naharam crowded together on both sides. They closed in behind him, cutting off any chance of escape. Sweet scents, musky odors, indescribable aromas, and the stench of partially digested fish hung in the warm air.

Ariphema, his silent judge, stood on the platform. The distance to the center seemed much longer than David remembered. Near the platform stood Mojar, Daphema, and others from the desert village. Rammar nodded when David saw him. Across the platform, where the haranda were assembled, Hurc caught his eye. Every naharam David had met seemed present except for Gilyen and Gyra.

Philoah and Brusaka wore solemn expressions as they escorted David. Whispering to Philoah, David asked, "What am I supposed to do? Are there any customs I need to know?"

"Don't worry. We'll guide you through the ceremonies," Philoah answered.

The quiet was eerie. Not a cough, wheeze, or sniffle. Just the patter of his own footsteps and clatter of his friends' nails. When they reached the platform, Philoah turned to him. "Stop here," he directed in a low voice. David waited.

Ariphema eyed him for an embarrassingly long time. "David, human from Trenara, you are here for two reasons. First, we must question you regarding the serious injuries sustained by the phantera Panagyra. If he was deliberately attacked, we want to know who did it and why. Attempted murder is a capital offense. Second, if you are cleared of all guilt, we would like you to tell us about the state of Trenara.

"We will begin with the first item: What is your testimony concerning Panagyra's injuries? Was he attacked?"

David's mouth went dry as leather. Voices rose in a commotion at the edge of the room. The doors opened and the crowd stirred as some newcomers forced their way in. Lifting a regal brow, Ariphema spoke in a commanding voice, "Clear the path, and let them come!"

It was difficult for the naharam to squeeze back into the sidelines and several feet, tails, and tentacles were trampled in the process. A phantera kept shouting something, but the murmuring, undulating crowd made it difficult to hear.

Gilyen's head bounced up and down as he pressed forward, crying, "He's innocent! He's innocent!" A second voice cut through the air and the naharam quieted down to listen.

Scowling, Brusaka said, "I hear Gilyen saying 'He's innocent,' but I do not understand the second voice at all. What is it saying?"

David plunged into the crowd. *He* understood the words.

"You don't have to worry, David! I will tell them it's okay!" the second voice shouted in flawless English.

"David! Come back here!" Philoah called.

"Gyra!" David yelled. How could he find his friend in this rookery of birds and aliens?

"*Over here!*" came the English words.

The crowd parted and they saw each other. Lunging, David threw his arms around the phantera and wept with abandon. He didn't care if all the naharam in the universe watched.

"It's okay," Gyra soothed as yellow tears fell from his eyes. "I'm fine now. I just took a long time to heal. I woke up four days ago. Mojar wanted to keep me longer for observation, but I had to be here for your trial. Although I knew you'd be cleared, I couldn't bear the distress it might cause you."

"For days I didn't even know if you were alive!" David cried as his long-held grief surfaced like a great whale. With watery eyes, he saw Philoah's blurred form run up.

"Panagyra! *Hoowah!*"

"Philoah!" Gyra cried.

Standing aside, David wiped his eyes as the two brothers embraced. Yellow tears ran down their feathers as they squeezed each other, hopping up and down.

The three turned and walked to the platform. David stopped before Ariphema. "Shalar David if I offended you by running away. It was very important for me to greet my friend."

A corner of Ariphema's mouth turned up. "No offense taken. I am familiar with the custom."

"You speak Ramatera well!" Gyra spoke in a low voice.

"I had a good teacher," David whispered back, pointing to Philoah.

"Panagyra, do you wish to testify about how you were wounded?" Pendaram Ariphema asked.

"I do." Gyra mounted the platform. "I also wish to testify about what I have seen and learned about Trenara, if I may be permitted."

Ariphema gestured with his head. "Please, tell us."

"David is innocent of harming me. He has been a faithful friend and risked his life to save me, covering me with his wings. But before I go into that, let me tell you what I discovered. What happened to me on Trenara is insignificant by comparison."

Pendaram Ariphema's scalp feathers rose. "Speak what is on your heart, Panagyra."

"May I invite David to stand with me? He has been called to share this news."

"He may join you."

With pounding heart, David ascended the platform. *Jesus, give me courage.* Standing beside his friend, a gentle calmness descended on David.

Gyra looked out at the multitude. "Naharam of Yavana, hear me. You all know of the history of Trenara. You also know the veiled prophecies we received concerning her and Vashua. I tell you that the mystery of Vashua has been revealed on Trenara!"

Murmurs raced through the great crowd and Rammar's black head nodded. Watching the assembly, Gyra continued. "From the time of the Great Disaster until the Second Prophetic Age, we paid blood sacrifices to Yavana. Our ancestors knew that killing chelra and dalam would not clear naharam of their guilt or heal their dark nature. We sacrificed over and over, coloring the ground and the waters with blood. Looking to Yavana to help us, we offered our sacrifices because that was all we had.

"The time came when Yavana spoke once more through Dalamar the Prophet. To our bewilderment, we were forbidden to sacrifice any more chelra or dalam to Yavana. We were told to stop, but we didn't know why. Now you shall know why."

Turning to David, Gyra said, "Tell them why the sacrifices were stopped."

A sense of awe descended on David as he gazed out at the sea of alert eyes and expectant faces. Like a swimmer preparing for a strenuous dive, he drew in a deep breath.

"Yavana Himself has provided a sacrifice for us. This sacrifice was perfect because He is perfect. This sacrifice was complete because He is complete. This sacrifice was eternal because He is eternal. This sacrifice was...Vashua!"

"Vashua!" Ariphema exclaimed. The assembly clamored.

Gyra quoted portions of phantera Scriptures. "'Vashua will bleed...Vashua will be poured out like a bowl of falatirah upon the ground, upon Trenara's ground...Yavana Himself will touch her face.' How can Vashua bleed? How can He be poured out? How would Yavana touch Trenara's face? Tell them, David!" The echo from Gyra's words merged into the expectant silence of the vast chamber. The great longing of the assembled naharam was almost tangible, the inaudible cry of three thousand creatures to hear the fulfillment of ancient mysteries.

"I will tell you how," David said, gazing at the living sea all around him. "Vashua became a naharam."

It took a moment for the words to sink in, but when they did, the voices rose to a roar until Ariphema quieted the crowd. Raising his purple hands, Gyra leveled his gaze at the eager crowd before him. "Vashua became a naharam on Trenara, a *human* naharam, like my friend."

All eyes returned to David. He bowed his head, humbled because Vashua chose to clothe Himself in human flesh. *Lord, we are so unworthy.* Releasing a deep breath, David raised his head and spoke. "Trenara's children have been at war with themselves since the Great Disaster. Humans and mel-humans live on the same continents, in the same cities, in the same villages. Sometimes it is hard to tell who is mel and who is not.

"Vashua was born and lived among humans and mel-humans. He stayed with them for thirty-three of Trenara's circuits. He called the mel-humans to return to Yavana. At the end of thirty-three circuits, they tortured Vashua and killed him."

The chamber became as still as a morgue. Rammar's wail sliced into the silence. He was joined by a great bellowing haranda. Others added their voices until the room resounded with howls, screams, clicks, and moans.

David gave the naharam time to mourn, covering his ears as Brusaka shrieked below him. Ariphema's bill lowered onto his chest. His tears turned from blue to purple, growing redder by the moment.

"No Pendaram Ariphema!" Gyra cried, embracing his leader. "Don't weep so dangerously. You must live to hear the hope!" Ariphema blinked rapidly as the flow of tears diminished. He raised his hands. The noise died to quiet whimpers, moans, and hissing.

Uncovering his ears, David continued. "Vashua died, but His death was not in vain. He died willingly, becoming our sacrifice! And to prove that His sacrifice was perfect, complete, and eternal, three days later Naphema raised Him from the dead! Vashua lived among the humans a little while longer and then returned to Yavana. Then Vashua sent Naphema to dwell in all who follow Yavana. Now, we can know Yavana in a way we never could before. We can know Him through Vashua!"

A low rumble filled the room and the floor trembled. "Who's shaking the building?" David asked in alarm.

"Yavana!" Brusaka cried. "Yavana the Mighty One!"

A fiery light burst into the air above their heads, dancing and rippling like an aurora. "Naphema comes, just as he did on Trenara!" proclaimed Gyra.

Reaching upward with his hands, Philoah shouted, "*Hoowah!* Consume me, fire of Yavana!" The entire assembly broke into spontaneous praise.

"Harana Yavana! Praise Your name! Master of all life, You have opened a way to Your presence by the strength of Your right hand." The words flowed from David's mouth as he spoke Ramatera like a native tongue.

Brusaka cried out, "Thank you, Lord, for Your indescribable gift! Thank You for giving us Jesus and making Him known to us!"

With a shock, David realized Brusaka was speaking in English. He focused on the voices around him.

"*Gloria Dios!*" cried a slender haranda.

"*Du bist unser Herr und Gott! Du hast alle Dinge gemacht,*" a silver phantera declared.

"*O Panginoon ko, buong puso kitang pasasalamatan,*" bellowed Hurc.

Listening, David realized many of the naharam were speaking languages from Earth. He was participating in a naharam Pentecost! The love and the joy that filled him, overwhelmed him, and burst through him was unlike anything he had ever experienced. Kneeling on the platform, he worshipped in awe.

A haranda broke into song, followed by a phantera. A slender blue alien joined in as the song grew in volume. Saturating the air, it echoed off the domed ceiling as each individual carried a different intricate part. Harmonies wove in and out of melodies and countermelodies–an audio version of a cathedral's rose window. It was a glorious majestic symphony of worship.

Feeling as if his heart had been given a voice, David sang with all his might. Heaven itself had come down to join them. He knew he would never hear a choir like this again until he stood before the throne of Yavana with the hosts of heaven.

When the divine song finally faded away, Gyra turned to David and asked, "Did you bring the books?"

"Dala." David took his bag from Philoah and passed it to Gyra.

Smiling Gyra said, "I'm still not used to seeing a human speak Ramatera." He peered into the bag. "David, your Bible is here."

"I know. Todd must have slipped it in when I wasn't looking."

Gyra's bill snapped softly. "May Yavana protect Todd. I miss him."

"I do too." Sighing, David looked up at the domed ceiling. "I miss all my friends and family, but Yavana has given me a task."

"Philoah," Gyra called. "Take these books to the copying center. Tell them to scan each page and send them to the chamber projection unit so we can assimilate them here."

Taking the bag, Philoah faced the unenviable task of worming through the crowd to reach an exit.

"Pendaram Ariphema, may I speak?" Gyra entreated. The pendaram nodded.

"I have a plan," Gyra said. "It is vital that we spread this Great Revelation as fast and as far as possible. Philoah is making copies of Trenara's Scriptures and the languages they were written in. I made an incomplete translation of Trenara's Scriptures in Ramatera.

"But David brought a complete copy of Trenara's Scriptures in English. If I used rhutaram on the delaram leaders, English could spread from the delaram to the village leaders, to the fathers, and on to the families. We could cover Arana as fast as a shartara! Let us call a Council of Pendarams so they, too, can hear the Great Revelation and take it to their planets."

With bright eyes, Ariphema said, "Agreed."

Gyra spread his hands. "Let us send out phantera to all the naharam planets so the mighty work of Vashua may be proclaimed throughout the universe!"

"Ramara Yavana!" Ariphema raised his hands. "I pledge all of Arana's phantera to this great and glorious task!"

A giant haranda wiggled onto the platform. He did not ask Ariphema for permission to approach.

"Who's that?" David whispered in English.

"Halora, pendaram of the haranda," explained Gyra. "He has even more authority than Pendaram Ariphema because this is his home planet. All the haranda delaram leaders are here too. They knew this would be an important meeting!"

Addressing the phantera ruler, Halora said, "Pendaram Ariphema, the haranda have been guardians of a prophecy. One of our prophets declared that Arana was an unlit torch. When the light-bearer came, Arana would be lit with a holy flame, destined to spread beyond our world. Today, we have seen the holy flame. Therefore, we wish to participate in the spread of this Great Revelation and are willing to take it to the water naharam who speak Ramatera."

"Ramara, Pendaram Halora. We are grateful for your service," Ariphema replied with a nod. "Your help will allow us to concentrate on other naharam and speed our task."

Rammar approached the platform and waited. The phantera pendaram motioned for the old prophet to join him. Mounting the platform, Rammar's fiery-orange eyes swept the assembly until everyone was still. "Halora is right in saying the haranda's prophecy has been fulfilled. The light-bearer has a name among the phantera as well."

Rammar approached David and circled him. The room grew so quiet David could hear his own heart. Stopping, the black phantera held a hand above David's head. "What I have spoken in the street, I now declare in this solemn assembly. This *is* the vadelah!"

David cast a cautious eye toward Gyra, wondering how his friend would react.

"David, I'm so honored to know you!" Gyra spoke with reverence. "I suspected it the night you gave me your Bible."

"Gyra, what does this mean?" David whispered in an urgent voice.

"You were chosen by Yavana to bring the Great Revelation," Gyra said with a broad smile—broad for a phantera.

"Dala. Panagyra is right," Rammar declared. "You brought the Revelation of Vashua to Panagyra and to us. You have been given the honor of being Vashua's messenger, but you are not finished yet. The phantera and the haranda will faithfully accomplish the task for the naharam. You must go where the phantera and haranda cannot go."

David secretly hoped Rammar would tell him to return to Earth, but suspected that wasn't to be. Extending his arm over David once more, Rammar spread his long purple fingers. "You, David, human naharam from Trenara, are to plant the seeds of light in the soils of darkness. You are to go to the three dark worlds of the mel-naharam."

"Rammar, are you sure?" Ariphema cried. "It will be like sending a lampar to a melcat! Yavana hamoth David!"

The phantera prophet raised both hands and bore into David with his eyes. "These are the words Naphema gave me long ago:

The three dark planets shall receive the vadelah.
To the mel-balahrane shine the light without
    deception.
To the mel-dijetara fill the emptiness.
To the mel-hanor show no fear and stand your
    ground,
Expose their slavery to passion.

Gyra's eye-rings paled. "Oh, David, be strong! You've been given a task none of us could hope to complete."

Still feeling the power of the naharam Pentecost within him, David replied, "If it is Yavana's will to go, I will go. It would be a glorious thing to die for."

Ariphema stared at Rammar. "Is it possible for the mel-naharam of the three dark worlds to follow Yavana? They have hated Him since the Great Disaster!"

Turning his burning eyes toward David, Rammar said, "I believe the vadelah knows the answer to that question."

23. Battle Plans

David closed his eyes a moment to focus before he spoke. "On Trenara Vashua extends His love to any who would come to Him. He has the power to change a mel into a servant of Yavana. His sacrifice cleanses even the worst mel-humans if they seek Him and ask for *shalar*. There was a human named Paul who hated and killed Vashua's followers, yet Vashua turned him into a mighty servant, a vadelah to many humans.

"I received my knowledge of the Great Revelation through a long line of humans touched by this man. Although Vadelah Paul is dead, his message is still penetrating the darker areas of my planet."

Ariphema lowered his feathered brows. "You have had this knowledge for a long time. Surely all of Trenara is familiar with this news."

Hanging his head, David replied, "I'm ashamed to say there are still many places where the very name of *Jesus*, Vashua to you, has never been heard. The battle on Trenara is fierce. We have many, many languages and it is hard for us to learn new ones."

Philoah nodded vigorously as he made his way back through the assembly.

David released a great sigh. "Still, you are right, Pendaram Ariphema. We *should* have filled Trenara with this knowledge, but many of Yavana's servants are lazy or do not have the vision to spread the Great Revelation. Vashua said He will not return to Trenara until the Great

Revelation has reached every group of people. We are divided by distance, language, custom, and even skin color."

Turning to Philoah, Gyra whispered, "Are they ready to begin?" Philoah bobbed his head.

Pendaram Ariphema spoke to Gyra. "Please prepare the room." He turned to Halora. "You and your people may find this tedious. I recommend a recess for the haranda and visiting naharam until tomorrow."

Halora agreed. Waddling off the platform, he slid across the floor and disappeared into the pool. The rest of the haranda followed him. Stepping up to the podium, Gyra pressed a few buttons. Rectangles of light flicked onto the walls and ceiling, like a dozen slide projectors. The air grew fresher with half the occupants gone.

Gyra addressed the phantera crowd. "Once we have finished viewing these books, we will assimilate English through rhutaram."

Brusaka nibbled the air as if sampling a tasty morsel. "How long will this take?"

"You'll be done before sunset," Philoah answered him.

"You have seen them!" the black phantera accused.

"Dala, but I don't know English very well." Philoah eyed David. "I need to ask Ariphema to release me from my vow, or I will have to wait a long time!"

Brusaka's scalp feathers undulated. "I am not under a vow, but do not worry. I will allow you the honor of learning before me."

Snapping his bill lightly, Philoah said, "Ariphema will be busy for a while."

"Daphema is here," David offered. "Can't he release you from your vow?"

"Dala, David!" Philoah scurried off to find Daphema.

Brusaka frowned. "He better hurry. They are almost ready to begin. Daphema will be too preoccupied once they start."

Sensing he was no longer needed, David retreated off the platform. Philoah's dainty feet pranced back. The first page hit the screens and the room went silent. The phantera watched, engrossed as page after page flicked by. David marveled at the speed and accuracy of the phantera's memory. Someone tapped his shoulder.

Philoah held up a waiting hand. Nodding, David bowed his head. As the hand rested on his scalp, he felt the familiar prickling sensation.

Philoah seized David's hand and led him away, treading delicately around the silent still phantera. It was like sneaking through a museum or a taxidermy shop except the eyes of the birds blinked occasionally.

Philoah pushed the doors and they swung open silently. Once in the hall, David realized he'd been holding his breath. Exhaling, he relished his profound relief.

"I thought you'd find that boring," Philoah explained as they strolled down the hall. "And since I've already seen it, why don't we go for a walk?"

"I'd love to, but don't I need Pendaram Ariphema's permission?"

"Myute, David, he has no authority over you now. He will do nothing unless you endanger his naharam. The same is true with Pendaram Halora."

David rubbed his moist forehead. "I don't understand."

"Panagyra cleared you. Ariphema has no authority over a naharam from another planet. He will only act if his flock is threatened."

"So, I'm a free man?" David said in English.

Philoah laughed. "Did we really treat you so bad?"

"No, you were quite kind. I'm afraid Trenara's children would not have acted as hospitably toward a phantera. So, what do I do now?"

Eyeing him, Philoah declared, "You are the vadelah, yet you ask me what you should be doing?"

"I know I'm to go to the mel-naharam of the three dark worlds—"

"Yavana hamoth David!" Philoah cried. "I really did miss a lot when I left! You're to go to the mel-naharam? Why?"

Shrugging his shoulders, David replied, "Gyra said none of you could do it."

"Dala, he's right about that! The mel-naharam would 'shoot first and ask questions later.'"

David laughed.

Cocking his feathered head, Philoah asked, "Did I say it wrong?"

"No, it's just I haven't heard English in months, and it's a shock to hear it from you. If the mel-naharam are so hostile, what chance do I have of speaking to them?"

The phantera scratched his neck. "The mels may be curious. They've never seen a human before and might assume you're a mel-human. You do come from Trenara."

"You make me feel like I came from the 'wrong side of town.'" David teased.

"That was not my intent. I only meant that the mels know that evil originated on Earth and they might associate you with it." Philoah lapsed in and out of English, toying with his new tongue.

"Well, that makes me feel even better!" David retorted.

Snapping his jaw hard, Philoah said, "I still don't understand why you're going. What do you plan to tell them?"

"The same things I told you." Stepping outside, David drank in the fresh air.

"But they are mel and will not listen! They have been rebellious from the beginning!"

"And the sacrifice of Yavana was not good enough?" David cut in. "Vashua's blood is not powerful enough to cleanse them? His love is not great enough to offer them a chance? Don't you wonder *why* Yavana didn't annihilate the mel-naharam?"

Blinking, Philoah cocked his head first one way and then the other. "Thank you, David. You have expanded my mind to see new things. I was focusing on the mel-naharam's wickedness, but you have shown me to focus on Yavana's greatness."

They walked in silence across the spongy pink lawn. David drank in the fragrant ocean breeze as it caressed his face and hair. A lone duca soared out from the foothills, folded its wings, and dove.

"It is Gilyen's duca," Philoah noted. "But I do not know why he has come down from the hills." The giant chelra grew larger, but instead of trumpeting a greeting, the duca released a high-pitched keen.

Philoah's eye-rings paled. "This is not good."

Landing in rough haste, the duca emitting a rapid succession of rumbles, clicks, and whistles. "Oh no!" Philoah leaped and flew for a delah parked nearby.

David ran after his friend. "What's going on? Speak to me!"

The phantera warbled a command and the delah's door slid open. He landed and sprang through the opening.

By the time David entered the ship, Philoah was strapped to his seat and looking at his instruments. "David! This is no place for—never mind. Hang on!" The door shut and the delah burst from the ground like a flushed quail. David fell, pinned to the blue-green floor as his vision darkened.

Philoah emitted a quick series of clicks. The floor moved like an animal beneath David. Rolling onto his back, his vision returned. The hard, yet fluid-like, material molded itself into a chair. David dug his fingers into the armrests.

Slowing, the delah hovered over the mountains. "Quick, strap yourself in with those belts in the storage panel to your right." Philoah urged.

David obeyed. Gripping the armrests once more, he asked, "*Now* will you tell me what's going on?"

"Arana is about to be attacked." Philoah watched his monitor. "Here they come!"

David stared at the screen as several dozen crullahs appeared. High above the atmosphere, Arana Patrol engaged them in battle, but three crullahs slipped by. The dark ships dove for the surface.

Philoah scowled. "Are they going to attack the Pendaram's City or Zun Drevash, the southern port?"

"How did the duca know—"

"Hold on!" warned Philoah as he spun the delah around. David thought he would lose his breakfast. Three dark ray-shaped ships flew toward them in tight formation. "These are our attackers!" Philoah declared. Charging his quarry, he blasted away. The first crullah exploded and slammed into a mountain. The other two veered off. Philoah pursued one and kept an eye on the scanner for the second.

"Is our delah the only one around?" David asked.

"For now. It will be a few minutes before reinforcements come. I was hoping to take out two in the first sweep, but they just weren't lined up right. Yavana, give me skill!" Philoah prayed.

"How did they get here so fast? Couldn't the mining base on Agaria warn Arana Patrol?"

"Crullahs use *trelemar*."

David scowled. "What's that?"

"You have no English words for it. *Warp speed* doesn't come close. Trelemar is a form of instantaneous travel."

David remembered his instantaneous trip from Trenara to Arana.

Pairing up, the two crullahs swung back for the Pendaram's City. "Oh, no you don't!" Philoah cried. Containers rattled and panels squeaked as the delah hit turbulent air. Feathers rising on his scalp, Philoah snapped his jaw several times. "I don't think I can overtake them before they reach the city."

"Where are the other delahs? I don't see another ship for miles!" David asked in frustration.

Philoah glanced at his computer screen. "Most of them are in orbit, overhead. By the time reinforcements arrive, the crullahs will have struck the city. We may see a lot of casualties."

David's pulse pounded in his veins. "Yavana, don't let Your people be butchered—especially after all that has happened! This day should be a day of praise, not a day of mourning!"

Flying side by side, the crullahs headed straight for the council chambers.

"They're getting ready to fire," Philoah said in a solemn voice. "Yavana, have mercy."

A crullah exploded. Its shower of debris battered the second crullah as it fired, causing the laser to merely graze the council chambers. The remaining crullah darted out to sea, trailing smoke from a wingtip.

Dodging the deadly rain, Philoah followed the crullah's trail. "Hoowah!" he whooped as he gained on his wounded enemy. Laser beams burst from their delah, striking the crullah with deadly accuracy.

The black ship erupted into a fiery light, spewing molten metal and blazing shards. Philoah sent out a query. "Delah Philoah: Whose beautiful ship foiled the crullah's attack?"

"Delah Rammar: Yavana gave me the honor. Although I preferred Naphema's firestorm, this one wasn't bad. Ramara Yavana!"

After their ship landed, David and Philoah hopped out and walked over to Rammar's delah. The old black phantera poked his head out.

"How did you know there was trouble?" Philoah asked.

With a subtle smile, Rammar said, "It really wasn't that difficult. There was a duca in distress, so I left to find out why. Once I heard the news, I just sat in my delah and waited for the enemy to come."

Philoah laughed. "You always did have the sharpest ears!"

"Whenever Yavana gives a wonderful gift, the mel-aradelah try to steal it!" Rammar stated.

"Do you think the mel-aradelah told the crullahs where to attack?" David asked.

Turning his uncomfortable gaze on David, Rammar answered, "Dala, and these crullahs were piloted by the mel-balahrane, who worship the mel-aradelah."

Scores of phantera poured out of the council chambers, jabbering and bobbing their heads like pistons.

"We heard explosions," Gyra said as he ran up. "What happened?"

Raising his aged hands, Rammar looked up at the creeping trail of smoke left from the wounded crullah. His eyes seemed fixed upon something beyond the gray smoke, beyond the sky itself. "We have drawn up the battle plan for delivering the Great Revelation. Now the war is upon us."

Fast Facts

Classes of Life-forms

Aradelah: Spiritual beings. Angels (**mel-aradelah:** Demons)*
Naharam: Mortal sentient life-forms*
Chelra: Creatures on a level between animals and naharam, possessing crude language skills
Dalam: Animals without developed language skills
Tearel: Plant life

*The plural forms of aradelah and naharam do not use an *s*

Ramatera–English Dictionary

ab (ahb). Or
adrana (uh-**drah**-nuh). Sea
Agaria (uh-**gair**-ee-uh). The large white moon of Arana. Literally, "big light"
agera (uh-**gair**-uh). Large
aireah (**air**-ee-uh). An artificial overhead light
Alamar (**ah**-lah-mar). Arana's sun
alawa (**ah**-lah-wah). A spongy turf-forming plant that grows in pink or lavender. Native to Arana
aradelah (air-uh-**del**-uh). Angels. Also see mel-aradelah
Arana (uh-**rah**-nah). Home world of the haranda. Also home to a large colony of phantera
awal (uh-**wal**). Hot
ayeen (ah-**yeen**). Pain. May also be spoken to express discomfort. Often shortened to "ayee" Literally, "Oww!"
ba (bah). A word that forms the plural of the noun it follows
balute (bah-**loot**). Why?
barune (bah-**roon**). To open
boosah (**boo**-zuh). An expression of disgust, akin to "gross" or "yuck"
bot (bot). To stop
caleah (kah-**lee**-uh). To eat or drink
caruk (kah-**ruk**). A versatile laser tool and weapon

charane (cha-**rayn**). To come

chelra (**chel**-ruh). A group of life-forms possessing crude language skills. One level of intelligence below naharam, and one level above dalam

crealin (**kree**-uh-lin). A vital phantera organ that can rupture and cause death during a time of intense mourning. Used to perform falarn and rhutaram

crullah (**krul**-luh). A spaceship built by the mel-dijetara, used by the mel-naharam for space travel. Literally, "dark ship"

dala (**dah**-luh). Yes

dalam (duh-**lahm**). Any animal that has no developed language skills

dalaphar (**dah**-luh-far). Bonding covenant, e.g., marriage. Literally, "yes covenant"

Dalena (dah-**lee**-nuh). Home world of the phantera

dee (dee). To bring, send, or give

del (del). A message

delah (**dee**-luh). A spaceship built by the coralana, used by the phantera and other naharam for interplanetary travel

delaram (**del**-uh-rahm). Leaders who traverse large areas of a planet to ensure the well-being of their subjects. The next level of authority under the pendaram. Literally, "traveling rulers"

Dilari (dih-**lahr**-ee). The small red moon of Arana. Literally, "little light"

dilu (**dee**-loo). Small

Doiyal (**doy**-ahl). The first phantera female, their "Eve"

doloom (doh-**loom**). A cave. Also an enormous system of caverns under the great Arana desert

dowel (**dow**-wel). A stick with a lighted orb on top

drea (**dree**-uh). Water

duca (**doo**-kah). A very large flying bird, resembling a giant duck with a bony crest. The phantera's chelra

elah (**el**-ah). A cry for assistance. Help!

fala (**fah**-lah). A sweet purple fruit grown on Arana

falarn (fuh-**larn**). The phantera ability to share the current thoughts of another naharam

falatirah (fah-lah-**teer**-uh). A drink made from the fala fruit

hamjea (hahm-**jee**-uh). The protective third eyelid of a phantera

hamoth (**hahm**-oth). To protect

harana (ha-**rah**-nah). To give praise

haranda (ha-**ron**-dah). An aquatic seal-like naharam whose home world is Arana

hoowah (hoo-**wah**). A phantera expression of joy, similar to a cowboy's hoot

horlah (**hor**-lah). A chalky tan vegetable found on Arana

jarune (juh-**roon**). Cold

lampar (**lam**-pahr). A large, deer-like dalam found on Arana

lar (lahr). The same as. Equal to

loomar (**loo**-mar). An edible fish found in the great caverns (dolooms) of Arana

maha (mah-**hah**). Who?

manar (mah-**nar**). What?

marana (mah-**rah**-nah). Where?

marza (**mar**-zah). A rare element used to make very strong alloys

matrel (mah-**trel**). When?

mel (mel). Those who rebel against Yavana. Unbelievers

mel-aradelah (mel-air-uh-**del**-uh). Demons

mel-balahrane (mel-bah-lah-**rayn**). A mel-naharam whose home world is Wicara

mel-dijetara (mel-dih-jeh-**tar**-uh). A mel-naharam whose home world is Cruskada

mel-hanor (mel-hah-**nor**). A mel-naharam whose home world is Morsala

mel-naharam (mel-nah-ha-**rom**). Mortal intelligent life-forms who do not serve Yavana

melcat (**mel**-kat). A giant arachnid dalam native to Arana's deserts

myute (mee-**yoot**). No

nachel (**nah**-chel). Children of naharam

nadrea (nah-**dree**-uh). A large marine mammal on Arana. The haranda's chelra

naharam (nah-ha-**rom**). Mortal intelligent life-forms, e.g., humans and other species. Also used specifically for those who serve Yavana

najaran (nah-**jar**-ron). Truth

nal (nahl). And

Naphema (nah-fee-mah). The "True Spirit" of Yavana

patu (**pah**-too). Mine. Belonging to me

pendaram (**pen**-dar-rom). The ruling leaders of the phantera. These twelve are each responsible for the phantera populations on their planets. Also used by other naharam as a title for their highest leaders

phantera (**fan**-tair-uh). An avian naharam whose home world is Dalena

phema (**fee**-muh). Spirit

pinnah (**pin**-nuh). Five

ramara (ruh-**mar**-uh). To give thanks. Literally, "Thank you"

Ramara nal harana sa Yavana (ruh-**mar**-uh nahl ha-**rah**-nah sah yah-**vah**-nah). A formal blessing for a meal. Literally, "Thanks and praise to God"

Ramara sa Yavana (ruh-**mar**-uh sah yah-**vah**-nah). An informal blessing for a meal. Literally, "Thanks be to God." In the company of close friends "sa" may be dropped

Ramatera (ram-uh-**tair**-uh). The language of the flexible tongues. Spoken by most naharam and mel-naharam (except humans) who have the ability to form words

rhutaram (roo-**tar**-um). The phantera ability to learn a foreign language instantaneously through contact with a naharam's head

rusoph (**roo**-sof). To learn

sa (sah). To

salan (sah-**lon**). To go

Sanor (**san**-or). The name for Earth's sun

sarena (sah-**ree**-nuh). Peace. Often spoken as a blessing

shalar (sha-**lar**). To forgive

shar (shar). To mix, stir, or agitate. Used to describe a storm

shartara (shar-**tar**-uh). A sandstorm

steen (steen). To close

ta (tah). Is

talaram (**tah**-lah-rom). The main leader of a naharam village. This is the next level of authority under the delaram

tara (**tar**-uh). Sand or dirt

tearel (teer-**el**). Plant life

teayoo (tee-**yoo**). Down

toorah (**too**-ruh). Door

tor (tor). From

tren (tren). One

trelemar (**trel**-uh-mar). A form of deep space travel discovered by the coralana. It allows one to jump from one point in space to another with no lapse in time

Trenara (tren-**ar**-uh). Earth, the home world of humans. Literally, "first planet"

vadelah (vuh-**dee**-luh). Literally, "Vashua's messenger"

Vashua (vah-**shoo**-uh). Known as "the Mystery," "the Provision," and "the Restoring One"

Yal (yahl). The first phantera male, their "Adam"

Yaram (yah-**rom**). Father God

yarama (yah-**rom**-ah). A naharam father

yatala (yah-**tal**-ah). Family

Yavana (yah-**vah**-nah). The Creator of all naharam. Combination of Yaram—Father, Vashua—the Mystery, and Naphema—the True Spirit

Julie Rollins resides in Washington State with her husband and their three daughters. In addition to writing, her interests include canoeing, painting, and raising ducks. An active member of her church, she sings on the worship team, composes worship songs, and leads a home group. After teaching in a Christian high school for eight years, she now homeschools her children. She has a BA in Art and holds a commercial pilot's rating. This is her first novel.

COMING SOON...

BOOK 2 OF THE VADELAH CHRONICLES

Would you risk your life to take a message of hope to your enemies?

David Decker nearly got killed during his stay on Arana, and that was a *friendly* planet. Now he must go to three hostile worlds that are sworn enemies to everything he holds dear. Will anyone listen to him? He knows one thing for certain: his message has the power to heal their lives or stir up their murderous rage.

FOLLOWED BY...

BOOK 3 OF THE VADELAH CHRONICLES

David and Gyra must return to face a nightmare: Earth. They tremble at the pronouncement, but Rammar the Prophet has spoken: only David can sever Earth's secret link with the dangerous mel-naharam, and Gyra must help him. Who are the humans involved on Earth? How will David stop the contact? Will he come out alive? David doesn't know. But Rammar has warned that David will suffer...greatly.

Want More?

Be sure to visit the author's colorful and informative website at **www.JulieRollins.com** for

- **Vadelah Chronicles** alien "photo gallery" with computer screensavers
- Bonus chapters (not in printed books)
- Short stories by the author
- Book descriptions and release dates
- Feedback and questions to the author
- Links to order books

Or you can order books in the **Vadelah Chronicles** series by contacting the publisher directly at

Essence Publishing
20 Hanna Court
Belleville, Ontario, Canada K8P 5J2
Toll-free: (800) 238-6376 ext. 7575
Fax: (613) 962-3055
Email: publishing@essencegroup.com
www.essencebookstore.com